"*Astonishing. . .*
A novel that haunts your mind. . .
Dennis McFarland displays the powers of imagination and craftsmanship that can transform news trivia into timeless fiction."
—*The Seattle Times*

"A journey of self-discovery . . . The many story lines are enough to make this novel good reading, but they are only one part of the magic McFarland weaves. Here his mastery of language manifests itself in imagery about seeing, in both the literal and figurative senses."
—*The San Diego Union Tribune*

"Imaginative and understated . . . This book is hard to classify, as a detective novel or as serious fiction. But it sneaks up on you. So carefully unplotted it keeps you guessing how it can possibly work out, it's one of the most inventive suspense novels I've read in a long time."
—*The Detroit News*

"Dennis McFarland combines the familiarity of the police procedural with the unsettling dream images of literary fiction. Trying to solve inexplicable deaths, his characters stumble upon clues to their own lives."
—*The Asheville Citizen-Times*

Also by Dennis McFarland:

THE MUSIC ROOM

SCHOOL FOR THE BLIND

Dennis McFarland

IVY BOOKS • NEW YORK

Ivy Books
Published by Ballantine Books
Copyright © 1994 by Dennis McFarland

I am grateful to Dr. Karen Victor, Det. George Lotti, Bob Metafora, Mary Glasspool, Jeff Jacoby, and John Traficonte, for their invaluable help and advice; Harry Colt and Bill Brower, for guiding me on a tour of the Perkins School for the Blind; and the friars of St. Joseph's Monastery, for their hospitality. Some of the photographs described in this book are derived from the work of Robert Capa and Clara Sipprell, to whom I mean to pay homage. The material from Anton Chekhov is taken from his great story "Gusev," translated here by Constance Garnett. The detective novel from which Deirdre reads to Francis is *Maigret and the Informer*, by Georges Simenon. Finally, for their generosity, encouragement, and incisive editing skills, I'm deeply grateful to Larry Cooper and John Sterling, and, for far more than the sum of these gifts, to my wife, Michelle Blake Simons.

—D. McF.

Library of Congress Catalog Card Number: 93-49831

ISBN 0-8041-1350-5

First published by Houghton Mifflin Company.

This edition reprinted by special arrangement with Houghton Mifflin Company.

Manufactured in the United States of America

First Ballantine Books Edition: May 1995

10 9 8 7 6 5 4 3 2 1

*To Katharine and Sam
and to Michelle*

WITH ALL MY LOVE

No one ever told me that grief
felt so like fear.

—*C. S. LEWIS*

Part I

One

HIS LIFE'S WORK and ambition fulfilled, Francis Brimm believed the only metamorphosis left him was a slow, affable decline toward death, and so at the age of seventy-three he returned to the town of his youth to retire. He had been a news photographer—a witness, a messenger amid the world's fire and ashes—and he figured he had earned not only the right to let the world go, but also the poise to let it go with authority. He would read, write, sleep, visit the beach, fish, garden a bit, whatever he pleased—the pastimes, he imagined, of solitary old people of some accomplishment. The medley of images he assembled for this retirement included a cottage with a porch on which he might sit and muse over the prospects of the very next hour, but soon after he had settled into just such a place, he found himself absorbed in entirely different, unexpected ways.

Everything seemed to begin with the gulls that awakened him around 4 A.M. with their ethereal, light-greeting symphony, two or three mornings a week, out on the nearby golf course. The crying and cawing continued usually for about twenty minutes, during which Brimm, in a state of partial sleep, would open his eyes and see a pale radiance wash across the ceiling of his bedroom. At first he thought it some phenomenon of aging eyes (he'd had "floaters," tiny shapes like pieces of lint, troubling his vision since his late forties), but soon a face began emerging out of these bursts of dull light on the ceiling, the face of a young woman he had once photographed almost fifty years ago in Normandy, and he knew that more than aging eyes was involved.

The cottage he'd purchased was on a quiet street in a turn-of-the-century neighborhood that abutted the golf course, and if you walked the short distance to the course's highest point—what passed for a hill in this low-lying plain known as Florida—you could see the Gulf Coast town of Pines, spread out like an immense barge of colorful crates about to be launched into the bay. In the south end of town, near the college and the mouth of the Yustaga River, you could see the roof of the red brick house where Brimm had spent his youth and where his unmarried sister, Muriel, lived to this day. You could see the ugly college gymnasium with its two different architectures; the whitewashed armory, long used for theatrical events; and atop the entrance to the Creighton Tunnel, the olive-drab statue of the conquistador Hernando de Soto astride a horse. Everywhere you would see the pines for which the town was named, and behind you that was practically all you would see—the forest that was the protracted setting of Brimm's new neighborhood, a few country homes (the Dills, the Tutwilers, the Coopers), an important county road, the winding Yustaga, and the Raphael School for the Blind, its stone tower rising medievally out of the evergreens.

"The French girl, yes," said Muriel. "Of course I remember her. The *collaboratrice*."

It was late enough in the day—after seven-thirty in the evening, in summer—for them to stroll to the top of the hill without rousing the fury of any late golfers. Brimm had walked a bit ahead; he stopped and turned to wait for her to catch up. She was older by five years, and she had recently cut her white hair very short, making her large gray eyes all the stronger. He had photographed her many times over the years, mainly because of the eyes, and watching her now, under the dome of near-twilight, her impractical shoes making her traverse the rough with her arms out-

4

stretched like a tightrope walker's, he acknowledged to himself that he had always been a little in love with his sister. These days he found himself yielding to such sentimental, disagreeable truths like somebody who'd completely lost his mettle.

"Yes," he said, "the French girl. It ran in *Picture Post* a hundred years ago. She'd had a baby by a German soldier."

"That's right," said Muriel, reaching for his hand. "Hold me up, Frankie. I'm going barefoot."

This he'd done before, held Muriel's hand while she bent to remove her shoes. She'd always, always worn the wrong shoes, an excuse, he imagined, for going barefoot eventually. Muriel, unmarried, unselfconscious, removing her shoes: for some time Brimm had thought there was no longer any pure memory, only memories of memories, recollections of things once recollected. And some of them had gone so abstract, like this shoe-removing of Muriel's, that you couldn't legitimately call it memory—more like a vague recognition of something once known better.

"They shaved her head," he said. "And marched her through the streets, carrying the baby in her arms. She was just a kid herself."

Muriel, shoes in hand, stood erect and looked at him. "Francis," she said. "There are tears in your eyes."

He waved a hand at the sky and headed for the top of the hill, where there was a tee with a bench. The fairway stretched out toward town and the bay. Brimm watched a black dog digging in a bunker down to the right of the visible green.

"I don't know," he said after they were seated. "This thing is happening to me."

"What do you mean," said Muriel, " 'this thing'?"

"I'm not sure," he said. "It's my mind, I suppose."

"Well, of course it's your mind," she said. "At your age."

"Oh, it's nothing," he said. "Forget it."

"Okay," Muriel said. She peered down the fairway, bringing a hand to her forehead. "I think that Labrador retriever may be mad," she said. "Look at the way he's digging up that sand trap."

They both watched the dog in the distance for a moment. Then Muriel said, "Only, if it was nothing, why did you mention it? I wonder where she is today, that girl. I wonder what happened to the baby."

Without thinking it through, Brimm said quietly: "I see her."

Muriel looked at him askance. "You see her," she said.

"Yes," he said. "On my bedroom ceiling. At night."

"Okay," she said, nodding. She cleared her throat, paused. "You see her," she said. "Okay. I think I know what you mean. You mean you see her on the bedroom ceiling. Of course. At night. I think—"

"Oh, shut up," said Brimm.

"I'm sorry, Frankie," she said. "Tell me, please, what do you mean?"

"I mean what I said. The gulls wake me up before dawn and then I see that girl's face, as big as a . . . well, I don't know exactly how big. But there she is, recognizable."

"But I mean is it like a ghost?" said Muriel. "Like a projection? Or like a bas-relief?"

"You really can't stop yourself from patronizing me, can you," he said.

He stood, turned, and began walking away, down toward the strip of pines that separated his street from the golf course. He got through the trees and all the way to the house before he even thought about looking back.

Then, there she was, an old woman picking her way through the floor of pine needles in the dusk, barefoot. He waited for her on the porch step.

"You realize," she called from the middle of the street, squinting at him, waving one shoe in the air in his direction, "that I might have been attacked by a rabid dog out on that golf course."

Brimm shrugged.

When she reached him, she said, "Oh, well, Frankie,"

and took his arm. "I'm sorry, but I think you should consider yourself lucky, really. I never see anything at all on my bedroom ceiling."

"Go home, Muriel," he said.

"I *am* going home," she said, releasing him. "You bet I'm going home. You're in no mood."

She walked to the red Volkswagen she'd had forever and threw her shoes in through the open window. (She called the car by name, Ruby—husbandless, childless, she made pets of practically everything, even thc kitchen appliances. "Roo-bee, roo-bay, this little tiny car," she would croon as she cranked the engine. "Bye-bye, roo-bee, roo-bay.") "Get a cat, Frankie," she called, once she was behind the wheel. "You're much too alone here."

"If I'd wanted to live with cats," he said, "I would've moved in with you."

"Then come to church with me on Sunday," she said. "You've got to find some company for yourself."

He rolled his eyes and hitched up his pants, pulling on his belt loops. "Church," he said, wholly disgruntled.

She looked at him for a long moment. "I just realized something," she said. "You've always been a hermit, haven't you. All that world travel, all that mission . . . just a front, a way to be alone."

"Go home," he repeated.

"Well, at least take something up. Write your memoirs. Make some headway."

"*You* make some headway," said Brimm, motioning the car forward along the street.

"Come to church," she said, smiling. "We've got a marvelous new preacher."

Then she drove away.

He watched the old car until it disappeared around the bend at the end of the block, thinking suddenly that they hadn't talked about what he'd called her over there to talk about. He had meant to ask her again about their father, about a certain Sunday when their father forbade a trip to the beach, and about several other things as well. He went inside the cottage and switched on the swing-arm lamp by his reading chair. He said aloud, "Dinner," a word that so defeated him, he sagged into the chair and closed his eyes.

After a minute of blankness, he reached into a cardboard crate near his feet and pulled out the old *Picture Post*, which now fell open automatically to the famous photograph: the camera aimed straight down the village street, victory banners hung from the windows of the buildings on either side, the street filled with throngs of people—mostly women and girls in summer dresses, and a few old men— all moving rapidly forward over the cobblestones. The girl with the baby, the young mother, is the focus of all the others in the picture: they are marching her home after having publicly shaved her head. Everyone jockeys for position to get a look at her, to get in a jeer. Two gendarmes flank the girl, one with a leering grin. She herself, wearing a checked dress under a white apron, concentrates on the face of the swaddled baby in her arms—perhaps the baby is crying— and this priority, the baby, whose German father might be already dead, or imprisoned, or simply gone forever, seems to render the young mother impervious to the crowd's amused scorn. How had she collaborated? Did she turn in Jews to the enemy, or merely fall in love with the wrong man? The photograph didn't reveal anything new—it remained the same—yet Brimm noticed for the first time how gay the floral prints on the schoolgirls were, and how old-fashioned everyone's shoes.

He rested the magazine closed in his lap, then reached into the box for a yellowed eight-by-ten of Muriel. On the back, in his own handwriting, "M.B., 1950." Wearing some kind of Chinese number, sleeveless, and large pearls on her ears, her black hair pulled back, her arms crossed, she looks away to the right side, where a curved stem of a geranium plant enters the frame. You can see the darkly painted nails of one hand, and on the plain white wall behind her, her diffused shadow. Saint Muriel of the Pines, Brimm thought

8

almost with affection, Muriel and her faith, Muriel and her preachers. Brimm supposed she developed attachments to men of the cloth because she failed to develop attachments to other men. It was one of the things that made the church so unsavory, all those lonely women gaping worshipfully at the pulpit, all that earthbound, fleshly reverence, all that confusion between ordinary secular neediness and spiritual longing. He held the picture closer to the light for a moment. It too revealed nothing new—only Muriel in her mid-thirties, youth lingering exotically in her eyes, and Brimm couldn't think where in the world she might be standing.

Two

MURIEL HAD LONG ago turned the back parlor downstairs into a bedroom for herself, forgoing the steep climb up to the second floor, and now, suddenly, after all this time, those upper rooms had begun to represent the past. She thought this odd and she blamed her brother Francis for it. She had never been the least bit taken with the past. Only with Francis's return to Pines had such things begun to occupy her. She was pleased, generally, about his coming home, but on three or four occasions in the last few weeks, she'd found herself standing at the base of the old stairs, one hand resting on the pineapple-adorned newel post, gazing upward like some woebegone character in a Tennessee Williams play.

She considered herself a classical woman with classical, pragmatic sensibilities. She acknowledged her passion for good, attractive shoes and colorful clothes, and her love of cats as merely symptoms of her poetical self. These were harmless traits; they brought warmth. But this blossoming of the past, this creeping vine of memory that had taken root with Francis's return was entirely another thing. Muriel felt certain that the apparition he claimed to be seeing on his bedroom ceiling was only a recurring dream, but if it turned out to be a sort of psychic or supernatural event, she wouldn't be surprised. Something as dramatic as that would be required in order to jar Francis. It appeared to Muriel that some long-dormant part of her brother had begun to awaken these last several weeks, and she thought this made some spiritual sense. If Francis's seventies were to be his era of feeling, of going back and sowing history with sentiment, that was fine and good. She was happy to observe it, even to help when she was able, but only as a kind of consultant, detached; she hadn't intended actually to become any kind of *player*. What had pleased her most about his return to Pines was that having him around had initially had the happy effect of taking her out of herself. But now she was being taken *into* herself instead, and she didn't like it.

Yesterday morning—the day of their evening walk on the golf course—Muriel's book club had been assembled and the discussion had reached a lively peak when Francis telephoned to ask her many questions about their mother and father. Why had Mother never finished school? Had she and Daddy really met on a train? How exactly had their father, a physician, lost the better part of his arm?

"Frankie, I have company," Muriel had said into the kitchen telephone. "You're interrupting my book club."

"Book club," he said. "Are *both* members in attendance today?"

"There's strength in many things other than numbers," she said. "Now I must go."

"When will you be done?" he asked.

Muriel looked at her watch and sighed heavily, directly into the receiver. "Ned and Billie are staying for lunch," she said. "Now you've flustered me. My mind's not as agile as it used to be, Francis. I can't have it leaping back to the nineteenth century when I still have lunch to do."

"Why didn't Father let us go to the beach that Sunday afternoon?" he said quickly.

"What Sunday afternoon?"

"You know the one I mean."

"Frankie, for heaven's sake, that was in nineteen twenty-*eight*."

"Yeah, so? Why did he stop us from going?"

"You're being rude," she told him.

11

"Call me back," he said.

"Maybe," she said.

And when she returned to the front parlor, Ned and Billie Otto, her good friends, were sitting in the two leather club chairs where she had left them, Billie now staring out the west window—at the blank white wall of their own house next door—and Ned clutching an old souvenir pillow with a picture of the Empire State Building on it, his eyes closed. When Billie saw Muriel, she brought her index finger to her lips and whispered, "Ned's fallen asleep."

"Wake up, Edward," said Muriel.

Ned, unstartled, opened his eyes and smiled, setting the pillow carefully aside. The barrier between sleep and wakefulness, always permeable, had become for him a mere gauze through which he passed back and forth without ceremony. Muriel recalled that Ned had possessed a certain charm in his younger years, and she felt acutely disappointed that he had let himself become such an old man.

Attempting to pick up some thread from ten minutes earlier, Billie Otto began chattering. "I was thinking," she said. "Isn't it odd the way the British people say 'in hospital' and we say 'in *the* hospital'? But then I thought, well, we say 'in school,' don't we? We wouldn't say, 'My children are in *the* school,' we'd say, 'My children are in school.' It's almost the same, isn't it?"

"The most amazing thing has just happened," said Muriel.

Ned moistened his lips with his tongue, a delicate, bright pink thing that Muriel would just as soon not be distracted by when she had something to say. "That was Francis on the line," she continued. "He just said to me, 'Why wouldn't Father let us go to the beach that Sunday afternoon?' and I said, 'Frankie, for heaven's sake, that was in nineteen twenty-eight.' "

The Ottos looked at Muriel, then at each other. Finally Billie, possibly peeved at having her own remarks ignored, said, "I think you'll have to explain, Muriel."

"Well, don't you see?" said Muriel. "The date just came to me. Just like that. How could I possibly have known the exact year?"

"Oh," said Billie.

The room fell silent. Outside a cloud passed briefly across the sun, dimming and restoring everything immediately. Then Ned nodded and also said, "Oh."

Late that afternoon, after the Ottos had gone home, Muriel drew the drapes and attempted to nap, but she lay in her bed for more than an hour, unable to fall asleep. She'd let the day go by without phoning Francis, and that meant he would be smoldering—she could smell the fumes clear across town. At nearly six o'clock, she turned on the bedside lamp and dialed his number.

To her surprise, he didn't seem the least bit focused on her having failed to call sooner. It was a lovely evening, he told her, not too hot, and if she would drive over, they could have a nice walk on the golf course.

It was a fifteen-minute drive, five minutes longer than usual because the most convenient bridge across the Yustaga River had washed out in a recent cloudburst. All routes in that direction were familiar to Muriel, since she'd developed a variety of approaches to the Raphael School for the Blind during her several decades of service there in the school library.

Francis had been right, it was a lovely evening, and along the river, despite the bright flare of the sun, the air seemed pleasantly cooled by the water and the shade of the pines. On the old stone bridge that connected the county road to the smaller one that led into Francis's new neighborhood, Muriel met a group of six or eight students from the Raphael School who were having an outing. The bridge was narrow, not much wider than one lane, and she had to proceed slowly. Briefly, Muriel was saddened at not recognizing any of the students; surely everyone she might have known was long gone from the Raphael School. But the children—teenagers, actually, a group of girls—looked decidedly cheerful as they walked in pairs across the bridge, the ones nearer the wall tapping their white canes against the stones. And then Muriel did see someone she knew, their sighted companion bringing up the rear, Joe Letson. How long it had been—five or six years at least—and she'd been fond of Joe, a kind, balding, middle-aged man who would frequently drop by the circulation desk with an amusing story. She waved enthusiastically as he passed the open window of the Volkswagen, but, oddly, he seemed so shocked to see her that he quickly averted his eyes to the glaring river, cutting off any possibility that she might stop and say hello.

The moment left Muriel rattled, and the rest of the way to Francis's she was unable to resist interpreting it symbolically. That face from the past, so disagreeably astonished and unhappy to see her, seemed to signify just how friendly the past intended to be to her should she allow it in. She entered a dark, sheltered interval of pine woods and was angered to note that for an instant she actually felt afraid.

As she gained Francis's street, she resolved to shake whatever gloom this was and to try to give herself for the next hour entirely to her brother. But then, right away, during their walk on the golf course, Francis had brought up that business about the "vision" on his bedroom ceiling.

"Consider yourself lucky," she'd said to him, unable to take it as seriously as he did, and they'd had a less than cordial parting. "Come to church," she'd told him, but it didn't seem likely that he would.

Then today, after her morning coffee, she returned to her parlor-bedroom to discover that something about the large oval mirror over her vanity made her feel vaguely remorseful, a blurry kind of heartache she would later describe as adolescent, since it reminded her of a youthful, hormonal confusion in which one feels loss without being able to name what is lost. The mirror's shape and presence, the *fact* of the mirror, had brought on the feeling, and not anything reflected in it. There was a word for that sort of thing, when an object irrationally triggered an emotion, but she couldn't think what it was. The confusion was fleeting, but when she turned and walked through the front parlor into the hall, she stopped, placed one hand on the newel post, and began gazing up the stairs.

Annoyed, she collected herself and went directly to the back porch and called through the screen to Billie Otto.

A few minutes later, in Muriel's kitchen, Billie asked, "What do you mean, this thing is happening to you?"

They were seated at the counter, drinking coffee. "My mind," said Muriel.

"Oh, goodness, that's nothing to worry about," said Billie. "You're old, Muriel. It's to be expected."

It did not escape Muriel that she and Billie had practically duplicated a bit of yesterday's conversation with Francis on the golf course, and she resolved to call him and tell him just how she felt about this invasion of the past he'd brought with him to Pines. But at that very moment, as if summoned, the telephone rang on the wall near Muriel's left ear, startling her.

It was he, Francis, sounding simultaneously worn out and excited. "Muriel," he said. "You remember that dog we saw last evening on the golf course?"

"Certainly I do," said Muriel.

"Well, you'll never guess what it was digging up," he said.

"Oh, I bet I can," said Muriel. "An old bone."

"Ha!" said Francis. "But what kind of bone? That's the question. You better get over here right away."

"Don't be silly," she said. "I'm having coffee with Billie and I'm not even dressed."

"Come as you are, God won't have you any other way," he said—a wisecrack, since this was exactly the message of the glassed-in marquee on the lawn of Muriel's church.

Three

HE CLOSED HIS eyes and a memory began to unfold in precise detail, vivid as a flag—not what he'd expected, not from the days after the war, nothing to do with the French girl at all. He was thirteen, and the Oberammergau Passion players came to town that year. At that young age he'd already formed his earliest enduring conclusion about God—a sort of big bang theory of accountability, simply that all calamity in the world was God's fault because God after all had made life—and the play, to which he was taken by his mother, disclosed nothing to alter this view. On the contrary, the idea that calamity was God's fault fit the events of Christ's Passion like a Bowie knife its sheath. The Oberammergau Passion players would have had Francis believe that the Jews killed Jesus, but Francis had reflected on these events before and had come to understand Gethsemane as only a child could: everything that had befallen Christ was precisely what God (the Father) had wanted to befall Christ, and no amount of sweating midnight blood in the garden could change even the smallest detail.

In the dark armory, on whose stage only months earlier he witnessed a Cajun magician by the name of Jean-Louis Galhemo apparently eat a whole truck tire, his mother wept off and on during the last half hour of the Passion play, and once, when he innocently sniffled, she passed him a Kleenex. She'd handed it to him with a look of enormous empathy, and unmoved by the play, which had so far contained not a single amazing event, he felt demoralized. He crushed the tissue into a ball and tossed it back into her lap, snorting through his nose. The extremely thin Mrs. Brimm narrowed her eyes briefly, then straightened her spine and faced the stage, where, at that moment, Muriel, a high school senior and one among many in a crowd scene, was shouting, "Crucify him, crucify him, nail him to the cross!"

It was the custom of the Oberammergau people, wherever they went, to find extras from among the talent in the local communities, and Muriel, on hearing about the auditions to be held at the armory two weeks hence, had mounted a crash diet. She lost seven pounds, a loss visible only to herself, and won a part as a young townswoman in the famous scene where the Jews prefer the release of Barabbas, after which poor, frightened Pilate asks the multitude what he's to do with this other one, the one called King of the Jews, and the multitude demands Christ's execution. For ten days Muriel went about the house chomping on ribs of celery, chanting her one line, "Crucify him, crucify him, nail him to the cross!" as if it were a football cheer.

She also gave Frankie some inside dope on the play. She told him about how the people of Oberammergau, hundreds of years ago, had beseeched God to spare them the Black Death—about how they had negotiated with God, promising to develop this Passion play and take it to the corners of the earth for eternity. Frankie thought about calamity being God's fault—the notion often found its way to the front of his thinking—shrugged his shoulders, and said, "But everybody else in all the *other* towns died."

They were in Muriel's pine-paneled bedroom at the corner of their old brick house. She sat on the padded bench before her vanity mirror; he lay across her bed. Next she turned to his juvenile face of stone and described how the enigmatic young Bavarian who portrayed Christ in the Passion play would pace backstage in silence, never speaking

17

a word to anyone else in the cast, never for a second leaving his role.

"So?" Frankie said, rotating onto his back and staring up at the ceiling. "He's probably just practicing his lines."

"Most of them learned their lines by rote," said Muriel, this bit of information a throwaway. "Most of them don't actually speak English."

Finally impressed, Frankie had sat up quickly and said, "You mean they don't even understand what they're saying?"

And all through the play, stoical in the fifth row of the armory, he kept thinking about this oddity and how, vaguely, it conformed to his sense of the play as a kind of charade that confirmed God's treacheries. His mother had bowed her head, either in prayer or from an excess of passion. Christ was on the cross, languishing. Mrs. Brimm cleared her throat and lifted her head, facing the crucifixion in a resigned sort of way. She dabbed at her cheeks with the crumpled Kleenex, which she then dropped to the floor. Frankie looked down into the dark by his feet and watched the wad of tissue, freed from the constraint of his mother's hand, begin slowly to open, to blossom like a damp, milky flower.

After the walk on the golf course with Muriel, Brimm had sat in his armchair, mused over the two old photographs—one from the Normandy village, the other, of Muriel, from somewhere else unknown—and eventually he'd fallen asleep. The vivid memory of the Oberammergau play had mixed, in sleep, with his dreams. When he awakened, he thought maybe he'd dreamt of the young French girl. Several arresting impressions lingered: long white banners snapping in the wind, a pale man in a military uniform, sunlight on water changing to cobblestones. But in some way the dream had also been about food, strewn as it was with children eating, and kitchen aromas wafting out of open windows.

He had eaten no dinner, and it was almost ten o'clock. He roused himself, drove his Jeep out to a joint on the county road, ordered a burger and fries, and didn't return home until almost eleven.

The cottage greeted him in utter silence, and for a moment he wondered if the whole design, this return to the town of his roots, had been anything more than a sentimental scheme, doomed by its lack of specificity. His vision had failed him in regard to details. He had not, for example, imagined himself ordering food to go at a lively bar on the county road, then eating it alone in his car in the parking lot. Certainly he hadn't imagined himself standing in the dark at his living room window, as he'd taken to doing lately, hoping to get a glimpse of the beautiful young Cuban woman in the house next door. Objectively he considered neither of these shameful acts, yet he couldn't deny that shame was precisely what he'd felt while doing them, and especially right afterward.

Before bed, Brimm read from a book of stories by Anton Chekhov given him by Muriel, selected by her for improving his mind. It seemed to him that Chekhov was overly concerned with old men and young girls, and the stories were rather dry and understated. Yet Brimm also found that they had a good cumulative effect, and he read for almost two hours. When he finally went to bed, images from a story about an old man dying at sea haunted him and kept him awake: a corpse wrapped in sailcloth, resembling a carrot, slid off a plank into the deep. "Blessed be the Name of the Lord," intoned a priest. "As it was in the beginning, is now, and ever shall be."

It was warm, humid, and despite the night's windlessness, the awful stench of the paper mills up north had traveled down the coast and mixed with the more usual bay scents.

"About this face," Muriel said to Brimm in a fragment of dream, "does it speak to you?"

And then he was wide awake again.

He threw back the covers, rose from the bed, pulled on his trousers, shirt and slippers, and went back into the living room. He opened the front door and stood for a long minute staring out through the screen. He moved onto the porch and walked to its edge, where he could get a look at the sky, which was overcast, but with a moon up there somewhere brightening everything. "Oberammergau Passion players," he said aloud. That was something he would like to have a picture of—Muriel in her teens, on stage in a religious melodrama. He could almost hear Pontius Pilate speaking his tragic lines with great biblical and cosmopolitan dignity, followed by the multitude of locals shouting back at him in their boorish, gluey Southern drawls.

On one side of the cottage stood the big white colonial house, now completely dark, where the beautiful young Cuban woman lived with her scientist husband from the college. On the other side, piny woods, and more woods out back. Down at the end of the block, where a path led through the pines and onto the golf course, an incandescent streetlight still glowed, though the better part of its light had long been eclipsed by an intruding pine branch. A quiet, lonely place—a place, Brimm had noticed, popular with college kids, who parked under the pines on weekends. He had seen the cars (there were never more than two at a time), and though in the dark it was impossible to see anything other than the cars themselves, Brimm had sometimes stood on the porch or at a cottage window watching for long stretches, as though these vigils might connect him somehow to whatever liveliness went on inside the cars. It was no wonder he felt ashamed, since these acts of voyeurism, and of isolation, were the acts of a lonely man. Wasn't it, after all, shameful to be lonely? Shameful to have ended up lonely?

Part of the problem, he realized, was that he hadn't managed to become the least bit interested in doing any of the things he'd imagined himself doing. He'd been to the seed store, for example, spent a fortune on seeds, but the preparation of the soil and getting down on one's hands and knees in the dirt—it all seemed like something he should hire someone to do. He'd purchased a rod and reel, which now stood in a corner of the garage, but he hadn't yet organized a tackle box. Organization was what seemed to daunt him. The idea of most things amply appealed, but the required arrangements always raised the question of whether the reward could possibly justify the effort.

He scrutinized the sky again, which reminded him suddenly of a black-and-white shot developing in the tray, just as the first gray starts to fade in, before any specific shape materializes. As he stepped off the porch and walked into the dark street, he told himself, I have had an original thought, and he resolved to tell Muriel about it.

He walked down the street to the path's entrance and stood under the streetlight's amorphous pool. He thought of Jimmy Durante, closing his television show, moving from one spotlight to the next, tipping his hat, saying, "Good night, Mrs. Calabash, wherever you are."

On the path through the woods he kicked a beer can into the darkness, and when he emerged onto the fairway, he saw what he'd had in mind to see: sleeping on the gentle dome of the hill, a large gathering of white and gray gulls.

"My old friends," Brimm said as he started up the slight incline.

None of the birds stirred until he was quite close, and even then none took flight. Reluctantly, they simply stood and moved away, clearing a narrow trail for him to pass through. Briefly Brimm thought of Moses. Then he felt happy, imagining with his photographer's eye the spectacle of an old man crossing through an ocean of gulls under diffused moonlight.

At the top of the hill he stood gazing at the sparse lights of downtown and at the isolated, shimmering pinpoints of light in the bay—shrimp boats, which, with the horizon invisible at this hour, seemed to float in midair. As he headed down toward the green and the bunker where earlier that evening he and Muriel had seen the dog madly digging in the sand, Brimm found himself again fixated by images from the Chekhov story: iron weights had been sewn into the sailcloth with the corpse, to make it heavier . . . soldiers and crewmen stood around with bared heads, crossing themselves and looking away at the waves . . . "It was strange that a man should be sewn up in sailcloth and should soon be flying into the sea," Chekhov observed. "Was it possible that such a thing might happen to anyone?"

And that was when Brimm saw the bones, which appeared almost to glow in the moonlight, strewn about near the spot where the dog had been digging. "Quite a little cache," he said aloud, stopping several feet from the edge of the bunker and then turning back in the direction of the path home.

As he entered the dark patch of trees near his street, he acknowledged that it was of course his own death, the prospect of it, that was at the bottom of his preoccupation with Chekhov's gloomy story. He had never had a suitable picture for his own death, nothing that rang quite true, and now that he seemed to have found one, how unlikely it was: a coarse-white carrot-shaped cadaver flying through the air toward water.

Four

WHAT COULD BE so urgent about an old bone Muriel couldn't begin to imagine. When she arrived at the cottage, at almost ten, she found him in an agitated state and not a little bit exhausted. That was what agitation did to you when you were old. When you were young, excitement could bring a certain vibrancy, but when you were old, it only made you tired, as if the vehicle could no longer bear the load. When she saw Francis, the first thing she thought was how old he looked.

Earlier that morning, before he had telephoned, she'd hoped to sort out her thoughts, over coffee with Billie. Billie had a knack for putting things in perspective, probably a consequence of her long marriage to Ned, an affliction that made philosophical crises pale by comparison. (Muriel wasn't sure that a philosophical crisis was what she herself was having, but it felt like one.) "You're old, Muriel," Billie had said over coffee, and that, for Billie at least, was the last word. It was typical of Billie to say something undeniably true, but it had left Muriel feeling dismissed, and later, while she was getting dressed to go over to Francis's, Muriel thought Billie's terseness on this subject, and on a few others lately, showed her less pithy than merely abrupt. She hadn't even given Muriel a chance to tell about the strange business with the vanity mirror, or about the beckoning upstairs rooms.

After Billie went back home, Muriel forced herself to sit at the vanity as she brushed her hair and applied her modest makeup, mentally daring the mirror's broad oval to conjure anything the least bit unusual. But then, when the mirror behaved itself, obeying her as it were, she felt oddly, keenly disappointed. As she went out through the front door, inserting her key in the lock and turning it, she thought she faintly heard her mother's voice, suggesting that she, Muriel, needed to have her head examined. The echo of this imperative (one of her mother's favorites) seemed to linger with her on the short drive over to Francis's, and she bravely allowed herself to imagine going up the stairs and into each of the upper rooms of the old house. She thought this was, after all, the kind of exercise an analyst would put her through were she actually to go to one. "Where are you now?" she imagined the therapist (a kind, older woman) saying.

"I'm standing at the nursery door."

"Don't be afraid to look inside, Muriel. What do you see?"

"Nothing," Muriel answered. "It's empty."

Muriel did this for each room, five in all, the answer always coming back the same. Empty rooms, precisely as she had expected. By the time she arrived at Francis's cottage, she was in a much better frame of mind.

"Have you been drinking?" she said to him from the concrete walkway that cut his small front yard in two.

He sat, out of the already hot sun, in a rocker on the porch. "Come up here at once and sit down, Muriel," he said to her, patting the seat of a ladder-back chair next to him. "I have much to tell."

She sat next to him. "What have you been doing, Francis?" she asked him.

"I don't know what you mean," he said.

"I mean that if you haven't been drinking, you've been doing something else," she said. "You look terrible."

"Well, I'm not terrible," he said. "In fact I've never been better. You can read all about it in the afternoon paper."

"What *are* you talking about?" she asked.

"Something extraordinary has happened, Muriel," he said, sliding forward onto the edge of his seat.

She looked at him. How was it possible that she could see in this creased, drooping countenance the excitement of a young boy as he barged into her pine-paneled bedroom, shouting some sad news about the mysterious poisoning of a neighbor's cat, a tragic drowning in the bay, a train wreck? Calamity had always fascinated and thrilled him, the more colossal the better. The most gruesome of his photographs, expertly crafted, showed soldiers in foxholes with untreated wounds quickened by infection, sick or injured children in hospital beds, anguished women prostrate over coffins.

Muriel breathed deeply and said to him, "It was a human bone, wasn't it?"

He raised his eyebrows, apparently impressed. "Four, to be precise," he said. "Three vertebrae and *part* of a femur."

"How ghastly! Where are they now?"

"Well of course the police have been here and taken them away," said Francis. "You've missed everything, Muriel. The reporters, the photographers, the—"

"I'm ashamed of you, Francis. You're actually giddy over this."

"You're not ashamed of me," he said. "You're jealous."

"Don't be ridiculous," she said.

Francis gazed out at the pines across the street. After another moment he said, "I confess that I feel somehow ... somehow chosen for this."

"What on earth can you possibly mean by that?" said Muriel, surprising even herself with her sudden sharpness.

"I guess you wouldn't understand," he said at last, sliding back into the seat of the rocker and beginning to rock thoughtfully.

Muriel allowed a long silence to pass between them, and then, looking straight out at the street in front of her, said, "Don't be so glum, Frankie. Of course I understand."

He smiled at her warmly and began telling all that had

25

happened—how he'd been unable to sleep and so decided to take a walk on the golf course; about the gulls sleeping on the hill; and about noticing but not paying any mind to the bones near the bunker. Later, back at the cottage and sound asleep, he'd been wakened at around 4 a.m. by the gulls, and when he opened his eyes the face of the young French girl was already fully formed (in color, he noted), strangely constant yet changing with every moment, like something seen through water. As usual, she lingered only for a few seconds and then was gone, always gone before he achieved full wakefulness. He had rubbed his eyes and listened for a minute to the gulls' plaintive recital, then sat up on the edge of the bed.

"I can't explain exactly how," he said to Muriel, "but I feel that somehow she left me this insight. She *imparted* it to me."

"What insight?" asked Muriel.

"Well," he said, "that the bones I'd seen a while earlier were human bones. It hadn't occurred to me until then. And I'll tell you something else—"

"Wait," said Muriel. "Don't tell me anything else. How exactly did she impart it to you, Frankie?"

"I don't know," he said. "That's what I'm telling you—I can't say exactly, but I'm sure that she was . . . instrumental."

"Instrumental." Muriel repeated the word, nodding. Then, looking at him pitifully, a bit urgently, she said, "Frankie. You didn't tell any of this to the police, did you? Or to the papers."

"Of course not," he said. "Not about my girl on the ceiling. Don't worry, Muriel. I haven't sullied the family name."

Relieved, Muriel rose to go into the house. "Well, I think I'll make us some tea," she said, an excuse for getting away from him.

On her way through Francis's small living room, she noticed the cardboard crate sitting on the floor next to his armchair. Lying on top was an old *Picture Post*, opened to the famous photograph of the Normandy village street after the armistice. Muriel, bracing herself on the wide arm of the chair, knelt to the floor and examined the picture. "Yes, there you are," she said to the young woman with the shaved head and the baby in her arms. But then, as Muriel lifted the magazine to get a closer look, she discovered beneath it a yellowed eight-by-ten of herself, in which she wore a sleeveless dress of black silk she'd bought in Chinatown while she'd been visiting Francis in New York. It had to have been forty years ago at least. She quickly put the magazine aside and took the picture gingerly in both hands, drawing it to her face and meeting, as it were, her own eyes. Suddenly she felt quite dizzy, laid it aside too, and pulled herself up off the floor into the chair as best she could. Francis appeared at the screen door and asked through the screen, "Are you all right?"

Muriel, slouched half in and half out of the big chair, heaved herself up straighter. "I'm fine," she said.

"You're pale as a ghost," he said.

"I'm fine," she repeated with emphasis.

And thank God he moved back away from the door then, because Muriel had just begun to notice how lovely Francis's little room was—quiet, peaceful, welcoming—and though it didn't entirely make sense to think of a room this way, she had just thought of the room as compassionate, which was something like the way she had felt looking at her younger self in the Chinese dress a moment ago, and she was about to cry.

Five

MURIEL SAT WITH the cats in the parlor's front window seat, looking out at the empty lot across the boulevard. The cats, the immense striped alley cat and the younger, smaller Siamese, often played their stalking games over there among the high weeds, but what had begun as a sunny day had changed in the afternoon to rain, the kind of thunder-showers off the Gulf that Muriel had once been fond of but that now made her joints ache. Many years ago, when she and Francis were growing up, a big, boisterous family of nine had lived across the way—seven children spanning ten or so years, all girls except for the two youngest, twin boys. Fayson had been the family name, now all trace of them, including the huge old clapboard house itself, long gone. The children had dispersed to other Florida towns or cities, the house, which had sat empty for a number of years, eventually burned by an arsonist and cleared away, leaving the abandoned lot to overgrow with cornflowers and goldenrod. Previously, Muriel had recalled the Faysons as she had perceived them in her youth, as a contented family without flaw: the handsome father on the front lawn tosses one of the happily squealing twins into the air; in the porch swing, the younger girls play a rhyming game, laugh and tease one another good-naturedly; the mother, dressed in a smart blue suit, emerges from the front door with her parasol and handbag, off to an important luncheon; the aroma of baking bread drifts out from the kitchen windows as, inside, one of the older girls sings "I Won't Say I Will."

The Faysons had put that side of themselves forward, an animated felicity, but Muriel now assumed—as she hadn't when she was a girl—that she had idealized them, and that every family had its troubles. Scratch the surface of any family and you would find the ugly source of pain and disappointment: the middle child can't learn to read, the oldest daughter has to be secreted away for an abortion, the father drinks too much, the mother's a hypochondriac. Experience had taught Muriel this bit of wisdom, and she knew it to be mostly true, yet if indeed the Faysons had suffered any of these problems that all families suffer, she had never chosen to see it. On those rare occasions when she looked across the boulevard, beyond the median strip's crape myrtles and into the past, she saw the twin boys in short pants climbing over the porch railing, calling out to her cheerfully in their high voices as she walked along on the opposite side, "Where's your shoes, Muriel? Where's your shoes?"

But today—after a morning beginning with Billie's off-hand remarks over coffee and ending at Francis's cottage, a morning so unsettling to her that she had lapsed into generalizing, more than once thinking stupidly, after lunch, that *life* was unsettling; and after drawing the drapes for a nap but kept awake by thunder and lightning—she had moved to the window seat, stroked the cats absent-mindedly for a while, and begun looking out at the empty lot across the way. Now she pressed the heels of her palms against her eyes and said aloud, "Oh, I give up!" By which she meant that she would succumb to the undertow of recollection prompted recently by Francis and summon that Sunday afternoon when Dr. Brimm had made such a scene about her and Frankie's going to the beach with the Faysons.

The bishop had visited the church that day, she recalled. While the congregation stood and faced the back of the nave, the bishop knocked loudly on the door three times, then entered, wearing his bright red robes and tall white miter, blessing the building and everyone in it. Quite a long service ensued, full of "smells and bells," as Dr. Brimm used to say, and including the Great Thanksgiving and a rambling sermon. Muriel appreciated the bishop's visit and the pomp it brought, but she also worried that the Faysons, with whom she and Frankie were to go to the beach that afternoon, and who attended the Presbyterian church with its short, pared-down service, would be kept waiting. When at last the Eucharist was over, Muriel was given permission to skip coffee hour and run home with Frankie. Once there, she told Frankie to hurry up and change, and she herself slipped into her swimsuit and terry-cloth beach coat. She could recall the swimsuit she wore: a red and green floral print that tied behind the neck.

Frankie remained in the Faysons' front yard with the twins as Muriel ran inside to announce her and Frankie's readiness and to apologize for the delay. But she found no one waiting impatiently inside the parlor. She smelled tobacco smoke and followed it to the kitchen door. There she saw the handsome father, who had served in the navy and was called Captain Fayson, sitting alone at the breakfast table smoking a cigar. He greeted her with his usual warmth. The captain's warmth was restorative to Muriel in a general way, and she had found herself thinking about it occasionally that summer as she sunbathed on a bamboo chaise longue in her own backyard. Considering his warmth, she excused the cigar and the tattoos of mermaids on Captain Fayson's arms, and as he opened those arms toward her that Sunday, greeting her, she naturally stepped into them. Once there, she saw that her standing and his sitting put her at some unusual intersections, and she was comforted when he turned her around and drew her down into his lap. He kissed her cheek and began bouncing her up and down, saying, "Why, Muriel, you look today as if you're just about ready for anything!"—which made her think briefly of summer sports, tennis, swimming, and so on, and in any case she was happy to be understood as ready, since only minutes ago readiness was what she'd been most worried about.

30

No explanation was ever given for Dr. Brimm's extreme behavior that afternoon. Muriel recalled her father's silhouette in the Fayson kitchen's screen door, and the way his red necktie seemed to bleed into view as he entered and quickly—too quickly—approached. She remembered him jerking her rudely away by the wrist, Captain Fayson's plea ("Henry, don't go blowing up over nothing"), the scraping of chair legs across the linoleum, and most shocking of all, Dr. Brimm's taking a swing at the captain with his one good arm.

At home, she was sent to her room, in tears, where she spent the afternoon on her bed reading, never changing out of her swimsuit. At dinner, she went to the table still wearing the swimsuit—as a kind of vague protest—and was sent back upstairs to change.

This occurred in the summer of 1928. The Pines Roxy had yet to show its first talkie. The *Graf Zeppelin* had yet to cross the Atlantic. Muriel was thirteen, an age at which two girls she knew from school, who came from the poor white section of Pines, had actually got married and soon had babies.

Now it seemed to Muriel that she'd almost seen these events as she recalled them, as if they were painted on the silver canvas of the rain outside the window—an expression that so pleased her when she thought of it that she slipped into a meditation about why she had never realized her youthful dream of becoming a novelist. Clearly she lacked the novelist's temperament, though she might have been able to develop it had she tried. She definitely had the artist's keen eye. She'd always been one to tell what things looked like—a talent she'd employed often at the Raphael School—an exceptional ability to describe a thing so a blind friend could tell what she meant. Blind friend—there was a surprising, nearly charming phrase too. Well, that was how she'd thought of them; never as underlings of any sort, but as friends. And these friendships were as good as anyone could want. Strange, though, that none had ever continued past graduation. That had been the dominant rhythm at the Raphael School: you formed connections of a finite duration and stood in place as the annual commencement exercises down by the riverbank quietly severed them. But Muriel steered her mind past this craggy spot and back to her ability to describe things, thinking that she was happy at least to have been useful in this lifetime, and that she would just have to contribute to the literary stream in another.

She pulled the big striped alley cat into her lap, softly pronouncing its name, Henry, after her stern father, the general practitioner. Outside the window, the Ottos were struggling through the downpour toward Muriel's porch, sharing a single beige raincoat held like a tarpaulin over their heads. Muriel caught sight of them just as Billie wrenched the coat away from Ned and Ned wrenched it back, a variation on the comic territorial battle involving bedcovers. She went to the door smiling, pleased at their arrival—she would be taken out of herself again—but also surprised that she had emerged from these last few minutes of reverie and reflection not nearly so disagreeably as she might have expected.

"Well!" Billie shouted in the entry hall, shaking the fingers of both hands rapidly down toward the floor.

"Yes, well!" said Ned. He slung the wet coat over the newel post, produced from the back pocket of his trousers a rain-speckled copy of the Pines *Crier* (the afternoon paper), unfurled it, and held it up so that Muriel stared directly into her brother Francis's nearly life-size, black-and-white face, under which a caption read: "Pines Native Uncovers Bones, Grisly Scenario."

The next few minutes were spent clearing the Ottos' fogged eyeglasses, and Muriel made a pot of coffee—decaffeinated, since it was already past four. (Even Ned, who dozed at all odd hours, had trouble sleeping at the proper times.) When Ned had confronted Muriel with the *Crier*, she'd tried to give back to him her best poker face, but she hadn't quite managed. She'd said, "Oh, that's Francis," a stupid thing to say, which had delighted Ned, since he'd apparently seen in it his success at startling her.

While the coffee brewed, Muriel remained alone in the kitchen and read the short newspaper article. The reporter had described Francis as a "noted photojournalist, now retired," and "brother to lifetime Pines resident Muriel Brimm." Her own claim to fame, Muriel thought: having stayed in one place for three quarters of a century.

She loaded up a wooden tray with the coffee things but discovered that, once loaded, it was too heavy for her to carry into the parlor. Out of some feminine habit, she called Ned in to do it, but since Ned's stroke three years earlier, his hands shook so that he had trouble enough managing a cup, let alone a tray.

Billie, the most robust of them, had no trouble at all. *"Grisly,"* she said, placing the tray on the table in the parlor and moving the newspaper off the tray onto the arm of a nearby chair.

"Yes," said Ned to Muriel, widening his eyes ridiculously. "And to think that it could have been one of us."

This had not in the course of things occurred to Muriel. In fact she realized she hadn't given much thought at all to the victim whose bones Francis had found, except briefly when she'd scolded him about his giddiness over it.

"Don't be silly, Ned," she said. "Why would you say such a thing?"

"Well, why not?" he said, slighted at being deemed unqualified as a victim of fatal dismemberment.

"I just don't see why your mind would leap to such a thing," she said to him. "I mean, I suppose you can read any article in the paper, any at all, and say it could have been one of us."

"I think what Ned means," said Billie, passing Muriel a cup with a spoon resting in its saucer, "is that when this sort of thing happens, one always thinks, There but for the grace of God go I."

"That's not at all what I always think," said Muriel.

"You were *on* that golf course," said Ned. "Just last evening." He pointed to the newspaper whose article referred to the walk that Francis and Muriel had taken yesterday evening.

"Yes, well, I suppose hundreds of people were on the golf course in the last few weeks."

"Yes," said Ned, "and it could have been any one of them."

Muriel rolled her eyes. "I think we should change the subject," she said.

"Change the subject?" said Ned. "Why do you think we're over here? We came over here to talk about the murder."

"Wasn't it smart of Francis to recognize the bones as human?" said Billie, taking the available leather club chair, where she could see her own house out the side window. "I'm not at all sure that I would have. If it had been me, I would have just thought *bones* and let it go at that. I think if it had been me, I would have . . ."

Muriel heard only the first of Billie's remarks, about Francis's being smart, which caused her to reflect on what Francis had told her—that in fact he hadn't recognized the bones as human, but that the vision of the French girl had somehow "imparted" this insight to him—and it now seemed clear to Muriel that she had been too hasty to conjecture, originally, that this phenomenon on the bedroom ceiling, whatever it was, might make some spiritual sense, that in fact it made no sense at all, spiritual or otherwise, and that it really wasn't very different from an old man in a *home* somewhere thinking he was Napoleon Bonaparte.

"Good heavens, Muriel," she heard Billie saying, "you're a thousand miles away. Ned, will you answer the door. Muriel's a thousand miles away. Muriel, there's someone at the door."

* * *

Muriel had forgotten that Deirdre, the girl who came three days a week to help out around the house, had changed one of her days to Saturday. At nineteen, Deirdre, who seemed to have skipped childhood entirely, had already embarked on what she called her new life, which consisted of staying away from drugs, alcohol, and men; putting herself through college; and never letting herself become too hungry, angry, lonely, or tired (a formula from one of her "programs" for overcoming addictions). When she arrived in the rain, she was greeted by Ned, who immediately inquired as to whether or not she had heard about the hideous murder.

"Yeah, I heard about it," Deirdre said.

"Aren't you frightened?" said Billie from the parlor.

"Not much," she said, whipping her long brown hair out of a plastic rain cap she'd been wearing.

Ned said, "There's a maniac running loose. It could easily have been *you* who was killed out on that golf course."

"I doubt it," Deirdre said in her worldly-wise way. "I haven't come this far to end up in somebody's homemade stew."

The bit about the stew visibly shocked both Ned and Billie, but made Muriel smile.

That night at bedtime, it made Muriel smile again as, lying on her back, she reached for the switch to turn off the lamp. She had just finished reading the Scripture lessons for tomorrow's church service, one of which was the passage in Proverbs that included the verse "Forsake the foolish, and live; and go in the way of understanding," advice that young Deirdre seemed already to be exemplifying.

Dreamily, Muriel resolved to make an appointment for Francis to talk to the new rector of the church; it was necessary for him to get some spiritual advice.

Then she allowed her thoughts to follow a thread having to do with forsaking foolishness, and before long she found herself absolutely alone in the world, without friends, without church, without even herself; she stood somewhere dark

35

and confined, her arms pressed tightly to her sides, unable with certainty to recall her own name, mumbling something about foolishness being all we've got . . .

This small terror, dredged up by her subconscious, returned her to full wakefulness so that she might better abide the loneliness it left behind. On her way to the medicine chest, she chastised herself for her rainy-afternoon, window-seat reveries. When she had been Deirdre's age, she was hopelessly in love with the cigar-smoking, tattooed father of seven children who lived across the street. It annoyed her now to think that perhaps that sad situation had had its roots, its rebellious seed, in her own father—not just in what he'd withheld from her as his daughter, but most vigorously in his disapproval of Captain Fayson. Muriel had *known* that something like this night-owl dejectedness would be the result of her letting in the past—she'd seen it quite clearly yesterday, on the unwelcoming face of Joe Letson as she crossed the Little Yustaga Bridge.

She took one of the Seconal capsules that were so effective at knocking her out and returned to bed. Soon she fell into a deep, dreamless sleep. But near dawn, as the drug wore off, she dreamt she was sitting in the old armory downtown, among a throng of people who had come to see Jesus, who was back on earth. Jesus, already seated in a lotus position near the middle of the flower-strewn stage, was surrounded by Eastern-looking holy men. He himself looked like an Eastern holy man, something like a hippie, white-robed and feminine, with long, flowing hair. Muriel watched as a woman with a young child approached the rim of the stage, carrying what appeared to be a bouquet of flowers wrapped in white paper twisted into a cone. When the woman reached the place where Jesus sat, she turned the point of the cone toward him, thrust her hand into the flowers, and pulled the trigger of a revolver that was hidden there, spattering fragments of Jesus's brain against the back wall of the stage. Muriel started instantly awake, not at so horrible a sight but at the amazing sound of the gun blast.

She had never heard anything so loud. There had never *been* anything so loud, not since the beginning of the universe, pieces of which were still flying apart.

Six

THE PHOTOGRAPH WAS a horror, a hodgepodge of fleshy pouches, debatably human, but Francis found the caption evocative: *Native* and *Bones* together gave it a nice jungle flavor; add to that *Grisly Scenario*, and you had something with a jungle flavor that would one day be playing at the cinema multiplex.

"Keep me informed" had been his last words to the policeman who'd shown up at the front door early that morning. The detective, a young man with thick glasses, who looked to Brimm like a black version of the ninety-seven-pound weakling in the old Charles Atlas ads, had nodded his assent, but now, when Brimm thought back, he felt certain that the young man had been humoring him. In reality, the police had no further use for Brimm, and by afternoon (after Muriel's queer visit) his high had worn off. By supper he was thinking how this single day had been, in miniature, like his career: a brief moment of notoriety (in the late 1940s, with his scores of photographs of the armistice revelry in England and France), followed by each subsequent effort falling into what he called "the world's great yawn" (a New York museum had brought out a book of his work in the sixties, but only a handful sold). Now, as he stood in the dark at the cottage window, looking out at the windows of the house next door, he saw that his desperate sense of "chosenness" in the morning had become, at night, something like self-pity.

Keep me informed, indeed.

The windows of the house next door glowed with great enthusiasm, as if a party were going on inside, but Brimm had ascertained that the young Cuban woman was, as she was so often, alone. Shortly after arriving in Pines, Brimm had read in the *Crier* that the Cuban woman's husband, the scientist, had apparently come into his own at the ripe and reasonable age of about sixty-five—that he'd been one of many astronomers who had witnessed, a year earlier, an enormous solar flare erupt from a group of sunspots on the east limb of the sun, a flare that released more energy in about nine minutes than humans had consumed throughout all of history, and now he'd abandoned his post at the college to travel around the country talking about it. Why he didn't take his beautiful young wife with him on these travels Brimm didn't know, but Brimm had deduced from observation that she might have refused to go, and that she was possibly a woman whose refusals were not easily challenged. From Brimm's distance, she appeared fairly independent-minded—like him, a kind of loner. As far as he could tell, she had no particular work of her own, and left the house mainly on shopping ventures, to the market or to the department stores in the mall downtown. He had never seen her visited by any friend, male or female. Every Tuesday morning, a crew of college boys arrived with lawn mowers and rakes to tend the yard, and she would often stroll out onto the front lawn to speak to them, not to be sociable but to give instructions. She would usually wear a long silky dressing gown, her raven hair already pulled back severely into a bun, and as she turned to reenter the house, the boys would exchange glances, raise their eyebrows, remove their baseball caps and fan themselves.

Brimm thought his large investment for so small a return was the most humiliating aspect of his voyeurism in her direction—he waited for such long stretches of time for no more than a glimpse. And since the whole exercise was only vaguely sexual—the kitchen and dining room windows were all that were accessible to him—he wasn't sure what exactly he was after. Mostly he'd seen her passing fully clothed through the dining room, and sometimes, late at night, using a bright silver watering can on a few plants in the kitchen windows. Occasionally, at dusk, he had seen her set the dining room table, a task accomplished, to his thinking, with unusual grace.

He easily recognized his behavior in this matter as vestigial of his bygone profession, but he was less quick to acknowledge that he'd never felt lonely or ashamed behind the lens of a camera. Intrusive, invasive, impertinent, even exploitative, yes, but in the service of a higher cause, and not lonely or shameful. He moved away from the window and through the dark to his own kitchen, turned on the overhead light, and went to the cabinet over the refrigerator where he kept a good bottle of Armagnac. Of course, in the end, the spying was only a symptom of the truly mortifying thing, the firm yet unarticulated need behind it. He poured some brandy into a short glass, burned his throat with too large a gulp, then allowed himself to depict precisely in his thoughts what had only wafted through faintly in the afternoon: that the young woman next door, seeing his photograph in the newspaper, would grow curious and be drawn to him. Even while he felt degraded by this childish wish, he was glad somehow for having made it distinct in his own thinking.

At bedtime he read a long, terrible story in the Chekhov collection, a bleak, indefinite tale that ended with the drowning of a baby. As he drifted to sleep, his mind wandered on to the human skeleton, to the naming of the bones, and soon the Latin terms seemed to refer to rooms in an enormous building somewhere. A woman's voice asked him to walk on through the cranium, where there were numerous potted plants, and to wait for the doctor in the east mandible.

Near dawn, the gulls out on the golf course awakened him. When he opened his eyes, he saw the face of the bald girl on the ceiling. He felt her penetrating sadness pass through him, like something cold and thick in his blood, and he sat up quickly, lowering his feet to the floor and wiping his eyes. When he looked again, the girl's face had gone, as if startled away, and Brimm lay down on his back, placing one hand over his heart, which pumped so hard it seemed to shake the bed.

He slept deeply into the morning. It was only after he'd awakened, gone into the kitchen, and started the coffee that he recalled the unsettling experience of the early hours, the immense sadness of the poor girl with the baby. When the telephone rang near where he stood, he shuddered for a moment before answering with the words "Yes, Muriel?"

"Why Frankie, how did you know it was me?" she said, obviously pleased.

"Because you're the only one who ever calls me, Muriel," he said.

"Well, you needn't sound quite so disappointed," she said. "I have some good news."

"What is that?"

"I've just come from the early service at church and our new rector has agreed to talk to you tomorrow morning. That's Monday. If for any reason you're unable to—"

"What on earth are you talking about, Muriel?"

"Francis," she said, "I'm talking about spiritual advice. Of which you are in dire need."

"Spiritual advice," he said.

"Yes," she said. "Spiritual advice."

Following a long pause, during which Brimm observed, as if from a distance, his feelings advance from resentment, through resignation, and on to gratitude, he said, "What time in the morning?"

"At eight-thirty, Frankie," Muriel said, plainly stunned by his easy acquiescence. After a pause, she asked him if he would like her to bring him some lunch today.

"I wouldn't mind your bringing me some breakfast, actually."

"Breakfast?" she said.

"Yes," he said. "I had a bad night."

She volunteered cinnamon rolls from the bakery in town, which he said would be acceptable.

A clergyman wouldn't have been his first choice (nor cinnamon rolls, for that matter), but charity was charity, he did feel ready for a confidential setting, and Muriel happened to have caught him at the right moment. Immediately, his prejudices about priests began surfacing—they were vain, ambitious, latently homosexual or womanizing, meddlesome, alcoholic—but Brimm resolved to strive for disinterestedness. After all, there were exceptions in every category, he himself representative in the category of septuagenarians. He had not become an old geezer, for example, who told war stories, gazing into space, grasping for details, and wearing a listener's patience thin. When he saw the priest tomorrow, he would say what he had to say in an objective style and listen objectively to the response. Brimm had been around enough to know that even Mozart was something of a jackass, that useful things came from unlikely sources.

He took a cup of coffee to the front porch. Yesterday's storms had left behind a cloudless blue sky and a pleasant breeze blowing off the bay. The Sunday paper lay folded on the sidewalk, near the street. Brimm stood at the edge of the porch wearing his robe and slippers, squinting and breathing in the morning's piny scent.

Before looking at the newspaper, he wanted to organize his thoughts on the subject of the golf course business. First, it was obvious that the victim had been dismembered somewhere else and carried in pieces to the golf course for a speedy burial; the sand trap was chosen because it could be dug easily and quickly, and because the sand wouldn't show a fresh grave. Second, it was likely that the rest of the skeleton would be found nearby. Third, the size of the dissevered femur suggested that the victim was either a woman or a young person. And fourth (this was pure instinct), there was a good chance that an excavation of the golf course would reveal the bones of more than one victim. One thing eluded him, however. If the body or body parts had been buried in the bunker long enough for all flesh to decompose, leaving bare bones, why had the dog (or some other animal) only just now discovered it? That detail made no sense.

When Brimm opened the paper, he scanned the story while still standing on the sidewalk; there was only a rehashing of what had already been reported the day before, with no new information. On page 14, where the story continued from the front page, was a small photograph of Brimm, even more unflattering than yesterday's and so much like a mug shot that readers were bound at first glance to take Brimm for the apprehended psychopathic killer. As he turned back toward the cottage, a black-and-white police car cruised slowly by on the street. Its driver, uniformed, though otherwise looking like a teenager with a crewcut, waved to Brimm and smiled. Something about this overly congenial greeting echoed yesterday's unlikely detective, who had patronized Brimm at the end of the interview, and Brimm decided to go inside and dress; Muriel would be disgraced to find him outdoors in his pajamas on a Sunday morning. As he mounted the porch, he thought he heard piano music in the distance—Chopin or Liszt—but when he paused to listen, it was gone.

"I never formally forgave you," said Muriel to Brimm a while later on the porch. She referred to an ugly episode of nearly thirty years ago in which she thought her brother had sided against her with the enemy.

"As I recall," said Brimm, "I only attempted to interject a grain of reality, and you treated me like a criminal, a Judas."

"Oh, good Lord, Francis," she said, "I do hope you aren't about to tell me that you were right and I was wrong. You'll make me angry all over again."

Brimm thought she looked much better today. Yesterday,

when he'd stepped to the screen door and seen her kneeling on his living room floor, looking at an old picture and about to cry, he thought maybe her demise had finally set in. He considered Muriel's demise in imminent terms—it could begin any day, at any hour—and, overdue, it was apt to be sudden and steep. This was exactly opposite to how he envisioned his own, which was something like the evenly spaced tones of a descending musical scale, perfectly pitched. Brimm's punctual withdrawal from the screen door yesterday had been polite, deferential, but driven, too, by fear: when Muriel's demise set in, he hoped it wouldn't be on his living room floor.

He was glad to see some color back in her face, but he was sorry to have brought up the subject of her obsession with the clergy. He'd only meant to tease her, and hadn't foreseen her taking off on the incident of so long ago. She'd been about fifty then. She'd become overly devoted to the man who was rector at St. Matthew and the Redeemer, in Pines, and the man's wife, stoked by wine, had confronted Muriel at a wedding reception in St. Matthew's fellowship hall. Everyone had been humiliated by the incident, even the unlucky bride and groom, but Muriel by far the most deeply. The letter she wrote to Brimm, who was on assignment in Jakarta in 1965, prompted him to telephone her once he was back in New York. He had sympathized vastly. But when he tried to show Muriel how some of her behavior toward the priest, even as she herself described it, might be misconstrued, she reacted with the bottomless sense of betrayal peculiar to a person running from the truth. She stayed away from church for almost four full years, until the priest and his wife moved on, a period she later referred to as her time in the wilderness, her exile.

"No, no," Brimm said now. "I wouldn't dare suggest that you were wrong about anything, Muriel. Not thirty years ago, not fifty years ago, not ever."

"Good," she said, and passed him the plate with the rolls. After a pause she said, "Frankie, I've been thinking. The

44

Ottos are all worked up over these bones you found. Do you think we're ... I mean, you and I specifically ... do you think we're in any kind of danger?"

"Danger?" he said. "Why would we be in danger?"

"Well, that's what I said, but then I got to thinking. Our names were in the newspaper after all, for everyone to see."

"But we didn't witness any part of the crime," said Brimm. "He's got no reason to bump *us* off. Besides, I found bones, not a corpse. This had to have happened ages ago. The killer's probably long gone."

"But what if he *isn't* long gone?" said Muriel. "And what if he just enjoys this sort of thing? What if he's just not a very nice person?"

"It wouldn't surprise me if he turned out not to be a nice person," said Brimm.

"Frankie," she said after a moment, "my feelings for that priest were entirely proper. I resent your making me out to be some kind of repressed, neurotic old spinster who—"

"I think," said Brimm, "that it was your actions that brought your feelings into question. I'm afraid people—"

"Oh, what do *people* know?" she said, waving her hand at him in dismissal. "Don't talk to me about *people*."

"Okay," he said, smiling. "I'll ask you a question about us non-people, me and you."

"What?" she said.

Brimm watched a gray squirrel across the street scampering expertly along an electric cable, the considerable distance from one creosote power pole to the next. "I was just wondering," he said. "Do you ever get the feeling that the ground has shifted under your feet and suddenly things aren't what they were even a minute ago?"

She looked at him as if he'd spoken in an unknown tongue, as if he'd said something important but incomprehensible. Finally she said, "I'm really glad you're going to talk to the rector tomorrow, Francis."

"You didn't answer my question," he said.

Now she looked past him, into the distance. "Well, no,"

45

she said irritably. "I don't ever get that feeling. Of course I don't get that feeling. Now, who is that beautiful woman and child walking this way?"

Seven

AS THE YOUNG woman with the boy turned into Francis's walkway, Muriel observed the expression on Francis's face. The old photographer's scrutiny was there, but something else too: he looked as if a dream were coming true.

You couldn't help but admire the young woman's beauty, though she clearly spent a lot of time and money on herself. Her hair was just so, black and twisted somehow, pulled into a neat bun at the nape of her neck, her white sundress and gold sandals expensive looking. In Muriel's opinion, the pink camellia behind one ear was too studied—my lady is beautiful, it said, and Caribbean, and sensual. Muriel thought she noticed a faint aroma of incense as the young woman drew near the porch.

Francis had always been a little odd about women. Fortunately, Muriel hadn't witnessed most of this oddness, since she'd been the steady beacon, ever lighting the way home while he roamed the globe. But in his letters he would sometimes mention that he'd "met a girl," usually a native of whatever place he was visiting. He might add a sentence or two about how lovely the girl was, or how intelligent, or, once or twice, how rich. In some cases he would include a bromide about the depth of his love, the immutability of his devotion. Then he would never again mention the girl and simply ignore any of Muriel's subsequent inquiries. From these symptoms in his letter writing, Muriel deduced a love life for her brother that was promiscuous, including French and Asian prostitutes, and lacking even the dimmest effort toward any kind of commitment. On those occasions when Muriel had visited Francis in New York (where he'd always kept an apartment), she had seen him go slack-jawed over waitresses, shop clerks, and strange women in the streets, but the look in his eye had always been that of a voyeur—he viewed a woman sexually as he viewed her photographically, as an interesting way to pass a few hours. Over the years, whenever Muriel questioned his nomadism in romantic matters, he blamed his general nomadism and quickly changed the subject.

At the edge of the porch, the young woman introduced herself as Claudia Callejas. She soon revealed that she'd been a concert pianist back in Havana, and though she'd recently married the American scientist next door, she'd kept her professional name.

"And what a beautiful name!" Francis exclaimed, and repeated it aloud, reverently. "Isn't that a beautiful name?" he said to Muriel.

"Yes," Muriel said, giving him a sidelong glance.

"And this is my nephew," said Claudia, smiling and placing a hand on each shoulder of the boy, who looked to be about eight or nine. "Nicolás."

"Nicolás!" said Francis.

The boy, she explained, lived in Miami, but would be staying with her for a while in Pines.

"Welcome," said Francis, and stepped to the edge of the porch to shake the boy's hand. "Welcome, my boy!"

Turning to Muriel, Claudia said, "I'm sorry, but my husband told me that Mr. Brimm was not married."

"Your husband told you correctly," said Muriel. "I'm Francis's sister."

"Ah," said the woman. "You are brother and sister."

"Yes," said Muriel.

"We saw your photograph in the newspaper yesterday," she said to Francis, "and I promised Nicolás I would bring him over to meet you."

48

Muriel reflected that the young woman couldn't have read the newspaper article very carefully or she would have known that Francis and she were brother and sister; the article had said so.

Francis asked—you could almost say beseeched—them to stay and have coffee, but Claudia declined, saying she'd also promised the boy a trip to the wharves downtown. As soon as they left, Muriel quietly said, "Really, Francis."

"What do you mean by that?" he said.

"The way you transformed in that young woman's presence."

"Oh, Muriel," he said, "I did not transform."

"You did," she said. "You transformed. You should have seen yourself."

"Oh, but Muriel, tell me truthfully," he said. "Did you ever see a more beautiful woman?"

If she had, she couldn't think of any.

Driving home a bit later, however, she made a more searching effort. If you discounted movie stars and only allowed people you'd actually met or known, there was Marietta Fayson, the youngest daughter of Captain and Mrs. Fayson, who had gone unnoticed in that large family until about the age of seventeen, when she returned home from a summer in the Florida Keys suddenly ravishing. And there had been Mrs. Fayson herself, who had that noble air about her, and wonderful clothes. And exotic Mrs. Schwaub, of the dry goods store on Palmetto Street, in her prime. And Winnie Tutwiler, the soprano who'd sung "Panis Angelicus" in the armory ten Christmases ago. And . . .

Maneuvering the car onto the narrow Little Yustaga Bridge required Muriel's concentration for a moment. In any case—she thought, once on the bridge—it was plain that all was definitely not right with Claudia Callejas's family. Muriel had seen trouble in the young woman's eyes when she explained about the boy's staying with her for a while. School would be starting in another week or two, a strange time for the boy to be embarking on a long visit away from home.

As Muriel slowly steered the car over the bridge, it seemed the day had suddenly become unpleasantly hot, the river unpleasantly muddy, and she noticed something down below, snagged in the middle of the water, something that looked distinctly like a bowler hat. She pulled the Volkswagen into the turnaround on the far side of the bridge and got out. She couldn't have said why she stopped to investigate, except that she hadn't seen a bowler hat in many years, and certainly she'd never seen anything resembling a bowler hat floating in the Yustaga River. A rugged path led down from the corner of the bridge to the water's edge, but Muriel didn't dare try it. All she needed was to slip and twist an ankle and she might be stranded for hours. Besides, she only meant to get a more careful look, not necessarily a closer one.

As she walked toward the center of the old stone bridge, she eyed the bowler hat in midstream, speaking to it in the kind of high voice usually reserved for speaking to young children. "Now, what in the world are you doing down there in that muddy water?" she said, and as if responding to her question, the dark brown hat appeared to turn itself inside out, sending a chill up Muriel's spine. Then the thing in the water collapsed on itself grotesquely, elongated into something hairy and unseemly, and swam away under the bridge.

"A river otter," said Ned a few minutes later in Muriel's parlor. "Or maybe a nutria, something like that."

"Yes," said Billie. "Nothing to worry about, I'm sure, Muriel."

"Worry?" said Muriel. "Do I seem worried?"

"Well, frankly, yes," said Billie. "You do."

"Well, I'm certainly not worried."

"Good," said Billie. "I'm glad. I might be concerned if I thought your screeching into the driveway and running straight to the telephone and calling us to come over here double quick was just because you'd seen a wild animal in the river. I might think you needed to call Dr. Van Buren and see about getting him to adjust your medication."

With this last sentence, Billie cast a glance at Ned, indicating that something like this had already been discussed between the two of them on a prior occasion.

"I did not screech into any driveway," Muriel said. "And just what are you trying to imply about my medication?"

"Imply?" said Billie. "I'm not implying anything."

Later, when Muriel considered this disagreeable scene with Billie, she couldn't think what might have been her own next move had the telephone not rung at that moment. It was Deirdre, calling to say that she had misplaced an amethyst ring and thought she might have left it on the windowsill behind the sink in the kitchen; she sometimes removed it and put it there when she was scrubbing the drip plates of the stove. When Muriel went into the kitchen to check, she found the Siamese cat perched in the windowsill, but no amethyst ring. She returned to the telephone and said as much to Deirdre.

"I wonder, would you mind if I just came over there and looked for it myself?" said Deirdre. "I have a feeling it's in the house somewhere. It's not an expensive ring, but my sponsor in AA gave it to me and I'm having dinner with her tonight."

"Of course you can come look," said Muriel. "I'll help you if you like."

Muriel had hoped the Ottos would take her announcement of Deirdre's imminent arrival as their cue to go home—if she'd known in advance about Billie's foul humor, she'd never have called them over—but when they heard the girl's name, they exchanged another of their tawdry, collusive glances. Billie walked to one of the parlor windows like some actress in an old movie and looked out pensively at the sunshine in the boulevard. "There's something unsavory about that girl," she said dramatically, her back to the room.

"Oh, Billie, really," said Muriel, "I'm afraid you and Ned really must go."

"Did you hear that remark yesterday about the home-made stew?" said Ned. "A warped mind at work there."

"Of course we'll go," said Billie, already aimed at the front door. "Ned," she said, very loud, as if Ned were hard of hearing, which he wasn't, "*now* Muriel wants us to *leave*."

"Beck and call, beck and call," Ned said, straining up out of the club chair.

"God, it's hot!" Muriel heard Billie exclaim out on the sidewalk.

As soon as she closed the door, she turned and placed one hand on the newel post, gazing up the stairs and thinking how stifling it must be up there in those rooms without air conditioning.

She felt tired and regretted Deirdre's coming. She only wanted to draw the drapes, shut out the world, and sleep. She went into the bedroom, and as she passed toward the window, glimpsed herself in the vanity mirror. It seemed a primary and irreparable failing that at midafternoon on a Sunday she'd still not managed to change out of her church clothes. If she were now to lie down in her best summer suit, it would have to be taken to the cleaners for pressing. She directed the vents of the old clattering window unit at the bed, and lay down anyway.

Francis had stated it precisely. The ground had shifted under her feet and things were not what they had been even a moment ago. The unusual experience on the bridge had frightened her—irrationally, she knew, like something in a dream—but she should have kept the whole thing to herself. It occurred to her that Billie had used up her store of empathy on Ned over the years, and now had none left to give to anyone else. Muriel had entered into some kind of uncharted region these last few days, and Billie was simply too unreflective a person, too unrefined in her sensibilities to help Muriel navigate now; she wasn't any longer a person to confide in, and that was too bad. But lying on her back, with the air conditioner blowing directly on her, Muriel moved swiftly down the tunnel of this loss and arrived unexpectedly (and delightedly) at an admiration for her own powers of invention: her previous exchange with the imaginary psychotherapist had been fruitful, so once again she allowed the therapist to conduct a brief interview. In a kind, compassionate voice she asks, "Where are you now, Muriel?"

"I'm upstairs in the hallway," Muriel answers in her imagination, after a brief pause. "But all the doors are closed. It's very warm up here."

"Don't be afraid to open them, Muriel. We'll do one at a time. I'll be with you every step of the way. Now where would you like to begin?"

"I'm not afraid," says Muriel, her eyes closed so that she can see better. "I'll start with my folks' room."

"Maybe we should leave that one until later," says the woman, and Muriel, her eyes still closed, imagines that the woman is reaching out her hand, to console. She wonders why the woman thinks she's so in need of consoling.

"I'm not afraid," says Muriel again, and opens the door.

"Okay," says the therapist. "What do you see inside?"

"Nothing," says Muriel. "It's completely empty."

"Good. Shall we move on?"

"Yes." Muriel opens the next door, Frankie's room, which used to be the nursery.

"What do you see?"

"Nothing," says Muriel. "Empty."

"And the next?"

"Empty."

"And the next?"

"Empty, yes. Completely empty."

"And what about your own room, Muriel?" the therapist asks. "Is it empty too?"

"Yes," says Muriel at first, then, "I think—"

"Can't you see yourself there?" asks the therapist gently, without prodding.

"No," says Muriel at last. "The room is empty."

When Deirdre arrived, she found the ring easily, in the soap dish in the powder room under the front stairs. Then, to Muriel's surprise, the girl threw herself into one of the leather club chairs in the parlor, as if she meant to recuperate from the strain of an arduous journey.

Muriel, standing at the door to the parlor, said, "How are you, Deirdre?"

"Well," Deirdre said, slumped in the chair, "I'm not dead."

"That's good," said Muriel.

"And I'm not in jail."

"That's very good," said Muriel.

"But, it so happens . . . I'm pregnant."

"Oh," said Muriel. "Oh, dear."

"Yeah, that's what I said," said Deirdre. "Or some version thereof."

"Let me get you something to drink and we'll have a talk."

"That would be lovely," Deirdre said. "Do you have any single-malt, twelve-year-old Scotch in the house?"

"I certainly do not," said Muriel.

"Harvey's Bristol Cream?"

"Certainly not."

"A little dessert wine maybe?" asked Deirdre. "Cooking sherry?"

"I'll get you a glass of tea," said Muriel, and went to the kitchen.

Deirdre followed her and sat on one of the stools at the counter, resting her chin in her palms.

"But I thought you'd given all that up," Muriel said to her. "Men, I mean."

"That's just it," Deirdre said. "I have. This is my sordid past coming back to haunt me."

54

"I don't understand," said Muriel.

"Well, I mean this happened three *months* ago."

"Oh," said Muriel. "And what about the father? What does he say about it?"

"The father doesn't have much to say on very many subjects," said Deirdre. "You might say he's kind of post-verbal."

"You have told him, haven't you?"

"I told him," said Deirdre. "But you have to understand, Miss Brimm. He's an on-again off-again drunk. Every once in a while, in a fit of sobriety, he comes to an AA meeting to pick up women. I made the mistake of calling him on the telephone to tell him about the baby, and without actually seeing me he couldn't remember who I was. I had to describe myself in some detail, which was very humiliating under the circumstances."

"Yes, I guess so," said Muriel.

"A light finally went on in his head and he mumbled something unintelligible. I thought he said 'No regrets,' which kind of surprised me. But when I asked him to please repeat what he'd said, it turned out to be 'No rug rats.' "

"No rug rats?"

"Children," said Deirdre. "You know, babies crawling around on the floor. Rug rats."

"Oh," said Muriel. "Deirdre, I guess I just don't understand how you could end up with somebody like that."

"Well, I didn't end up with him. I just went to bed with him. One time."

"But I don't understand how," said Muriel.

Deirdre looked at Muriel carefully, craning her neck. "I'm not sure what you're asking."

"I mean *why*?" said Muriel.

"Oh," said Deirdre. "He was irresistible, Miss Brimm. Unavailable, unemotional, uncommunicative, half brain-dead. Loafers with no socks. Kitchen match stuck between his teeth. I'm a pushover for that sort."

Muriel passed the girl her glass of tea. "What are you going to do, Deirdre?"

Deirdre emptied the glass in one long drink, pumping her throat four or five times. "Thanks," she said, setting the glass down on the counter and standing up. "It wasn't my plan, and it surely isn't my schedule, but I guess I'm going to have a baby." She looked deeply into Muriel's eyes and smiled, then shrugged her shoulders. "The Lord moves in mysterious ways, right?"

The next moment, Muriel was a bit surprised to find herself embracing her young housekeeper in the kitchen, but it felt the natural thing to do, the charitable thing to do for a girl who apparently hadn't forsaken all foolishness to the degree that one imagined.

Muriel couldn't bring herself actually to recite the failures of heart and temperamental weaknesses that impelled her to confession at the end of the day—confession such as it was, to God alone, in her parlor-bedroom—but her shortcomings were well organized in her mind and eager to chant their dark song of remorse. Making an appointment with the rector for Francis that morning, she'd felt outrageously superior to her brother. Greeting the young Cuban woman and her nephew, she'd coveted the attention the woman, and even the boy, directed toward Francis, and she'd been unduly intrigued to note the trouble in the young woman's eyes. She'd been impatient with the Ottos, when all they'd done was answer her bidding. And this by far the worst, she'd felt repulsed by Deirdre and her plight, and philanthropic when consoling the girl. Muriel didn't say any of this aloud—that would have smacked too much of masochism—but in bed she spoke open-eyed to the ceiling. "Most merciful God," she said, ". . . if you are merciful, and I think you are . . . I *hope* you are . . . I confess that I have sinned against you in thought—especially in thought—and in feeling, but also in word and deed, by what I have done, and by what I have left undone. I have not loved you with my whole heart; and quite obviously I have not loved my neighbors as myself. I am truly sorry and I humbly repent. For the sake of your Son Jesus Christ, have mercy on me and forgive me; that I may delight in your will, and walk in your ways ..." She paused here, thinking, Walk in your ways, now there's a tall order. She was sure that if she contemplated it further, she would grow hopeless, so after another moment of silence she shrugged her shoulders and said aloud, "... to the glory of your Name."

She had reflected before that real, deeply felt confession was almost as good as Seconal. She slept soundly into the early morning hours, but was startled awake at around four-thirty by the telephone.

"Muriel Brimm?" the voice said, a youthful, very nasal, backwoodsy voice.

"Yes?"

"You know, Miss Brimm," said the voice, "what's buried ought to stay buried."

"But I—" Muriel began to say, and the line went dead.

She dialed Francis immediately, expecting to rouse him from sleep, but when he answered, after only one ring, he was obviously wide awake.

"Francis," she said. "I've just had the most terrible—"

"Phone call?" he said. "Me too. 'What's buried should stay buried.' "

"Yes," said Muriel, and noticed that the receiver was trembling in her hand. "Frankie," she said, "I'm very frightened."

57

Eight

"YOU SEE, FRANKIE," Muriel said a while later in her kitchen, "I've actually been angry at you these last weeks."

He sat at the counter drinking coffee as she cooked them some breakfast. It was a little before 6 A.M., and Muriel had tied a red-and-white-striped apron over her blue kimono. A bit dumpy but patriotic, Brimm had thought when she greeted him at the door.

Now, at the Formica counter, he noted that the smell of bacon and coffee had filled him with a pleasant sense of belonging, even a kind of fondness for being human. Several times modified, this was the kitchen where he'd eaten breakfast as a boy; the mere fact, unremarked upon, struck him as remarkable.

"Why angry, Muriel?" he said, trying to stay engaged by what she meant to tell him.

He couldn't have explained exactly how or why it had happened, and the irrefutable truth of it embarrassed him, yet the appearance on his porch step yesterday of the concert pianist Claudia Callejas had wrought what felt like an all-encompassing change in his retirement. He'd gone to bed last night with the phrase "my girls" going through his head—by which his head referred to the three important female influences in his current life: the French girl on the bedroom ceiling (to whom he would have to give a name if she meant to take up such persistent residency), his sister Muriel, and now Claudia Callejas. It pleased him to have female influences in his life at this time, and it pleased him to think of them as influences, as emanations flowing toward him, altering the shape of what was left of his future. It seemed to Brimm increasingly certain that this last chapter, his retirement to Pines, had something of a spiritual character, and that spiritual character was by its nature female, like the sea. Despite the odd and unsettling circumstances under which he was awakened at dawn that morning, he had wondered, as he raised his bedroom shade, at his former blindness, not to have noticed the splendor of summer in Pines. Out the single unassuming rectangle of his window he could hear birdsong, the chattering of squirrels, and the occasional whispering of the pines. He could see a gold and silver range of cumulus clouds taking form, the welcoming shade of the woods with its mat of brown straw, a world abounding in order and reason, love, beauty, impending blue sky and sunshine. He'd been dead wrong to have thought himself, in his retirement, as letting go of the world. Plainly he was meant to connect with it in new, more fundamental ways, to probe the deeper connections the world invited when one achieved a slower pace, when one stopped doing something and stood still.

He'd also been mistaken in thinking, even briefly, that the past was the new frontier open to him in repose. What lure could it possibly hold compared with the elegance of the present moment? Getting dressed, he'd felt a kind of physical yearning that demanded exercise, and he resolved to walk downtown, stop in to see Muriel, then kick around a bit, maybe visit the docks.

"*You* are not the right pan for frying bacon in," Muriel was saying at the stove. "You're much too thin."

"Muriel," said Brimm, "if you'd rather talk to the frying pan, I could go in the other room."

"I don't suppose it's really your fault, Francis," she said, ignoring his last remark, "but since you came home, and especially with your constant questioning, I've been increasingly preoccupied with the past. I've never had much regard for the past, as you know. Now suddenly I'm starting to feel haunted by it."

"But Muriel," he said, "I'm all over that already."

"What do you mean?"

"I mean I'm not the least bit interested in the past," he said. "Unless you mean state history or something like that."

"You know very well I don't mean state history, Francis. I mean the *past*."

"It was just a phase I went through, Muriel," he said. "It's only natural that certain memories would start to surface for me back here in Pines, and—"

"Like what?" she said quickly.

"Oh, nothing important," he said.

"Like what?" she repeated.

"Oh, that Passion play you were in as a kid. Things like that."

"What about it?"

"Nothing about it, Muriel, for Christ's sake," he said. "I just recalled it, that's all. I didn't mean to. It just happened. I remembered you on the armory stage and Mother crying in the audience."

"Crying?" she said. "Why was she crying?"

"I don't know, Muriel. I think she found the story of Christ's Passion to be moving. Many people do, you know. But as I said, it was just a phase. My mind was too idle for a while, and now I'm over it."

"That's nice for you," she said.

"Yes," he said. "I find the present tense has recently grown very interesting."

"Wonderful," she said. "Just wonderful."

"What do you want from me, Muriel?" he said. "What would you like for me to do?"

"Nothing," she said, resolutely facing the wall behind the stove.

"Anyway," she said after a long silence, "when this . . . this . . . person called this morning and said what he said,

I thought he meant the stuff that's been going through my mind. You know, the past. Leave buried . . . what was it?"

Brimm did a perfect imitation of the caller's nasal, twangy voice—"What's buried should stay buried, Mr. Brimm"—and laughed.

She looked at him. "I don't see how you can laugh," she said. "I'm frightened, Frankie. The moment I realized who was on the other end of that line and what he was really referring to—"

"We don't actually know who it was," said Brimm. "It could have been anyone. A prank."

"That's true, I suppose," she said. "But maybe not, too. You said yesterday that we weren't in any danger."

"I don't think we are," he said.

"Well, in any case," said Muriel, "I think we should tell the police."

"I agree," he said. "I'll phone them after breakfast."

Brimm was confident that if he got out of the way of happenstance and proceeded with his life in a relaxed, optimistic manner, he would encounter Claudia Callejas again before the day was over. In his mental portrait of her, she wore a white sundress; bars of light fell across her bare arms as she swept pine needles from the flagstones in front of her house and hummed a Spanish serenade.

Detective Sergeant Connie Shoulders, the young policeman who had interviewed Brimm on Saturday, was not available when Brimm telephoned the station after breakfast, so Brimm left both his own and Muriel's numbers.

"That's an interesting name," said Muriel. "Oddly familiar." Now she sat at the counter drinking coffee as Brimm, wearing the red-striped apron, did the breakfast dishes.

"He's an odd-looking bird," said Brimm. "A young black man. You'd never guess he was a policeman. Looks more like a college student . . . a science major."

"And what does a science major look like?" Muriel asked.

"Oh, you know. Skinny. Thick glasses."

"Shoulders," said Muriel. "Very familiar."

Brimm rinsed the last dish and stood it in the drainer. "Well," he said for no special reason, and began to untie the apron strings.

"You best get going," Muriel said to him.

"I'm not in a hurry especially," he said.

"Well, you don't want to be late," she said. "You are going to change, aren't you?"

"Change for what?"

"Francis," she said. "You've forgotten your appointment with the rector."

"Oh, no," he said, having forgotten. "A priest is the last thing I'm in the mood for this morning."

"I don't think you need to be in any special mood," she said. "And it's a bit late to cancel now."

Irked, he turned without a word and walked out onto the porch at the back of the house, off the kitchen. A chameleon, a dull gray-brown, clung to the screen at eye level, and Brimm moved up close to study it: a female, lacking the male's identifying flap of skin on the throat; not a true chameleon, which was an Old World lizard, but properly a green anole, the kind that used to be sold for a nickel at the county fair in Brimm's boyhood. "You see," said Brimm to the lizard, "I've been seeing this vision on my bedroom ceiling."

Brimm had planned to take the photograph of the French girl with him to his meeting with the rector, which meant returning home for it first. Muriel drove him back to the cottage and dropped him off. She would have had him wear a jacket and tie to the church, but he said he was perfectly presentable in his polo shirt and khakis, and if he wasn't perfectly presentable, he didn't care.

Inside the cottage he found the old *Picture Post*, then set out for St. Matthew and the Redeemer on foot. If he cut across the golf course, he would be able to walk there and still be on time. Golfers would already be out at this early hour, and they would yell and wave their clubs at him, but it would be over quickly; if he could face a priest for the crime of seeing visions, he could bear the temporary reproach of strangers.

Turning into the path through the woods, he noted that his former euphoria—the splendor of summer in Pines and all that—had slunk quietly away. The birdsong of daybreak had now become the contentious squawking of scrub jays.

When he emerged from the pines, he was shocked to see a transformed golf course: a kind of vast burial ground, scores of dirt mounds scattered throughout, bunkers pitted with deep holes, some areas cordoned off with bright orange ribbon, a yellow power shovel parked inert just to the edge of the fairway. In the commotion, he'd forgotten the morning paper, which must have still been lying unnoticed in his small front yard, and it was impossible to interpret the golf course in its bizarre condition. From the extraordinary number of excavations, much could have turned up, or nothing at all. As Brimm continued across the course, it occurred to him for the first time that the Labrador might have found the bones somewhere else entirely and brought them there to bury in the sand trap. But why would the dog exhume the bones and then leave them lying out in the open, abandoned? Gaining the top of the rise, and then the bench on which he and Muriel had sat and observed the Labrador's digging, Brimm could see down the fairway three uniformed policemen on the distant green, one smoking a cigarette, one holding the flag stick, one putting a ball and, to the great amusement of the other two, just missing the cup.

Muriel had said that he should knock on the door of the rectory, which was to the right of the church proper and through an enclosed garden. Brimm noted the message on the marquee near the garden gate—"Come As You Are, God Won't Have You Any Other Way"—and took it as a point against Muriel, who'd earlier disparaged his attire. He also noted "The Rev. M. T. Whiteside, Pastor." Inside the garden, amid a half-dozen spindly camellias, stood an old granite pietà. Somewhere, he had a photograph of that piece of sculpture. He recalled having returned to Pines in the early fifties to attend his father's funeral, and there had been a freak snowfall that day; the photograph was of the pietà, in snow, and somehow Muriel had figured in it too, but he couldn't think how.

He was greeted at the rectory door by a slight young woman with very short hair, wearing jeans and a rugby shirt. Brimm told her that he was there to see the rector, and the young woman said, "You must be Francis Brimm."

"Yes," he said. "Most people call me Frank."

"Frank," she said, shaking his hand. She introduced herself as Mary Whiteside, and showed him into what Brimm took to be the rector's study, furnished with two or three upholstered chairs, many bookshelves, and an immense oak desk. The woman indicated that Brimm should take one of the upholstered chairs, and she offered him coffee, which he declined. Then she sat in the chair nearest him—facing his way, leaving the rector's chair empty behind the large desk—and smiled.

Brimm felt unduly impatient with this arrangement, probably on account of nerves, and after what felt like an interminable and awkward silence, he said, "I wonder, Mrs. Whiteside. Does the rector know I'm here?"

"Oh, my," the woman said. "I should say she does. I'm Mary Whiteside, the rector."

This surprise, which Brimm understood to have been prepared by Muriel, didn't strike him as particularly pleasant; it was never pleasant to have one's prejudices turned upside down. "You're the rector?" he said.

She nodded, smiling sympathetically.

"A woman?"

"As you can see," she said, opening her arms.

"Muriel might have told me," he said.

The young woman once again nodded and smiled, this time neutrally.

"Well," he said. "You're a priest?"

"Yes," she said. "Though I'm often taken for a nun, I am indeed a priest."

"What do people call you?" he said. "I don't imagine they call you Father."

"Most people call me Mary," she said.

"Oh," he said, and another long silence ensued, in which she was clearly waiting for him to get on with whatever business he was there for. He unrolled the *Picture Post*. "I brought something for you to see," he said, opening the magazine to the photograph.

"Oh, my," she said, leaning in to examine the picture. "Did you take this?"

"Yes," he said. "In the forties. Armistice."

"Oh, yes," she said. "I can see the American flag in the background. And the French . . ."

This was how Brimm began, and he spent quite some time discussing the photograph, its history, how he happened to be in the French village on that particular day, where he'd positioned himself in the street, the kind of camera he used, and so on, to the general effect of completely bewildering Mary Whiteside.

Eventually she interrupted him. "It's a very moving, wonderful picture, Frank," she said, "but is this why you've come? To show it to me?"

After a moment he said, "I think you can tell that I'm not senile."

"Yes," she said.

"I'm in full possession of my faculties," he added.

She nodded.

"I've always been a down-to-earth sort, and I'm not a religious man," he said. "In fact I would describe myself as irreligious."

She nodded again, earnestly.

"A few weeks ago . . ." He paused. Then, "Tell me, do

65

you believe people have visions? I mean, I know people had visions in the Bible, but I mean today. Do you think people have them today?"

"Oh, yes," she said. "Absolutely."

This response pleased Brimm and invited his confidence, but when the priest went on—"absolutely people have visions, Frank. All the time, not at all unusual. I've had one recently myself"—Brimm felt robbed of his singularity, his distinguishing experience reduced to a commonplace.

"Yes, well, good," he said, cutting her off.

"Have you had a vision, Frank?" she asked, widening her eyes.

"Of the woman in the picture," he answered.

She nodded knowingly, and it struck Brimm that the young female priest was completely insane. "Of the woman in the picture," she repeated back to him with exaggerated sincerity.

"Yes," he said, and went on to explain all the details—the seagulls, the light on the ceiling, and so forth. "I think it means something," he said when he was done. "I think I'm supposed to know something, or do something as a result of it. But I have no idea what."

"Does the woman ever speak to you in the vision?"

"No," he said.

She leaned forward and looked at him intently. "Frank," she said, "if she did speak to you, what do you think she would say?"

"If I could answer that question, I probably wouldn't be here now," he said. "I imagine that if she spoke to me, the message would be clear."

"It seems to me," she said after a moment, nodding again, "that you must empathize a great deal with the young woman. I wonder how you would feel about closing your eyes for a minute and trying to *become* her . . . trying to become the woman in the picture."

Brimm said that he would feel perfectly foolish about

that. "And besides," he said abruptly, "what does any of this have to do with spiritual advice."

"Is that what you've come for?" she asked. "Spiritual advice?"

"Yes," he said. "Muriel said I was in need of it and that I should come talk to you."

"Well, we *are* talking, Frank," she said. "I've taken very seriously the fact that you are having these visions, and you have said to me that you're fairly certain that there is a message in them for you. So my own sense of things is that you and I are talking about what that message might be."

"But you seem more like a shrink than a priest," he said, trying not to sound hostile.

She laughed, unperturbed. "Frank," she said, "would you like me to outline the Scriptural precedence for prophetic dreams and visions? Would that be the priestly thing to do? There's Joseph the father of Jesus, and Zachariah the father of John the Baptist, and the apostle Peter, and Pilate's wife, and Jacob of Jacob's ladder, and Joseph in Hebrew Scripture, who was a great reader of dreams. When the pharaoh—"

"I'm sorry," Brimm said. "I don't really know what I expected." He stood up, which apparently took her by surprise.

"Are you leaving?" she asked.

"I think so," he said. "Thank you for your time."

"Okay," she said, shrugging, and rose to see him to the outside door.

"Frank," she said as he paused on the stoop, "I have the impression there's something you're not telling me. I don't try to coerce people into telling me things they don't want to tell me, but I also feel sometimes a bit handicapped in being asked for assistance and then not having all the available information."

"I guess I thought you might recommend I see a doctor," he said.

"No," she said. "Not at all. Not unless you think you

67

need to see a doctor or want to see a doctor. Are you feeling all right physically?"

"Yes," he said. "I don't even take any medication, which is unusual for a man of my age."

"Then why see a doctor?" she said.

"So you just take it as truth that what I'm seeing is a bona fide vision?"

"Yes," she said. "Of course. Are you disappointed that I don't challenge that?"

He smiled. "I have to tell you, Reverend," he said. "I came here this morning with some apprehension that you might think I was crazy. Now I find myself leaving and thinking we both are."

She found this remark uproarious. "Stay with the vision, Frank," she said, recovering from her laughter. "And come back if you want to."

"You're not even going to try to get me to come to church?" he said.

"Nah," she said. "I think you know that you're always welcome."

As he left the garden, he recalled the day of his father's burial, something he'd not done more than a half-dozen times in forty years. That freak snowfall in the Florida panhandle, so symbolic-seeming on the day of the funeral, and Muriel furious at Brimm for bringing along his little Leica. Stoical, she'd called him, unfeeling. And they'd had more words, worse ones, about the "good doctor," as Brimm often sarcastically referred to their father. "He was a drunk, Muriel," he remembered saying to her in the car. "The good doctor was a miserable drunk. And a miserable loser." Cruel and cold-hearted, sadistic, she'd called Brimm, her cheeks streaked with tears, and he'd apologized finally. After the service they'd walked briefly in the church garden, the snow having stopped by then. Muriel had been distraught at the snow-dusted pietà, Brimm recalled. Had she actually climbed up onto the pedestal? "So cold," she had said, and Brimm snapped a picture.

* * *

A few minutes later, he sat on a green-slatted bench in Bonifay Square, downtown, thinking about what he had not told the young female priest at St. Matthew and the Redeemer. Only the business about his feeling that the woman in the picture—or the woman in the vision, whichever you preferred—seemed occasionally to communicate without words. He thought she'd imparted to him knowledge of the bones on the golf course, for example, and that most recently her sadness had seemed to reach him directly and powerfully. Those were the most crazy-sounding bits, and the most enigmatic, and he couldn't see how, lacking those, the priest should have been, to use her word, handicapped. He certainly hadn't intentionally withheld information, as she'd implied, in order to hinder her. Besides, the study in the rectory had been too warm and had a musty smell.

Here in the square, the air was cool, and as Brimm sat close enough to the imposing three-tiered fountain at its center, he felt comforted by the sound of the falling water. Odd that he should feel in need of comforting, and he couldn't begin to say why, but the water's quiet babble felt a kind of consolation nonetheless. The meeting with the rector had been . . . what? He supposed it had left him feeling, more than anything else, manipulated by Muriel. As far as he could tell, the meeting had been of no use to him, hadn't even the potential of usefulness. And was this what spiritual advice amounted to—close your eyes and try to become the woman on the ceiling? It bordered on sheer quackery, if you asked him, and what with Muriel deliberately withholding the fact that the rector was female, purposefully to disorganize him . . .

He gazed at the white concrete bandstand across the square with its fancy wrought-iron grillwork. He'd never known it to be used for any musical ceremony, though surely there must have been a time when that had been its function. Through an archway in the bandstand and down a curved staircase was a public restroom where, as a boy,

Brimm had found some important and memorable education in writing and diagrams on the walls. A place like that, in the basement of a bandstand in a public square, would be considered dangerous nowadays, and Brimm could see that like many such places, it had long been closed down, its archway the site of permanent iron bars.

He noted that a more colorful crowd visited the square than anything you encountered out in his neighborhood, which was known as Madison Heights—overly enthusiastically, since the highest height was just a couple hundred feet above sea level. Downtown Pines had been abandoned by the whites, and the blacks had flooded in (and now Cubans, who had found their way north from Miami). The chamber of commerce had decided to try to attract whites back by turning some of the streets into pedestrian malls with brick planter boxes and old-fashioned streetlamps, but it hadn't worked to any great extent. Most of the whites you saw were old people, like Muriel and the Ottos—those who'd remained and who'd been able to adapt to changing times. One such adaptable old person was seated on a bench just opposite Brimm, a white woman in a straw hat sitting next to a black woman of approximately equal age, obviously friends, chatting, shelling peanuts and throwing them to the pigeons gathered at their feet. A few years ago Brimm would have taken a picture of that. But a few years ago you wouldn't have seen it, not in Pines. The portrait, as he imagined it, would have had an inherent, understated hopefulness and wisdom.

This insight, or speculation, caused Brimm to open the *Picture Post* to the photograph of the French village, which did not have any inherent hopefulness or wisdom. He studied it for a long minute, again. He kept thinking there might be something to learn from it, something that had gone unnoticed for nearly half a century, some clue to what was going on in the wee hours of the morning on his bedroom ceiling. But as before, he found nothing new, nothing that seemed significant. The baby, who must have been born with quite a lot of hair, sucked its thumb. The gendarmes leered. A white-haired woman, amused, watched the parade from a second-story window. Brimm found himself examining the visible faces in the crowd. He was looking for a particular face, the one that might show distress at the young woman's misery—that acknowledged her unhappy fate, and the baby's, knowing that such acknowledgment didn't diminish whatever misery she might have fostered in her collaboration—a face chagrined at the timeless, compulsory turning of this wheel of shame. But Brimm found no such face among the villagers in the street. They had survived one of the world's greatest calamities and had not learned from it to forgive the mistakes of others. The war had ended, their side had won. But the war that still raged in their hearts, that had raged there before any arms were taken up anywhere, nobody even thought about winning. If that was what the head-shaven woman's visitation was meant to emphasize, if that was what she meant him to understand, why did she bother? He already understood this—it was what the picture meant to him, the theme of the story the picture told. In any case, the fountain's falling water had done its trick. He was calm. He rose from the bench and began walking away under the trees.

When Muriel, delighted to see him once again at her door, let him into the entryway, she said, "Guess who's here, out on the back porch having a glass of tea? Detective Sergeant Connie Shoulders. And I remembered who he is. It was ages ago, you see. She was a nurse or something at the hospital. A huge woman, as I recall."

"Who are you talking about, Muriel?" said Brimm.

"This woman, Shoulders," she said. "Such a terrible thing. Ages ago. I guess she wouldn't have been a nurse because I don't think they had black nurses at Memorial back then. But she worked there. And she was bitten by a snake, a coral snake, and she was taken to Memorial because it was so much closer to where she was bitten and she was refused treatment because she was a Negro and she died."

"My God," said Brimm. "I never heard that story."

"Oh, I think it was after you left," Muriel said. "Shoulders, I was sure that was the name. It turns out she was the detective's grandmother. I even remembered what we used to say about the coral snakes: Red touching yellow, dangerous fellow. Do you remember that, Frankie? About the rings on the coral snakes? Red touching yellow, dangerous fellow?"

Nine

EARLIER THAT MORNING, after leaving Francis at his cottage so that he might change for his visit with Mary Whiteside, Muriel had driven back into town. She stopped at the dry cleaners, where she dropped off her good linen suit for pressing, a soiled skirt, and two blouses. The dry cleaners—Peerless, it was called—had been owned and operated for the last ten or twelve years by a black family, and the old patriarch, who'd come to be known as Mr. Peerless (though that was not his real name), greeted customers as long-lost friends. "How grand to see you, Miss Brimm," he would say as Muriel entered the door. "You have brightened my morning."

Today, when Muriel's business at the counter was done, Mr. Peerless offered her a dish of candies in bright-colored foil wrappers. "We're grateful to you," he said.

"I beg your pardon?" said Muriel, for she'd understood him to say something about the candy, something about "gravel," and "chew."

"I said we are grateful to you," he repeated, enunciating each syllable.

"Oh, yes," she said. "Well, thank you."

"Take two," he urged.

"Thank you, Mr. Peerless. One is enough."

Outside, she leaned over the waist-high trash can at the curb to drop in the candy wrapper, and staring up at her from the grimy bottom of the can was Francis's face. She burst out laughing, then looked up to see Mr. Peerless watching her with a quizzical expression through the cleaners' plate-glass window. As if to explain herself, she pointed to the can, a gray-painted oil drum, but just then a sudden gust of wind blew something into her eye. Also, the piece of candy she'd just popped into her mouth had a terrible, rotten flavor. Disconcerted, she moved quickly toward her car, away from the cleaners and Mr. Peerless's observation.

It had been the front page of an old discarded *Crier*, the one with the large photograph of Francis from the other day, and though her first response had been laughter, there had been something chilling about it too, as if Francis himself had been thrown away, as if he were lost and abandoned in some dark pit, from which he gazed and longed for rescue. Once seated behind the steering wheel, Muriel leaned out the car door, discreetly lowering her head, and allowed the candy to fall from her mouth into the street. She took a Kleenex from the glove compartment and wiped her eye. It seemed she couldn't even leave the house these days without encountering some flustering, bizarre incident.

At home, she found Deirdre, who had let herself into the house with her own key and was already running the vacuum in the parlor. Muriel waved to Deirdre from the entryway, then went directly to the kitchen and opened the cabinet above the toaster, where she kept her bottles of pills. Her medication consisted of Naprosyn, twice a day, for the arthritis in her knees and hands; Dyazide and Lisinopril, once a day, for hypertension; and an over-the-counter stool softener, as needed. It was Monday, and Monday was the day she supplied her Ezy Dose Pill Reminder, the little plastic distributor case, with the week's medicine. When she was done with this procedure, she swallowed what she needed for the morning and recalled Billie Otto's unpleasant remark of the day before—Billie's implication that her medication needed adjusting.

Some time ago, Dr. Van Buren had put Muriel on a different blood pressure drug, something called Aldomet, and one Saturday, after taking the drug for a few days, Muriel had found herself having trouble negotiating the details of Billie Otto's excellent recipe for pound cake. Like many pound cake recipes, it called for a pound of butter. But there was a parenthetical option for a half-pound butter and a half-pound margarine, which seemed to Muriel, in the moment, a bewildering incongruity. She went to the telephone and struggled to recollect Billie's number. When finally she got her on the line, Billie was exasperated by Muriel's conspicuous, and uncharacteristic, dull-wittedness. A few more days of similar difficulties led Muriel back to Dr. Van Buren, where she learned that a "decrease in mental acuity" was indeed one of the possible side effects of Aldomet. He changed her drug to Lisinopril and it had been smooth sailing ever since.

All this was, to Muriel's thinking, a simple and brief progression of events, unfolding and resolving in an elementary fashion based on cause and effect. But apparently it was a progression that had had for Billie some mysterious resonance, causing her to file it away for future use: the small tactic, Muriel thought, of a small-minded person—and a disappointment in someone considered one's close friend for more than half a century.

This unpleasant conclusion happened to coincide with Billie's rapping at the back porch door, and when Muriel saw the face of her friend through the screen, it conjured in her a kind of fight-or-flight response. She had to close her eyes for several seconds and breathe very deeply in order to get back her proper bearings.

"I saw you standing there at the counter," said Billie when Muriel stepped onto the porch. "You were a thousand miles away."

Muriel moved up to the screen door but did not unlatch it. "Not at all," she said, smiling but feeling sinister at the same time. "I assure you my thoughts were quite local."

"Well, are you going to let me in?" Billie said, laughing a little.

When Muriel hesitated, Billie held up a heavy yellow music book. Smiling sweetly, sighing indulgingly, she said, "Piano?"

It was their custom on Monday mornings to play compositions arranged for four hands—Schubert marches, Strauss waltzes, Brahms's Hungarian Dances, music Billie referred to as "fun things."

"Oh, Billie," Muriel said through the screen, "I don't feel up to it this morning. Besides, Deirdre's not finished with cleaning the parlor."

Billie stood on the low wooden stoop outside the screen door and stared at Muriel for a long moment. She fanned away a bee that was buzzing around her head. She took one step back and said, "You're not yourself, Muriel."

"No," said Muriel, not averting her eyes.

The two women continued to stare at each other for another few seconds, one in sun, one in shade. Shaking her head slowly, Billie said again, "Not yourself," this time an inflected warning, and a reproach.

"No," Muriel repeated—neutral, impervious—and that was that.

Walking back through the kitchen, Muriel felt a pang of self-reproof and began to run a kind of moral inventory on her rejection of Billie at the screen door; but immediately she was reminded by the sound of Deirdre's vacuum in the other room that, after all, she'd only told the truth, a difficult thing to fault entirely, even when it slighted others. She *didn't* feel up to the piano, Deirdre *hadn't* finished with cleaning the parlor, and Muriel definitely *wasn't* herself.

When she arrived at the entry hall, she saw an odd sight: Deirdre, lying on the carpet, on her back, next to the still-running vacuum cleaner. The girl's eyes were closed, and one hand rested on her stomach, the other still clasping the vacuum's silver extension wand. Muriel didn't want to startle her, so instead of shouting over the noise of the machine, she tried lowering her voice and speaking deeply and firmly under the sound. "Deirdre, are you all right?" she said, but

76

wasn't heard. She walked over and switched off the vacuum with her toe. Deirdre's eyes opened.

"I'm all right," Deirdre said. "I don't know what came over me. I really haven't been sick at all. I suddenly just felt I'd better lie down. Just tired, really. A little dizzy."

"You need something in your stomach, I imagine," said Muriel, feeling rather like a giantess, towering over the girl on the floor.

"That's not all I need," said Deirdre.

"What do you mean?"

"I think I could use a husband."

"Oh."

"Forget I said that," Deirdre added quickly. "A moment of weakness."

Muriel offered her hand, but Deirdre got up on her own. "I'm really all right now," she said. "I feel much better."

"Come out to the kitchen and sit down," said Muriel. "You need toast, plain toast. And something to drink."

To her own amusement, Muriel found herself guiding Deirdre by the waist and elbow toward the kitchen, and saying, "Steady as she goes."

Deirdre gave Muriel an inquisitive look, and Muriel thought how fascinating it was that nautical language seemed so often to find its way into times of trouble (or when trouble was over)—an observation she thought she could work into one of her book club discussions.

"Miss Brimm," Deirdre said, "you think this is fun, don't you?"

"Well, Deirdre . . ." was all Muriel managed to say, caught out as she was.

She found some ginger ale and was pouring a glass for Deirdre, who sat at the counter, when Deirdre, noticing the dishes in the drainer, said, "You had company for breakfast this morning."

"My brother, Francis," Muriel said, but with such a faraway air that Deirdre said, "And did your brother hypnotize you?"

"Hypnotize me?" said Muriel, still far away. "What do you mean?"

"You seemed to go into a trance at the mention of his name, that's all."

"Oh, no," said Muriel. "It's just that you reminded me of something. Something I'd forgotten."

What she'd forgotten was to remain frightened over the strange telephone call in the wee hours. She realized that for the most part she'd been inexplicably jolly all morning, and she'd ridden those bumpy moments—Francis's face at the bottom of the oil drum, Billie's at the screen door—like something essentially buoyant; she thought of those red and white bobbers that fishermen use to suspend a baited hook from the water's surface (a particularly evocative image, she thought, though she didn't know for certain what it evoked).

As she served Deirdre's plain toasted white bread and ginger ale at the kitchen counter, she attempted to bring her emotions in line with what logic would dictate. She thought of being startled awake by the telephone at 4:30 A.M., of the receiver trembling in her hand, of the unpleasant nasal twang in the caller's voice. But fear seemed now to have deserted her (or she it) and wouldn't come back. All she could summon in the way of what seemed appropriate was the cloudy distress that attached to her original misinterpretation of the caller's words—"What's buried should stay buried"—as applied to her new preoccupation with the past. In that first mistaken moment, the words had felt like nothing less than an admonition from the Burning Bush, and she thought it credited her trust in God's love that she hadn't felt alarmed in her grogginess, but rather chastened, and penitent. Then, of course, all that had washed away in a mere second, replaced by wide-awake fear of earthly danger.

"Someone phoned here in the middle of the night," she

said to Deirdre. "I think it was the person who buried those bones that Francis found."

She went on to describe everything that had happened.

"Weird," said Deirdre when Muriel was done.

"Yes," said Muriel. "But now I realize that I'm not particularly bothered by it, not by the fact that a homicidal psychopath is phoning me in the middle of the night. It was the message that bothered me . . . that it seemed to be about *me*. Without his knowing it."

"I don't understand," said Deirdre.

Muriel explained about the recent intrusion of memory that had begun with Francis's return to Pines, and how at first, this morning, she'd thought "what's buried" referred to the past.

"Oh, that's just a coincidence, Miss Brimm," said Deirdre. "I mean, I admit it's a weird coincidence, but that's all it is."

"Well, I guess I know that," said Muriel. "But do you really believe in coincidences? Don't you often find providence in random events?"

"Yes," said Deirdre, thinking for a moment. "Yes, I do. But sometimes a cigar is just a cigar, too, if you know what I mean."

"I don't think I do exactly," said Muriel.

"I just mean that sometimes things mean something and sometimes they don't. I also think the more upset you are, or the more unhappy you are, the more you find hidden meanings in things. I can remember a few years ago, before I got out of my house. I was so miserable and desperate I was walking around thinking the pigeons in the *park* were trying to tell me something. You know what I mean?"

Muriel did know what Deirdre meant, but she didn't much like it. For some reason, she didn't like Deirdre's thinking of her as upset and unhappy.

"Anyway," Deirdre added, "I don't see how it could be providence when it's such bad advice."

"What do you mean?" Muriel asked.

"I mean . . . the past should stay buried . . . what a bad idea."

"Oh, I don't know about that," said Muriel. "Myself, I've never really seen what use it is."

"The past is prologue, Miss Brimm," Deirdre said. "Didn't you ever hear that?"

"That's a reference to history, Deirdre," said Muriel. "I'm not talking about history."

Deirdre continued to argue her point, with some clarifying remarks about personal history and child-as-father-of-the-man, but Muriel's mind wandered with a frightening thoroughness, not away from the subject so much as out of the room. Deirdre's attempt at instruction about personal history, when she herself had so little of it, struck Muriel as bold to say the least, and she felt annoyed at having a second conversation on this topic so early in the morning. These, however, were minor irritations noted in passing, for her mind, in leaving the room, had strayed for no apparent reason to the enclosed courtyard outside the rectory at St. Matthew and the Redeemer. Specifically, it had strayed to a moment long ago when she'd climbed aboard the courtyard's granite pietà and brushed snow out of Jesus's lap. She hadn't thought of it in years, but now this involuntary recollection felt quite whole. It had been the day of Dr. Brimm's funeral, and Francis, down from New York, had been brutal all morning, angry at their father—for having died, Muriel supposed—and dealing with Francis and his stupid camera (can you imagine bringing a camera to your own father's funeral?) had confused her grief. Francis seemed the cause of her tears rather than Dr. Brimm. Of course it made sense that Francis should be angry, Dr. Brimm's passing the way he did, but Muriel had needed companionship that day, not struggle. When the burial in the church cemetery was over and everyone had begun to leave, she and Francis, now mellowed and quiet at last, walked in the courtyard, and Muriel was able to feel what she was feeling: deep purposelessness, a loss of self, and a panicky need to do something. She would have to sort out this confusion—to distinguish her father's death from her own—but there would be plenty of time for that later. Right now she wanted an anchor, a cause, an *assignment*. And Jesus's snow-filled lap, a kind of natural desecration in ice and stone, had presented itself and furnished an opportunity for protest.

". . . let it out before you can let it go," Deirdre was saying. "Are you with me, Miss Brimm?"

"I'm sorry, Deirdre," Muriel said. "I was just thinking of Francis over at the church rectory. I've played a rather dirty trick on him, I'm afraid. I made an appointment for him to see Mary Whiteside and didn't tell him to expect a woman priest. It's the kind of thing that will throw him, and I knew it would, and I did it deliberately."

She looked at Deirdre, who was blank-faced, trying to accommodate this sudden shift of gears. After a pause, Deirdre said, "Will he be angry?"

"Oh, if I know Francis," said Muriel, "I'll never hear a word about it. He'll simply never mention it."

Deirdre stood. "Well, I feel much better," she said. "Thank you."

Muriel retrieved the plate and glass from the counter and carried them to the sink. She turned on the water, waited for it to get hot, then began rinsing the dishes. With her back to Deirdre, she said, "My father was a doctor. He was a doctor and he killed himself. I haven't said that to anyone for many years, and I don't know why I'm saying it now."

Deirdre moved next to Muriel and leaned inward, one arm on the counter next to the sink, so that she could see Muriel's face. This was the sort of information a girl like that could accept without batting an eye—it was, Muriel thought, the very language she spoke.

"Why'd he do it?" Deirdre asked.

"He went out one night," Muriel said, "and drove his car off the old Milligan Bridge. Right into the lagoon."

"But why?" Deirdre repeated.

"He was an unhappy, bitter man," Muriel said. "A drinker. Eaten up from inside."

"Sounds like my old man," Deirdre said. "*Just* like him, in fact."

When Muriel turned to her, she saw what looked like suspicion on the girl's face.

But then Detective Sergeant Connie Shoulders had shown up at the front door, and later Francis, and by the time Muriel was able to return to the look of suspicion on Deirdre's face, Deirdre had finished her work and left for her classes at the college.

Muriel had recognized the young detective in plain clothes at once, from Francis's earlier description of him.

"Shoulders," she said thoughtfully, once she'd got him seated at the table on the back porch with a glass of tea. "Now why is that so familiar?"

" 'Cause you have 'em maybe," said the detective, which Muriel thought terribly funny.

"No," she said. "Something else. You wait. It'll come to me."

The detective, thinner than she had noticed at first, wore a light straw-colored suit, which Muriel thought very handsome. The collar of his white dress shirt was too big, and though buttoned, stood out stiffly a good half inch from his neck. He'd turned sideways in his chair, so his long legs—crossed, with one dangling languidly—were not trapped beneath the small table. "In the meantime," he said, "how about telling me about these phone calls."

"Oh, that," said Muriel, surprising herself by waving her hand at him, a gesture of dismissal.

Detective Shoulders had received Francis's message earlier, and finding himself in Muriel's neighborhood, had decided to drop in and see what was what. Inquiring about the phone calls was, after all, why he was sitting on Muriel's porch. But Muriel had been having an unexpected and interesting morning, and Connie Shoulders struck her

82

as an unexpected and interesting guest. She felt bored with the phone calls, which was understandable, having rehashed it now twice already before ten o'clock. But when she waved her hand at the detective dismissively, she meant to put him at ease, encourage him to enjoy his glass of tea and not worry about such unpleasantness as murder and whatnot.

This, she realized, was utter nonsense. "Oh, yes," she said. "The calls. Well, as I said, I think it was the man who buried the bones on the golf course. He phoned Francis too."

"You're sure it was a man?"

"Well, now that you mention it," she said, "I guess I'm not really sure. I took it to be a man. It could have been a woman with a deep voice, I suppose. Or it could have been a woman imitating a man."

"Let's assume that it was a man," said the detective.

"I think we should," said Muriel.

"What did he say?" he asked.

"Francis could give you the exact words," she answered. "He can even imitate the voice. But it was something like, 'What's buried should stay buried.' "

And all at once it came to her: "I've got it!" she said.

"What?" he said.

"Shoulders," she said. "Many years ago there was a black woman by that name, bitten by a snake. A terrible thing. It gave Pines a bad name, as I recall."

The detective was smiling. "My grandmother," he said, raising his eyebrows. "Mind like a steel trap, Miss Brimm."

"Oh, well," she said. "Thank you."

"Roberta," he said.

"Roberta," she said excitedly. "Roberta Shoulders. She worked at the hospital, didn't she?"

"That's right."

"Oh, I'm so sorry," Muriel said. "Here I am delighted this way, when . . . I'm very sorry."

"It's okay," he said. "I wasn't born yet when she died."

"I was terrified of coral snakes as a child," she said. "My father made us learn that rhyme about them, you know, the one about the arrangement of the stripes."

"Rings," he said. "I think you'd say rings, not stripes. Otherwise it sounds like they run the length of the snake, you understand what I'm saying?"

"I suppose it does," Muriel said, liking this young detective more by the minute.

"Red touching yellow," he said.

"Yes," she said. "Dangerous fellow. I *knew* I knew that name."

"A lot of stories in my family about Granny Shoulders," he said.

"Some of us were so ashamed at the time," Muriel said. "People started to look around a little bit after that, I think. At the way we'd been living. At all we'd taken for granted. Mainly it was the out-of-town papers, though. They got hold of the story and people were ashamed that Pines had got this bad reputation. I remember the mayor . . ."

That was when Francis arrived at the front door. Muriel knew it was he, and even said, "Oh, how lucky, that'll be Francis," because of Francis's unmistakable ringing of the door bell—four short, emphatic sounds, equal in length, that seemed to suggest that a closed door was somehow an affront to him. Muriel thought perhaps it was an adjustment to be made, having to ask permission to enter the house where you grew up, so she was tolerant. Besides, she was excited to give him the news about Roberta Shoulders.

"No, I do not remember," he said when she asked him whether he remembered the little rhyme about the arrangement of the coral snake's rings. But she could tell, from the fleeting yet distinct light of recognition in his eyes, that in fact he did remember it.

Through the kitchen, on their way to the porch, he allowed Muriel to take his arm.

Once introductions were made, more tea poured, and the

three of them seated at the table, Muriel asked Francis to do for Detective Shoulders his imitation of the mysterious caller. Francis grimaced. "Oh, come on," she said. "You sent chills up my spine earlier this morning."

He grimaced again, and spoke to the detective. "I was on the golf course this morning," he said. "I wondered what you might have found?"

Muriel noted a moment's hesitation on the young detective's part and said, "That's an inappropriate question, Francis."

"Will you be quiet?" Francis said.

"I certainly will not."

"Actually," said the detective, "we haven't made anything public at this point, Mr. Brimm."

The detective glanced at Muriel in a way she couldn't interpret, then he asked again about the phone calls.

Francis confirmed the content of the caller's message, the approximate time of the calls, the general sound of the voice.

The detective made some notes in a small notebook. "So no kind of actual threat was made," he said.

"Well, I wouldn't say that," said Muriel. "Don't you think there's an implied threat in 'What's buried should stay buried'? I mean, he's saying to us that we did something wrong, do you see what I mean?"

"He called me Frankie-boy," said Francis.

"What?" said Muriel. "You never said that before."

"I just remembered it, Muriel. This instant."

"How could you forget that?" she said. "That's very threatening. The tone of it."

"I don't know if it's exactly threatening," said Francis. "But there's something ... well, who knows, after all? I doubt very seriously if it was actually the murderer."

"I'm sure it was," said Muriel, not knowing quite why she said this.

"Probably a prank call," said Francis.

Dennis McFarland

"Very unlikely if you ask me," said Muriel. "What do you think, Detective Shoulders?"

The phone rang in the kitchen, startling Muriel. Rising from her chair, she said, "Maybe that's him now."

On her way into the kitchen she heard Francis say, "She has a very dull life. This sort of thing amuses her."

It was Billie Otto, whom Muriel put off as quickly as she could, and which only intensified Billie's snit. When Muriel returned to the porch, Connie Shoulders was standing, ready to leave. He thanked her for the tea.

"Well, what are you going to do?" she said to him. "Aren't you going to put a trace on the line or something? That's what they do in the movies."

Francis said to her, "This is not a movie, Muriel," and the detective explained to her that she and Francis might never hear from the caller again. He said that when a thing like this happened, when a gruesome crime like this was reported in the papers, the police got calls from all sorts of people, people giving themselves up for murder and so on. He assured her that she needn't be afraid, that he would put a car outside the house. "If a pattern should develop," he said, "then we'll ask the phone company to monitor your lines." Then he wrote a telephone number, a direct line where he could always be reached, and gave it to Francis. He asked them to let him know right away should they get any more calls, and to Muriel's disappointment, he was soon out the door. She realized, once he was gone, that she felt a bit dazed.

"Well," she said to Francis in the parlor. "That's Roberta Shoulders's grandson. Wouldn't she be proud?"

But Francis, standing near the window seat, was silent, apparently deep in thought.

As usual, the day's events revisited her late at night, after she'd done her reading. She and the Ottos had decided to bring newly discovered poems by famous poets to their next meeting of the book club, and Muriel had been glanc-

86

ing through a volume of John Donne. Billie had assigned them each a poet, Donne for Muriel, Frost for Ned, and Dickinson for herself—which hadn't struck Muriel as much of a range somehow, and she knew Billie had given her Donne because he'd been a churchman, but she hadn't really minded; there was a logic to it. Once, before retiring, she'd glanced out the parlor window at the boulevard and seen a black-and-white squad car cruise by, which oddly made her feel more, rather than less, uneasy. In bed, she turned off the bedside lamp and closed her eyes. She saw that strange look of suspicion on Deirdre's face at the end of their conversation at the kitchen sink. She saw Francis, standing in her parlor, deep in thought after the detective's departure. And suddenly, tears welled up in her eyes, and then she was crying quite vigorously, not knowing why. It lasted for perhaps a full minute, and as she began to compose herself in the dark, Dr. Brimm entered the room through the vanity mirror. Or so it ridiculously seemed to her in her baffling, distraught state. She was able to step back for a moment and observe that something was going on in her subconscious, tricks were being played. She quickly resolved not to take a sleeping pill, no matter what, and it occurred to her to pray, and she would pray sooner or later, but right now the presence of her long-dead father precluded prayer. He would have approved of her praying—the preclusion was hers, not his—but she didn't feel safe letting him see her as a supplicant. She wondered what her father's airborne thoughts might have been, in the seconds between bridge and water. The water in the lagoon had been so shallow that the dark gray top of the old Pontiac shone bright and glistening just at the water's surface, like a whale's back. And how strangely at home he had seemed in that undeniably medical setting of the examiner's rooms, naked beneath a sheet on a cold table. Nothing horrifying about it, skin just the color and texture you would expect—fish, poached, taken from the refrigerator the next day, him and not him, a version of him. She'd

87

pulled the sheet down a bit farther, to expose the short, truncated arm. You brought yourself here, she did not say aloud, but said, not turning away, "That's my father."

In the volcanic image-spewing before real dreaming began, the huge square shoulders of the National Archives Building in Washington, D.C., loomed up high overhead with its deep-carved adages, the past is prologue and so forth. Out front, the magisterial giant from history sat on his throne. Only the names of those giants changed, from building to building, but all those mammoth edifices, those strongholds of power, seemed to have one—bearded or unbearded, the patriarch ready to judge or rule or merely ponder. And then here came Iowa, enormous, more vaguely Greek than Native American, woman of stone, in front of the state capitol in Des Moines . . . Distantly the thought, But I've never been to Des Moines, began to form in Muriel's mind, but no use. You could get lost and hide forever in the folds of her gown, Iowa, offering her breast to the nation.

Ten

FOUR DAYS LATER, in one of Brimm's more elaborate daydreams, Claudia Callejas asked him two questions, or challenges actually, that would have felt intrusive had Brimm not been flattered by the concern of a beautiful, much younger woman. Most comically, the two of them, Brimm and Claudia Callejas, sat on a billowy cloud high above the earth as they spoke, like angels in an old movie. She asked him why, in retirement, he had given up taking pictures altogether.

Brimm thought for a moment, looking down at the roof of his little cottage next to the Madison Heights golf course, and this quaint overview, removed from the litter of human life, provided a ready answer. It had been the simple thing to do, he told her, the simplest thing. If he was no longer functioning in the role of professional photographer, then in what role, camera in hand, would he be functioning? As an amateur? He could find no middle ground to stand on.

This answer pleased Brimm—he thought it had some of the elegance of an algebraic formula—though he had to confess to himself that it wasn't entirely honest. A large part of his decision to put down the camera had been his absolute lack of enthusiasm; the ambition that had driven his career had long been used up. But he feared this disclosure might sound impotent to Claudia, not the quality he wanted to invoke.

Then, more perturbingly, she asked him why he seemed to have no friends.

To this, he lied outright. He said he had left all his friends in New York.

Perhaps sensing deception in the air (as an angel surely would), Claudia Callejas vanished from the cloud.

Now Brimm sat in the rocker on his front porch. It was early morning. He found himself holding in both hands a still warm but empty coffee cup and stupidly smiling to himself. Briefly, he was amused at having wed fantasy and introspection in the form of this reverie, but he also found he'd purchased no real lifting of his spirits from it. As he stood and moved out toward the morning newspaper, which lay folded on the sidewalk, he thought about his not having carried forward into old age one good friend, and he deemed himself merely a victim of mood swings, a cliché on a cottage porch, possessing all the pathos of a Walter Mitty. What next? Hot and cold flashes? Unicorns in the garden?

He picked up the newspaper and stood in the sunshine out by the edge of the street. He was still wearing his white and blue pinstriped pajamas. When he turned back, shading his eyes with the folded newspaper, he stopped and stared in astonishment at his small rust-red house. He had always prided himself on his powers of observation, on his trained eye, and yet now he noticed for the first time that the object mounted to the exterior wall over the porch roof, which he'd taken to be steer horns, was actually an old wooden yoke for oxen, painted white. A small misapprehension really, but Brimm experienced its self-correction as humiliating and ominous. He went back inside, into the dark little living room, and sat in the armchair.

Contrary to his speculation earlier in the week at Muriel's kitchen counter, Brimm had not again seen Claudia Callejas, and not seeing her when he had thought that he would, coupled with this morning's pretentious and absurd reverie involving her, caused him to examine his foolishness regarding her. He'd been thinking of her as a kind of savior, as someone who might rescue him from loneliness and boredom, someone who might restore purpose to his life. He recognized this as a symptom of genuine obsession, a sickness of the mind. His angling for her (with his meager, pitiful methods, standing in the dark, staring at her windows) might keep him, he'd thought, from sinking to conventional pastimes of the aged such as gardening, birding, fishing, reading, watching TV, and sleeping. An infantile delusion, he now saw, unworthy of him.

Yesterday the boy, Nicolás, had dropped by and stood around listlessly, trying to make conversation while Brimm watered the small patch of lawn in front of the cottage.

"This used to be the gardener's house," Nicolás had said.

"That so," said Brimm, who, lacking much history in talking to children, thought some special technique was required.

What the boy meant was that Brimm's cottage and the large colonial house where the boy was now staying with his aunt had once belonged to the same estate. Brimm had not known this and might have found it an interesting detail had he not been incurious about children and had he been less taken with his cruel bombardment of a female velvet ant he'd managed to pin to the ground with the hard stream from the hose.

After the boy had gone away, Brimm felt cross at having failed to engage with him, at having been lazy in regard to Claudia Callejas, at having passed up an opportunity to nurse his own infantile delusion. How could he expect to befriend Claudia if he wouldn't even talk to Nicolás?

Now, resting in the armchair, and sobered (at least temporarily), he thought it was better to leave things as they were. He should stand in the dark staring at her windows like a common voyeur, and she should remain distant and unattainable. Weren't those their true and proper stations?

He bucked an impulse to return to bed. He forced himself to get dressed, and then returned to the porch to read the newspaper.

It was another fine day in a series of fine days, but Brimm was disappointed to see that once again no significant news had been reported about the golf course murders. Upon thinking it, the phrase "golf course murders" surprised him. Inaccurate in one way (since undoubtedly no murders had actually occurred on the golf course), the phrase, in another way, in its plural, hit the bull's-eye: Brimm had been sure from the beginning that the police would recover more than one victim. He was also certain that the police were withholding information from the papers in order to mislead the killer. If you believed the papers, which typically used clauses like "police are still baffled," there were no suspects, no identification of any victim, no clear motive, no leads of any kind.

Brimm was just thinking that the police could not withhold information indefinitely when a taxi came to a stop in front of the cottage. Curiously, he felt his heart speed up.

Sunlight struck the side windows of the cab in such a way that he couldn't see who was inside, but soon a brown wooden cane, rubber-tipped, emerged from the back door, pursued by Ned Otto. Ned, squinting in the sun, waved to Brimm on the porch, and Brimm, perplexed, waved back.

Ned, a likable but bland fellow, was the oldest of Muriel's friends, well into his eighties. He'd suffered a stroke a few years back, which had aged him enormously; his hands shook, he was known to drift midsentence into sleep, he never seemed to have enough saliva in his mouth. Brimm couldn't imagine what might have brought the man, especially without Billie, to his doorstep.

In a moment, Ned was climbing onto the porch and saying, "So these are your new digs, Frank. Charming. Quite nice."

A chair was found, coffee offered and declined, and then an odd conversation began in which Brimm tried in vain to discern the actual purpose of Ned's visit. Ned looked approvingly at the piny woods across Brimm's street. He inhaled and exhaled deeply, exaggeratedly. "I used to know somebody who lived out this way," he said at last.

Brimm had every right to think that this remark would be followed by the name of the person, but instead Ned fell silent. He'd obviously gone into a reverie of his own, and Brimm could tell from the look on Ned's face that the anonymous person, the subject of the reverie, was a woman.

"That so," Brimm said finally.

"Yes," said Ned.

"A woman," Brimm said.

"Yes. Just down the road there. On the river side. Very well-to-do family. Petroleum, phosphate, titanium, who knows what else. Gates was the name, and they had huge iron gates across the driveway. I imagine they're still there . . . not the family but the iron gates, you know."

Again Ned came to a long pause. He apparently needed regular prompting. "Gates," Brimm said.

Ned tilted his head back and closed his eyes, looking into the past. "Margaret Gates, yes," he said. "Maggie, and God, was I in love. Smitten to the core." He looked at Brimm. "But I was a Jew of course," he said. "The old man wouldn't let me anywhere near her. Which only made it all the more intriguing. All the more romantic, you know. Montagues and Capulets."

"What happened?" Brimm asked after another long silence.

"Oh, they moved away. Up north. We'd all been at the college together, you know. Billie and I had already been dating for a while when Maggie Gates came along. And I'm afraid my fixation on Maggie broke Billie's heart. Then when Maggie's family moved away I got a taste of the same medicine. My own heart broke, you see, and Billie and I looked at each other and it seemed the only thing to do was for us to get married. Both our hearts broken like that, we needed each other, if you know what I mean.

Maudlin, I guess. Pathetic, I guess, to someone like you, Frank—being the rogue. You've always known your way around a woman. I hope I haven't insulted you."

"No," said Brimm, truthfully, for Ned was constitutionally harmless, and *rogue* in this case was a misapplication, not a slight.

"I don't mean it in the sense of scoundrel," Ned added quickly. "I only mean it in the sense of broken away from the pack."

"Well, I certainly did that," said Brimm.

"Yes," said Ned. "Now, what do you think about this gruesome business on the golf course?"

"I think the police are withholding information is what I think."

"Me too. I said as much to Billie this morning. But why do you think they would do that—withhold information?"

"I imagine they're afraid that if they tell all they know, the killer might turn tail and run. Whereas if he thinks he's got them stumped, he might stick around to watch."

"That makes some sense," said Ned, "but if it's clear to you and me that the police are withholding information, why wouldn't it be clear to the killer?"

"Maybe he's not too bright."

"Oh, I doubt it. A psychopath like that. They're usually quite bright. Your sister says she thinks she knows who did it."

"Is that so?" said Brimm, and suddenly, intuitively, he knew that Muriel was somehow the real subject of Ned's visit.

Ned breathed deeply. "I've never liked the scent of pines," he said.

"Who does Muriel think did it?" Brimm asked.

"Oh, she doesn't say. She only says she knows who, but isn't telling."

"That's preposterous."

"Of course it is, Frank," said Ned, very pleased and encouraged by Brimm's reaction. "I don't mind telling you,

Frank, I'm worried about her. Billie and I are both worried about her. She's erratic."

"In what way?" asked Brimm.

"In any number of ways. Now why would anyone go around saying she knew who the killer was but wasn't telling. It's something a spoiled child might do. Last Sunday she called us over in a tizzy because she'd seen some animal in the river. She's on the verge of tears about half the time. She's rude. She drifts off into daydreams at the drop of a hat. Now she's going around asking everybody whether or not she's ever been to Des Moines, Iowa. Can you beat that? She calls me up at ten o'clock at night this week and says to me, 'Ned, have I ever been to Des Moines, Iowa, to your knowledge?' "

"To Des Moines?" said Brimm.

"Des Moines, Iowa," said Ned. "Now how in the world am I to know whether or not *she's* been to Iowa or not? I can hardly remember where I myself have been. And what the hell difference does it make anyway?"

Brimm noted that Ned had grown hot under the collar on the subject of Muriel, and he wondered: Was not wanting to grow old—not wanting to become an old person, that is— was it really a fear of death? Or were those two separate fears, growing old and dying, distinguishable each from the other?

Brimm learned that Ned had been dispatched over to the cottage by Billie, as a kind of ambassador, Ned's mission being to persuade Francis to come and talk to Muriel, and to help get to the bottom of what was going on with her. Brimm required no persuasion, idle as he was—it would be a diversion from trying to get to the bottom of what was going on with himself.

He offered Ned a ride home, and promised to have a chat with Muriel. As a reward, Ned promised to take Brimm deep-sea fishing on his son's charter boat.

Later, speaking over the hum of the air conditioner in her

95

parlor, Muriel asked Francis, "What was Ned Otto doing in your car?"

"Ned Otto?" said Brimm.

"I happened to be looking out the window when you drove up, Francis," she said. "I saw you let him off next door."

"Oh," said Francis. "He dropped by the cottage this morning. To visit. And I gave him a ride back over here."

"Visit?" she said. "Ned Otto? You?"

"Yes," he said. "Invited me to go deep-sea fishing with him sometime. And . . . asked me if I might have a chat with you."

"Ned wants you to have a chat with me?" she said. "About what?"

"He and Billie wanted me to talk to you. They think you've been behaving oddly."

She was sitting in one of the leather club chairs, and now she turned her head and gazed out the front window. "Well, I'm sure I have," she said, surprising him.

Brimm, following her gaze, saw that she was staring in an overly pensive manner at the vacant lot across the boulevard, the spot where a huge house had burned to the ground many years ago, a house belonging to a family Brimm had always referred to as the "phony Faysons"—a family, he recalled, that Muriel had been greatly enchanted by and infatuated with, incomprehensibly so, given that they were snobs. Looking at the vacant lot, which was now overgrown with weeds, Brimm could recall precisely the family's wild superiority. The father, a former officer in the navy, was called Captain both by the wife and by the children. The wife, whose family was the source of the money, passed for a socialite in Pines, something she could accomplish only in solo, since it was necessary to keep the spirited captain, with his tattoos and philandering, hidden away. The Faysons had represented something to Muriel, though Brimm never knew what exactly. One thing was clear: the captain, with his husky cheerfulness, and the mother, with her flamboyance, were striking opposites to the Brimm parents—the stern, alcoholic, corroding doctor with his missing left arm, the troubled, cowering, religious mother.

"What are you staring at?" Brimm said at last.

"Oh," said Muriel, a bit startled. "I was just looking at Henry over there, stalking in the weeds."

Henry was of course their father's name, which gave Muriel's remark an odd twist. Brimm looked again at the vacant lot but saw no cat in the weeds. ˎ

"Ned told me you were saying you knew who the golf course murderer was."

"That's a lie," she said, returning her gaze to the window. "I never said any such thing."

"He said you said you knew who it was but wouldn't tell."

"I said I *thought* I knew who it was. Which is the reason I wouldn't say the name." She looked at him. "You can't very well accuse someone without any evidence, can you?"

Brimm offered her a long silence in which he expected to be told the name, but Muriel instead returned to her window gazing. "Oh, Muriel, really," he said. "This mysteriousness is cheap."

"You don't know him," she said.

"Well, who is it?"

"I can't say. It wouldn't be right."

"Give me a hint."

"He works at the Raphael School. Now please stop badgering me."

"Okay then, what's all this business about Des Moines?"

She stood. "Honestly, I feel . . . I don't know what I feel . . ." she said, and strode out of the room.

Brimm followed her through the dining room, the kitchen, through the porch, and out into the back yard. He waited in the sunlight for a moment and watched her duck under the grape arbor at the back of the lot. Moving closer, he could see, beneath the curtain of leaves, that she had taken a seat in the arbor's wooden swing. She kicked off her shoes and dangled her bare feet, swaying gently back and forth in the swing. How was it possible, Brimm thought, that a woman approaching her ninth decade of life could still be such a girl in all the fundamental ways? There was something about that stubborn refusal to mature, an almost pathological arrestedness in her that was extremely unsettling. Somehow it undid you. Somehow it accused you, calling up your own cynicism and corruption and parading them out in front to look at. After a minute, he walked to the arbor and stood just outside the small dark clearing where Muriel had disappeared. "Muriel," he said. "Come out, will you?"

Silence.

"Muriel," he said. "Will you please come out now."

Then, in that sentimental voice she generally reserved for talking to appliances and machines and articles of clothing: "Why don't you come in, Frankie?"

Brimm sighed heavily, resigned to the inevitable, ducked his head down, and entered the coolness of the arbor, where the air was dark green and all one heard was the crackling skirmishes of lizards in the vines.

She patted the seat next to her in the swing.

"It'll break under the weight," said Brimm.

"Don't be silly," she said. "It's as strong as the day it was built."

He sighed again. She looked around the small enclosure, smiled, and said, "Takes you back, doesn't it?" but he was having no part of it.

"Muriel," he said, "I don't wish to be taken anywhere, back or otherwise. Your good friends and neighbors have expressed concern about you, and I have—"

"Francis," she interrupted. "Sit down."

He sat next to her in the swing.

"The man's name is Joe Letson," she said. "He works at the Raphael School, a kind, humorous man whom I was always fond of. Last week when I drove over to your place, I met up with him and some girls from the school as they

98

were crossing the Little Yustaga Bridge. I went to say hello to him but he averted his face, pretended not to know me. Now why in the world would he do that?"

"This is the man you suspect of being a homicidal maniac?"

"Yes," she said, "and I have no reason for doing so except that he averted his face that day on the bridge. Now wouldn't I sound silly saying this to Detective Connie Shoulders? He'd have me locked away in a home somewhere and throw away the key."

"I don't get it," said Brimm. "Why—"

"You aren't supposed to get it, Francis," said Muriel. "It isn't gettable, don't you see? Remember when you asked me if I ever felt that the ground had shifted under my feet? It's like that. It's a feeling. A feeling you can't explain. And the reason I asked Ned about Des Moines is that I had this memory I can't explain. I remembered seeing a giant statue of a woman. She was meant to represent the state of Iowa, the state of Iowa feeding the nation. I can see that statue clearly in my mind, I know it's in the city of Des Moines, and yet I don't know when I might have actually seen it. As far as I know, I've never been to Iowa. So how could I possibly have such a memory? Don't tell me I've seen a picture in a book, because it's not that kind of memory. You see, I can feel my own presence in the memory. I have a strong sense of being there."

"Well, you did go to Des Moines once," Brimm said, obviously shocking her.

"I did?"

"Yes," he said. "With Daddy."

"With Daddy?"

"Yes."

"I don't believe it. When?"

"I can't say exactly. I was just a baby at the time. I think I learned about it when I was older, either from you or Mother. There are pictures from the trip somewhere."

"Pictures?"

"Yes. Snapshots. I don't remember any statue, though."

"With Daddy?"

"Yes. He was on some kind of business trip, a medical convention of some kind, and he took you with him."

"That's impossible," Muriel said almost angrily.

He looked at her wide-eyed. "I'm only saying what I think to be the truth, Muriel," he said.

Late that night, however, lying in bed, unable to sleep, Brimm wondered whether he had in fact told the truth. Certainly he hadn't deliberately lied to Muriel—what possible motive could he have had for that? But now, in the dark, it seemed just as likely that he'd only imagined seeing old snapshots of a trip to Iowa. He noted that there had developed a subversive strain in his thinking lately, sounding the tones of second-guessing, wreaking a bit of havoc in his inner life.

He turned on the bedside lamp. He opened the book of Chekhov stories and reread the last paragraphs of the story about the old man who died and was buried at sea. There was something dreamy and surprising about the description of the body, wrapped in sailcloth and weighted with gridirons, zigzagging through a three-mile depth of water. A shark, almost cartoonlike, swims under the body, allows it to drift onto its back, then turns belly upward, "basking in the warm, transparent water." A school of small fish, harbor pilots, looks on, waiting to see what will happen next. "After playing a little with the body the shark nonchalantly puts its jaws under it, cautiously touches it with its teeth, and the sailcloth is rent its full length from head to foot." To Brimm, this journey through air and water into oblivion seemed much more appealing than the slow, claustrophobic route of coffin and earth. There was a handsomeness to it, a dignity, lacking the obscenity of decomposition.

In the front of the book, a bookplate depicted rabbits playing among pink lilies. Printed on the bookplate were the words "This book belongs to," and then, in Muriel's handwriting, "Muriel Brimm." Brimm didn't interpret Muriel's latest idiosyncrasies—her suspicion of the poor man at the school for the blind, her struggle to remember Des Moines—as ominously as the Ottos apparently did. These things taken alone did not amount to any slipping over the edge, though Brimm did sense an emotional undercurrent that seemed to be driving them forward. This, of course—the undercurrent—was much harder to get at.

Brimm closed his eyes and could see Muriel sitting in the parlor, gazing out at the vacant lot across the boulevard. Now, when he revisited the question of what that large family across the way had represented for Muriel, he thought surely it must have been a kind of escape, a refuge from their own parents' intensity and grim torpor. He himself had known, in that way children know these things, that he would leave Pines, bound for the larger world. As a boy he'd foreseen himself flying to the moon, fighting in wars, visiting the foreign lands he read about in encyclopedias. It was one of the things boys were given by the world, that deep, abiding sense of adventure and possible greatness; it could attach itself to any number of convenient dreams. But Muriel had had no such fantasies, not that Brimm knew of anyway. Her vision in this regard extended about as far as the other side of the street. The path of her deliverance defined itself in terms of relationships with others, with people, not with spacecraft, artillery, and exotic terrain. So it made sense that the Faysons, with their fancy airs and pleasures, with their sheer exuberance, would have found Muriel gazing across the boulevard. Brimm didn't think the Faysons had ever really taken her in, however. It seemed to him, without much detail, that Muriel's tie to the family was always probationary, experimental on their part, and he suddenly pictured her stranded on the boulevard's median strip, looking forward, looking back, not belonging fully home, not belonging fully away.

He turned off the lamp and tried again to sleep. His mind wandered into various territories—Claudia Callejas in her

Dennis McFarland

bright window, like a painting; Ned Otto, young and heart-broken, standing outside the great iron gates that barred him from his true love's estate; Connie Shoulders's grand-mother, foolishly going barefoot to the outhouse. "Such a snaky state, Florida," Brimm hears Muriel saying. "We've got every damned poisonous snake in America." And Con-nie Shoulders himself, last Monday, seizing the moment of privacy when Muriel had gone into the kitchen to answer the phone, sighing, shaking his head; "We've got ourselves a real arts and crafts job here, Mr. Brimm. Lots of cutting and—" Then Muriel suddenly reappearing at the door . . . In her study, the young female priest says, "I wonder how you would feel about closing your eyes and trying to *become* the woman in the picture." And then Brimm, Frankie, sways in the wooden swing under the arbor of grape vines, back and forth, dark green, dark green . . .

The crying of the seagulls is like that of human babies, urgent, imperative. The gendarme wearing the shiny helmet moves alongside the girl, putting his face close to hers. Does he whisper a kind word? The shuffling of hundreds of feet on cobblestones a sound of surf . . . A chant rises up from the walkways, the same brief phrase in French, over and over, an appellation aimed at the girl carrying the in-fant, a cadential epithet Brimm cannot quite make out. Be-hind him, just up the narrow street, soars the cathedral, its magnificent spire trained on a heaven recently filled with fire. The chanting spreads, garbled, louder, and Brimm, suddenly awake, sees the doughy face of the bald girl, an-drogynous, plain, sorrowful on the ceiling.

102

Eleven

BEFORE THE OTTOS arrived for the Friday morning meeting of the book club, Muriel prayed to be blessed with charity toward them. She hoped that with God's help, with His faculty for changing the human heart, she could at least begin to see the good intentions behind the Ottos' idle, reckless meddling. She took a few minutes to meditate on how she valued Billie and Ned, which proved a disillusioning exercise since all she came up with was loss upon loss, with how she'd once valued them and no longer did. Billie, once reliable, helpful, sympathetic, had become dismissive, skeptical, disloyal. Ned, once possessing charm and cheerfulness, now bellyached, belched, and nodded off in public, unthinkable in an earlier day. Still, this review of the Ottos' former merits enabled Muriel to greet them at the door with an open mind, if not a completely open heart.

No one, of course, even so much as alluded to Francis's visit earlier that same morning, or to its prompting. Through coffee, in the parlor, Muriel maintained a detached equilibrium, noting in passing some unusual tension in her jaw. Once the discussion began, however, and it became clear that Ned and Billie had each selected poems—Ned from Frost, Billie from Dickinson—that were meant somehow to instruct Muriel, Muriel began to falter. The old song lyric "In time, the Rockies may crumble . . ." passed through her mind, the Rockies here being her equilibrium, she supposed, though the effect of the "crumbling," counter to the metaphor, was a distinct pulling-in, a tightening. Listening to the Ottos' recitations, she even felt her eyes narrow, as if to let in less light was, in this case, to let in less darkness.

" 'The Armful,' " declaimed Ned broadly. " 'For every parcel I stoop down to seize, / I lose some other off my arms and knees.' "

Could he have been put up to this by Billie? The poem's implication—that somehow Muriel, in stooping to retrieve what might have been earlier dropped, would lose what she currently held—seemed almost too sophisticated for Ned. The choice of poem, like Ned's visiting Francis earlier that morning and prompting Francis to visit Muriel, must have been Billie's work.

Ned licked his lips, horribly. " 'I lose some other off my arms and knees.' "

"You already read that line," said Billie.

"Oh," he said, lowering his head and running his index finger across the page.

Actually, Muriel thought, it seemed almost too sophisticated even for Billie. When Ned was done, Muriel smiled, careful not to show any teeth.

They were evidently to treat the recitations as a kind of religious liturgy, proceeding one to the other without comment, for Billie began heralding the more pointed Dickinson at once. " 'To flee from memory / Had we the Wings / Many would fly / Inured to slower things / Birds with surprise / Would scan the cowering Van / Of men escaping / From the mind of man.' " With these last two lines, Billie cast Muriel what was surely meant to be a significant look, then said quickly, "I wonder why the birds are surprised. I mean, I like it, I like their being surprised. But it's not entirely clear to me."

"It says why right in the poem," said Muriel, trying not to sound bitter. "Because they're inured to slower things."

Billie looked down at the page of her book. "Oh," she said. "I think I see. But I thought that line referred to—"
104

"Will you excuse me?" Muriel interrupted, rising from her chair.

Billie and Ned shared a brisk, astounded look just before Muriel turned her back on them. Muriel went to the little powder room under the front stairs, closed the door, did not switch on the light, and therefore was enveloped in darkness. Groping, she made sure the lid to the toilet was down, and sat. She took a deep breath in an effort to slow her heart, which was racing.

It wasn't the poems that had sent her from the parlor; she had already felt herself happily gearing up for battle. What had sent her from the parlor was the sudden, terrifying thought that both Ned's and Billie's selections were innocent, originating from motives wholly their own, having nothing at all to do with Muriel; that Muriel was, in her definite insanity, reading into the poems all this paranoid narcissism; that mentally (and just as the Ottos suspected) she'd run amok.

She quickly concluded that Francis's visit must have upset her more than she realized. Earlier, when he had left the grape arbor, she'd felt only the relief of confession. She was glad to have explained herself to someone, and Francis had been, as was his nature, receptive, agreeable enough. But his suggestion that she, as a child, had been on a trip with her father to Iowa, that somewhere in the house there might actually be snapshots of such a trip, this had lodged somewhere near her heart with a little clock-tick of its own. One thing she knew: she was, at the present moment, expected to return to her parlor and read aloud John Donne's "Valediction: forbidding mourning," and that would not be possible. She wondered whether she should feign illness, play out her righteous indignation about the Ottos' pointed selections (even if that were a delusion), or simply return and say she had not done her homework. She struggled briefly with the options and then experienced a splendid, liberating insight: it made no difference what she did, for the Ottos already thought she had a screw loose. If she

105

wanted to, she could wait in the dark powder room until they gave up on her and went home. If she wanted to, she could take off all her clothes, return to the parlor stark naked, and pour more coffee.

She thought for another minute about what her real desires were, then returned to the parlor, composed.

She found Ned asleep, hugging a satin pillow. Billie, turning from staring out the window at the white wall of her own house, greeted Muriel with a persecuted What now? expression on her face.

Under the circumstances, it seemed to Muriel fortunate that Ned was sleeping, so she whispered to Billie, "Come out to the kitchen."

Once they were standing in the kitchen, Billie said, in full voice, "What's going on?"

Muriel looked at her. Billie, always stout, was losing weight. Muriel's scrutiny obviously made her feel awkward, and awkwardly she put one hand up against the refrigerator as if for support, then removed it and crossed her arms. Billie had been beautiful in her day, dark like Muriel but, unlike Muriel, also big. "You're losing weight, Billie," Muriel said.

"This is what you brought me out here to tell me?"

"I wondered if you might help me with something," Muriel said.

"What?"

"I had a visit from Francis this morning."

"Oh?"

"Don't be coy, Billie. For your information, he told me I did indeed make a trip to Iowa when I was a child. He said there were snapshots of the trip. I thought you might help me look for them."

When Ned awakened about an hour later, he called out the phrase "mattress sets!" loud enough for Muriel, who was rooting through a cedar chest in the upstairs hallway, to hear him distinctly. She walked to the top of the stairs and called down his name. Quietly, he appeared in the entry hall and leaned his head against the newel post's carved pineapple. Muriel looked at him: his head and the pineapple were about the same size. "Did you say 'mattress sets'?" she asked.

Ned closed his eyes, then opened them and answered, "Yes. But don't ask me why."

"Well, you certainly said it urgently, Ned," Muriel said, smiling.

"What the devil are you doing up there?" he asked. "And where is Billie?"

"Billie's up here with me," she said. "We're looking for something. Something dropped."

"What do you mean by that, dropped?"

"Never mind. Would you like to join us?"

Billie came out of one of the rooms carrying a shoebox full of old photos. "I just found these," she said. "Oh, Ned, you're awake."

"Such powers of observation!" he said, looked down and walked away, disgruntled, into the dining room.

Billie passed the shoebox of yellowed, scalloped-edged photos to Muriel. "I better take him home and feed him," said Billie. She paused for a long moment, as if she were giving Muriel a chance to respond to this remark, then added, "He gets awfully cranky."

Because the upstairs rooms were uncomfortably warm, Muriel hauled all the pictures downstairs to her bed. Also, she had to admit to herself that once Billie was gone, she did not feel quite safe upstairs alone. For another hour or so, she sorted through dozens of snapshots, a process, she noted, that seemed to turn her to stone. She told herself that this was natural, even a good thing—she couldn't possibly react emotionally to every image from her past. She found nothing that might have been from any trip to Iowa, and this outcome produced in her a very gray feeling, a confusion of disappointment and relief.

The morning—Francis's visit, the aborted book club meeting, the futile search through old photographs—had left her feeling a little sick, a little lightheaded and overtired. She had not eaten properly and . . .

She lay back on the bed, closed her eyes, and fell into a sleep that was like free-fall, rapid motion through blackness, and when she awakened (what seemed like a minute later) she had the cool, distinct sensation of wind in her ears. This proved to be a draft from the air conditioner. She lifted her head and looked at the clutter of photographs on the bed all around her. Then she caught sight of herself in the vanity's oval mirror, a solitary old woman lying on a bed surrounded by the disarray of her past. She felt instantly resigned to this image—somehow it seemed accurate—but a lingering glance revealed something more troublesome. The solitary old woman on the bed looked startlingly like Muriel's own mother, Louise Whitefield Brimm, the bleak religious fanatic. This of course was an irrational perception. Louise Whitefield, descendant of the Wesleyan evangelist George Whitefield, had never reached the age of the white-haired woman in the mirror.

She sat up on the edge of the bed, turning her back to the vanity, and swung her feet to the floor. She recalled that Francis had mentioned their mother, their mother's crying through the Passion play in the dark armory. Her mother had gone to every performance, escorting Muriel each night, obsessed with Muriel's punctual arrival. The silence and gravity that attended these escortings bordered on grotesque, and Muriel knew her mother had been privately fasting in order to achieve a new intensity—just like a drug addict. A drug addict was precisely what Mrs. Brimm had looked like, too, sitting in the armory a half hour before any other audience member arrived, stunned by hunger and prayer, waiting for Calvary to ravage her again, a haunted believer for whom, secretly, the Resurrection was anticlimactic.

Muriel lay back on the bed again, closing her eyes.

"Muriel, child," her mother whispers, leaning close to her, touching her brow. "Are you awake? Do you hear the wind? It's another storm."

"My mother," says Muriel to the kind therapist, "was a sleepwalker."

The therapist, surprised, says, "A sleepwalker?"

"Yes," says Muriel. "Somnambulant all her life. An interesting word, too, *somnambulant*. I looked it up once. 'Walking or addicted to walking while asleep,' the dictionary says. I always thought the stipulation of 'addicted' was interesting because that's how it seemed. And it was funny . . . My father was the drunk, the alcoholic, but in her own way my mother was truly addicted to all her aberrations."

"That *is* funny," says the therapist ironically.

"I've gone completely batty," said Muriel aloud, sitting up again. She gathered up the photographs, first with her forearms, then with her hands, and put them back into their boxes. She turned again toward the parlor, and as she looked through it to the light of the front windows, she recalled Billie Otto's standing next to her at the top of the stairs a while ago, Billie's saying, "I better take him home and feed him," followed by that odd, long pause. Billie had been enthusiastic about helping her look for the pictures, taking pleasure in having been needed and called on in so concrete a way. And Muriel had been too self-absorbed even to show gratitude with the offer of a sandwich. Of course. That was the meaning of Billie's pause between sentences—an opportunity for Muriel to invite them to lunch, and to begin to mend things between them.

She stood and took a deep breath, thinking that for all that, for all the strangeness of many days in a row, there was some good news: her morning prayer had been answered. For she had to acknowledge that her heart, over the course of the day, regarding the Ottos, had indeed changed.

Twelve

"I THINK YOU better call the sergeant, don't you?"

It was Francis's voice, Sunday morning, 6:45 A.M. by the clock on Muriel's night table.

"Francis," she said. "It's six forty-five A.M."

"I didn't wake you," he said, not a question.

"No," she said. "As it happens, I'm in bed reading today's lessons. But you *might* have waked me."

"Put down the Bible, Muriel, and pick up the newspaper."

"I told you, Francis, I'm still in bed. I haven't brought the newspaper in yet."

"Well, get out of bed," he said. "Put on your blue kimono and go fetch the paper. After you've read the front page, call me."

"Oh, you can be annoying, Francis," she said.

"You'll thank me in ten minutes," he said, and hung up.

In truth, she'd already finished reading the lessons a while ago, and young Connie Shoulders had just crossed Muriel's mind when the telephone rang. Supposedly she had been meditating on the Gospel, though now, interrupted, she reflected that her thoughts had taken a strange turn. Instead of dwelling on the message of the Gospel, she'd found herself considering Jesus's personality. In the passage from Saint John, Jesus had just shocked everyone in the synagogue at Capernaum—not only the Jews, but his own disciples as well—by suggesting that if they desired eternal life they would have to eat his flesh and drink his blood. As usual, he had been speaking metaphorically but not successfully so, and he had confused and repulsed everyone in his hearing. Muriel wondered, as she had wondered often, why Jesus couldn't have just *said* he was speaking metaphorically, why he couldn't have simply explained to them that he didn't literally mean they should eat his flesh and drink his blood. Instead—and this, too, was a pattern in Jesus's behavior—he had become peevish and sad about having been misunderstood. That of course would be Jesus's human side showing, but Muriel had to admit that sometimes when she read the Gospels lately, it aggravated her that Jesus himself didn't seem sure about what he was trying to say; sometimes his disappointment in the stupidity of others seemed a deflection, meant to mask his own uncertainty. Worse, his refusal to be clear appeared occasionally contrived to bring about the trouble he would get himself into later—like an affected plot device: if Jesus was to end up on the cross, crucified, it was necessary for him to be wildly misunderstood, and if he was to be wildly misunderstood, he had to be enigmatic.

Muriel didn't perceive these cerebral commentaries of hers as lapses in faith. She knew that doubt was the very rock upon which faith rested, and after all, God had given her the mind He had given her. The question that had her in its grip just now when the telephone rang was this: if Jesus were to show up on her doorstep and join her for breakfast this morning, would she enjoy his company? Would she actually like him? Would she like him as well as she had liked, say, Detective Sergeant Connie Shoulders?

That was why it had been uncanny that Francis should have phoned at that moment and said, "I think you better call the sergeant, don't you?"

She did get out of bed and pull on her blue kimono. She did go to the porch and fetch the newspaper. She did read, in horror and amazement, the banner headline and the front-page story, and then she phoned Francis.

"I guess you best come over here for breakfast," she said, feeling dazed.

"Give me twenty minutes," he said.

She left all the shades down on the parlor side of the house in hopes of averting the Ottos, who, once they had seen the newspaper, would be beating a path to her door.

At last, the *Crier* had revealed all that had been withheld for the past week. Parts of two bodies had been exhumed from the sand traps of the Madison Heights golf course. Both were female. Most of one corpse had been pieced together from what was found in the traps, and another corpse (missing its head and arms, which had been excavated from the golf course earlier) had washed up along the banks of the Yustaga River on Friday, about a mile north of the town line. The bones that Francis had discovered, as well as some others found later by the police, showed evidence of chemical applications—an acid had been used to eat away the flesh from the bones. There were also abrasions on the bones, suggesting a tool used to strip away flesh, perhaps a paint scraper or putty knife. What had prompted Francis's remark on the telephone about calling the sergeant was this: after lab tests were completed yesterday in Tallahassee, the two victims had been identified as students at the school for the blind. For four days the school had concealed from the police the fact of the missing students, and had been conducting its own private investigation in an attempt to keep its name out of the papers. The Raphael School's contrite spokesman, pictured on the jump page of the article, was Joe Letson.

"So, what do you think?" said Francis when he arrived. "Want to follow your intuitions now?"

"I don't know," Muriel said. "I suppose I could at least discuss it with him."

She was at the stove, scrambling eggs. Francis sat in his usual place next to the wall phone at the kitchen counter.

By "him" Muriel referred to Detective Sergeant Connie Shoulders.

"Just tell him what you told me," Francis said, reaching for the telephone. "He seems the kind of young man who could deal with that."

"But what about church?" she said.

"Muriel," he said. "What do you mean, what about church?"

"I mean, I can't see him this morning when there's church."

"How can you think about church at a time like this?"

"How can I not think about it?"

He seemed to understand her point without further explanation. He restored the telephone to its cradle and went to stand beside her at the stove. He took the spatula she was using from her hand and then waved it at her in a shooing gesture. "Well, go quickly then," he said, "and say a few prayers in your bedroom or something."

"I'll do no such thing," she said, taking back the spatula.

She watched in disbelief as Francis returned to the telephone, took out a small slip of paper from his shirt pocket, and began dialing the number written there.

She turned off the burner under the pan on the stove and moved to the other side of the counter. There was a long pause between Francis's dialing and his first words. She heard him ask for the sergeant and then say "Oh" in a rather befuddled way. After a moment, Francis gave his own name and Muriel's telephone number.

"Well?" she said.

He only stared at her, a mixture of frustration and disgust on his face.

"Well?" she repeated.

Francis looked as if she'd unfairly beat him at some game. "You'll be happy to know that he's at church."

Muriel was spared the shame of gloating by an urgent knock at the back door. "That'll be Ned and Billie," she said, and smiled.

* * *

"I wasn't *able* to eat anything," Ned said, watching Muriel and Francis eat their eggs.

They had moved to the back porch, where there were enough bamboo chairs for them all. Regrettably, Ned had worn, on a Sunday morning, baggy white shorts. Muriel noticed that his legs were thin and white, hairless, perfectly smooth with visible blue veins, like an alien's legs.

"Me neither," said Billie. "Good God, I can't imagine how any human being could do such a thing."

"What, eat?" said Muriel.

"No, of course not," said Billie. "I mean those things, those things in the paper."

"Here's what gets me," said Ned. "Whoever did these things, whoever he is, presumably he's living somewhere, maybe right here in Pines. He shops for groceries, has a family maybe ... maybe a job, a bank account ... goes to the laundromat, the dry cleaners. How could he be passing? How could he walk around passing for normal with that kind of stuff inside his head? With that kind of capacity? That's what gets me. He might be kneeling right next to you in church today, Muriel."

"Oh, I don't think he has dry cleaning," Muriel said. "And I'm sure he won't be in church."

"Well, why not?" said Ned. "Why not in church? Why not singing in the choir? Why not in the pulpit, for that matter?"

Muriel burst out laughing then, and the others—first Francis, then Billie, and finally even Ned—joined in. They all had a good laugh, and then as silence reclaimed the porch, they sat staring vacantly into the air as if they weren't sure what to do next.

Francis wiped his mouth with a paper napkin, stood, and went out quietly through the screen door into the yard.

"Where's he going?" asked Billie.

"The arbor, I imagine," Muriel said, and as she watched him moving slowly away toward the back of the yard and the arbor, she noticed his thwarted-seeming posture, his listless gait, and she suddenly heard her father's voice.

"Stand up straight!" it said, and Frankie, a boy of about nine in the dark kitchen, hands at his sides, eyes forward, struggled through the misspelling: s-e-p-e-r-a-t-i-o-n.

"Wrong," said Dr. Brimm. "You're wrong again, Francis."

Muriel, age seventy-eight, stood and said "Excuse me" to the once again bewildered Ottos and followed behind her brother out into the grape arbor, where she found him standing and staring at the old wooden swing. It occurred to her that Francis was thinking about the families of the slain girls, of the mothers and fathers who had lived through the heartbreak of having a child born blind, or born sighted and later blinded—Muriel herself had seen some of these parents when they visited the Raphael School—and how, over the years, the parents of the slain girls might have finally reached some resignation, some acceptance, even some peace, and perhaps only recently. It would be like Francis to think of that, like him eventually in all this horror to arrive there. But when he turned to her he said, "The people were chanting something . . . a name they had for her . . ."

"Who, Francis?" said Muriel, and noticed that his face was a terrible grayish color.

"The girl," he said. "They marched her down the street . . ."

"Your French girl," said Muriel. "Your girl on the ceiling."

". . . a name they had for her . . ."

"What name?"

She touched her hand to his forehead. His lips moved as if forming words but no sound came out.

"Francis," she said, "I believe you're running a fever."

"Yes," he said. "I don't feel at all well."

"You come inside at once," she said. "You must come inside and lie down. You're coming down with a flu."

"Yes," he said, and taking his arm, she guided him out of the arbor.

"Francis is ill," she called to the Ottos as they approached the porch. "I'm bringing him inside."

"You know, I'm not a bit surprised," Billie said, holding open the screen door. "I didn't think he looked quite right. He's very, very pale, you know."

Thirteen

MURIEL INSTALLED BRIMM in her own bed downstairs, between cream-colored sheets of satin, threw an extra cotton blanket over him, stood guard as he swallowed two aspirin tablets, and soon departed for the eleven o'clock service at St. Matthew and the Redeemer. For most of his life, Brimm had believed one's attitude to be the key thing in matters of health, and he regarded the illnesses of others as the result of mental or emotional, rather than physical, weakness. He thought that sick people, lacking a certain strength of character, embraced sickness, allowed sickness (like the wolf in a children's story) through the door.

"The prideful philosophy of a person who has been blessed with good health," Muriel had once said to him many years ago.

"Why prideful?" he had asked.

"Because you're trying to take credit for something God has given you through pure grace," she answered. "Garden-variety sin of pride. And intellectually beneath you as well."

Of course she had been right. Feverish and left alone among the silent rooms of his boyhood—the shades pulled down, the heavy drapes drawn—he knew that she had been right on all counts, and this small recognition seemed yet another surrender to some fatal design meant to undermine every good thought he'd ever had about himself. Surely it was the true purpose behind his returning to Pines: so that he might be taken apart, bit by bit.

Last night, he'd felt poorly after supper (now he understood why—he was getting sick) and had turned in early, around nine o'clock. He'd soon fallen asleep and dreamed again of the young Normandy girl carrying the baby through the village street; once again he'd heard the French and American flags snapping in the wind, the sea sound of footsteps on cobblestones, and the infernal, unintelligible chanting of the townspeople. He awakened just before midnight, parched, and went to the kitchen for cranberry juice. As he opened the refrigerator, spilling a bit of light into the room, he noticed, out the kitchen window, the bright windows of the house next door. In one of these—*her* kitchen, with the houseplants on glass shelves—he saw Claudia Callejas, who appeared to be having an animated conversation on the telephone—with her errant, scientific husband, Brimm imagined.

Her house and the oyster shell driveway were awash in moonlight. Brimm abandoned the refrigerator, moved up close to his own window, and stood watching her. After only a moment, Brimm saw that she was angry, shouting into the telephone, and now and then he could even hear her voice, faintly across the distance between the two houses. Soon the boy, Nicolás, appeared in the kitchen, wearing red pajamas and rubbing his eyes. Claudia put down the phone and began scolding him, pointing upward with one hand, toward the ceiling and the second floor. Apparently stunned, the boy turned and wandered back out of the room; Brimm could see him as he passed by the dining room window and then out of sight.

Claudia concluded her call quickly after that, perhaps even abruptly, and moved into the dining room herself, where Brimm could see her more clearly. Her long hair fell over her shoulders and down her back—*untamed* crossed Brimm's mind—and she wore a white dressing gown. She sat at the far side of the dining room table, facing Brimm's house, lowered her head into her hands, and began crying so vigorously that he could see her shoulders quake. This sight brought on a strange emotional confusion in Brimm, for he was at once moved by the young woman's sorrow and very nearly spellbound by the beauty of the golden tableau equally partitioned by the window's black mullions: Latin Woman Crying at Table. He thought it more than an erstwhile artist's dilemma, too—he wondered if men didn't always feel ambivalence at the sight of a woman's crying, if it didn't always stir something in them that was vaguely pleasurable.

A few minutes later, lying in his bed, humiliated, Brimm decided Claudia Callejas must have sensed his watching her, given the suddenness with which she had looked up and out into the night. He pulled away from the window swiftly, but—he was sure, given the brightness of the moon—not swiftly enough. When he looked again, he saw her standing precisely in the middle of the long dining room window, staring audaciously at his cottage. He stayed in the darkest part of the kitchen so as not to be seen, and after a few seconds passed, she moved away and extinguished all the lights in the house. Brimm remained frozen, aware of his own breathing. Then he saw her again, now in the moonlight, standing brazenly in the same window. Under the circumstances, the courageous thing, maybe even the honorable thing, would have been for him to move likewise into his own window, but he was too ashamed, and returned instead to his bedroom, noticing as he went the sad-looking rolled-up cuffs of his pajama pants.

Awake, lying on his back in the bed, he was possessed by two separate degradations, and he wondered which was the worse, having been discovered by Claudia Callejas to be a common voyeur (spying on her at midnight) or a common coward (slinking away from her dare). And what had she meant, standing like that in the window? It was clearly a challenge, but a challenge to what? What, exactly, was she inviting? What, exactly, had he passed up? It would be absurd for him to think even momentarily that this woman had been anything other than distraught and angry, made angrier still by the depraved old man next door, and daring the old man to show his face, to own up to his depravity.

Eventually Brimm drifted off, carrying into sleep a very low estimate of himself, and he awoke at daybreak in a funk.

With the arrival of the morning paper, however, everything changed. Its startling news took him cleanly and promptly out of himself. He noted that he'd been right about there being more than one murder victim, and after reading that the victims had been students at the Raphael School, he phoned Muriel and suggested that she contact Detective Connie Shoulders.

Later he joined Muriel for breakfast, the Ottos came to visit, they all had that good laugh over Ned's ridiculous musings about the murderer, a silence fell over the screen porch, and then a surprising thing happened. In the silence Brimm seemed to hear, across fifty years and thousands of miles, the jeering and chanting of the townspeople in his recurring dream. Not a bona fide auditory hallucination, he quickly comforted himself; more like recollected music, and the young woman's face . . . well, he no longer needed any visions on the ceiling for that. She had taken up residence, her visage looming before him at odd times throughout the day and night—rather like the face of a lover were it not for that doggedly neutral quality, that cold surgeon's demeanor.

In the grape arbor, Muriel had touched his forehead and explained to him helpfully that he was ill. Once she'd got him inside, into bed, and brought him the aspirin, she glared at him disapprovingly and said, "I don't like the way you look."

"What do you mean?" he said. "I'm sick."

"Yes, but there's something else," she said. "You don't like being cared for, do you?"

"Oh, go to church, Muriel," he said. "I'm sick and I don't feel like being analyzed."

"Well, then I'll pray for you," she said.

"Good," he said, meaning it, and for a brief moment she looked surprised.

She gathered her purse and white gloves from the vanity and left.

"Astute," Brimm said aloud once she was out the door. She had divined something about his state of mind. But what she couldn't know was that only a few minutes earlier, in the grape arbor, just before she had arrived at his side and put her hand to his brow, the jumbled chanting in Brimm's ears had found an unexpected unison, and the stars in the puzzling constellation of the last few weeks had lined up, chaos to order, nonsense to logic, obscurity to light and focus. *"Ange de la mort,"* the voices had said. That had been the villagers' name for the French girl, those had been the indecipherable words. Of course, angel of death, not really a surprise at all.

Fourteen

CONSIDERING THE REVELATION in the grape arbor, Brimm was thankful for the time alone, though spending it in his childhood home seemed almost fantastical. Once or twice he found himself close to tears, and he was in fact prepared, intellectually, to cry. The sensation of being about to cry, however, shook him each time in such a way as to ward off actual crying.

He lay under the blanket, flat on his back, his arms straight at his sides as if bracing for the next thing. One of Muriel's cats, the big alley cat, crept into the room, paused to size up the situation, then bounded onto the bed, settled on Brimm's stomach, and began to purr. The sheer weight of the animal, and soon its warmth, was comforting. It was Henry, Dr. Brimm's namesake, and being in his present frame of mind, Brimm allowed himself to imagine for a moment that the cat actually possessed the soul of his dead father; the absent patriarch had returned from the other side at this significant hour to solace his son. Dr. Brimm, a ghoul in life, was certainly more palatable here, now, in the form of a cat, though the pleasure Brimm took from his pretended visit was immediately unsettling and had the effect of forcing him to acknowledge what he considered to be a profound character flaw—that he, Brimm, had never really cared much for life. Buried beneath all his choices and actions, perhaps even driving some of them, had been a dominant conviction that life basically stunk, and that leaving it would not be such a bad thing. Oh, there had been times of joy and exuberance, even a sense of triumph, both felt and witnessed, around the world, in many languages. But hadn't even the best and strongest of these been fleeting protests against the vast, fixed, tyrannical truth that life basically stunk? In any case, the epistemology of it didn't finally matter. What mattered was that Brimm, by nature, perceived things this way, a condition that felt so ancient and deeply embedded that he suspected it hadn't been taught him by life but had come with him, whole and intact, at birth; it wasn't the result of anything that had happened to him, but rather something that he *was*, something he'd always been. If, as Muriel had often suggested over the years, he was running from something in all his running, it was from this. If, as she'd further suggested, he, with his camera, had been aiming always out and never in, it had been this he was aiming away from—though, he had to admit, not successfully so. Even the record of his life's work revealed it. Look at the picture of the Normandy village for only one example: a time of joy and triumph, barbaric cruelty at its heart.

Brimm placed his hand gingerly on top of the cat's head, not knowing for sure the proper way to touch a cat, and experienced an acute pang at never having owned a pet. Just then the doorbell rang, sending Henry into a high arc off the bed. That, Brimm thought, would be young Detective Connie Shoulders, who had decided to drop by rather than phone. Brimm threw back the covers and stood up. He felt lightheaded and decided to forgo the prospect of putting on shoes.

The bell rang once more before he reached the entry hall, and when he opened the door, he found not the policeman but a pretty young woman with long dark hair, wearing a white T-shirt and painter's overalls. She had a large leather bag, rather like a mailman's, slung over one shoulder.

"Oh," she said.

"Oh," he said back.

"I'm Deirdre," she said. "I work for Miss Brimm."

123

"Come in," he said.

"Is she here?" the girl asked, not moving.

"No, no," he said. "Muriel's at church, but you can still come in. I'm Muriel's brother, Frank, and despite what she may have told you, I don't bite."

She stepped inside, smiling. "It's just that I was surprised," she said.

"Me too," he said, closing the door. "I expected to see a policeman."

"A policeman? Has something happened?"

"You haven't seen the newspaper?"

"Oh, that," she said, slinging her large bag over the newel post.

Here, thought Brimm, is a girl completely bored by the trivial pursuits of a serial killer.

"Well, yes," he said. "That."

"Listen," she said, though he was already listening, "I left my ring here somewhere yesterday when I was cleaning. Do you mind if I look for it?"

"Of course not."

She moved past him into the dining room and out through the pantry, talking all the way. "I can't believe I did it again. I did the same thing last week. The same ring. It must be Freudian. Either it has to do with my needing to come back here—which doesn't really make sense, because I'm here already three times a week. Or it has something to do with this particular ring."

Brimm hadn't moved from the entry hall when she returned, holding up the finger with the ring on it.

"Right where I left it last time," she said. "In the soap dish. Isn't that crazy? My sponsor in AA gave it to me, so I guess you could say it kind of symbolizes my sobriety. So it could be that my forgetting it, leaving it, is like I'm trying to lose it, which could be me revealing my ambivalence about being sober. You know, like what I really want to lose is my sobriety."

They stared at each other for a moment in silence. Finally Brimm said, "Would you like to stay and have a cup of coffee?"

"Oh, God," she said, apparently noticing his rumpled appearance and stocking feet. "I bet you were sleeping. I'm so sorry."

"No, no," he said. "I wasn't sleeping. Stay and talk to me some more."

"Okay," she said.

He led the way to the kitchen. Trailing behind him, she continued: "But if that's the case, I guess it's actually healthy that I'm trying to lose the ring instead of losing my sobriety."

They were in the kitchen now and Brimm was pouring coffee into a cup. "None for me," she said. "No caffeine." She helped herself to a glass of ginger ale, and they sat at the small table on the back porch. She stared into the yard, seemingly engrossed in something she was seeing out there. Then she said, "Why did you think it was a policeman at the door?"

Brimm explained that earlier that morning he had phoned the homicide detective who was handling the golf course murders.

"You're the one who found the bones, right?" she said.

"Right," said Brimm, trying not to seem too pleased with himself.

"And you got one of those spooky phone calls too," she said, "in the middle of the night."

"Yes. You know about that?"

"Miss Brimm told me. She was a little bent out of shape about that."

The image of Muriel bent out of shape amused Brimm. "You can't blame her, can you?"

"No, of course not. We had an interesting conversation about the whole thing. She's going through some stuff, you know."

"What do you mean?"

"Well, I don't know if I should say any more. It's her

125

business after all, not mine. But she told me about your father and all."

"What do you mean, my father and all?"

"Uh-oh, I'm talking too much. I do it because I don't have anything else to do. I'm sorry."

"It's perfectly fine. I don't think you're talking too much at all."

"You know—I'm not smoking or drinking or doing drugs or anything. So I talk. I'm allowed to talk."

"Don't worry," he said. "What about my father?"

"Well, she told me, you know, about how he died."

"Oh," said Brimm. "Yes."

After a moment she said, "I was wondering why . . . why he did it."

Brimm hadn't thought about this question in many years. He took a deep breath, and despite a weakness in his chest, a symptom of his illness, he noticed in himself a new kind of calm he hadn't felt recently, as if he'd miraculously become a man with nothing to hide. He wondered if this young woman didn't have a certain charm, something intangible that made one feel this way.

"I think my father was extremely disappointed," he said at last, feeling a twinge of embarrassment at having given such an obvious answer.

"I guess," said Deirdre.

Later, Brimm would speculate about what else he might have said had Muriel's return from church not interrupted them. He supposed that his father, as a young man studying medicine, must have had plans. He must have had dreams about the kind of doctor he was going to be. Illustrious, bound for glory. But the Great War had come along, he was sent as a medic to the front, and he lost most of his left arm. When he came back home he developed, without much enthusiasm, a small practice, but that was all. He couldn't be a surgeon, which had been his intention. But he could do general medicine; there was little he couldn't do, really. People were wary of him, but not because of the missing arm. That would have required only a brief explanation, a small reassurance. It was Dr. Brimm's disconsolate air. His very presence exuded ruin. He was scary, like somebody who'd been locked away in an attic. He had been in his fifties when he drove his car off the bridge and drowned, and in a way it was surprising that he had waited that long. Of course he had also been a raging drunk—which could have delayed things, Brimm supposed. Brimm himself had been away for many years by then and didn't know much about what the doctor's life had become. Mrs. Brimm had died some years earlier, but Muriel was still there, living in the same house with the doctor, something Brimm found unimaginable. She even supported him, because he'd quit practicing long ago.

It also occurred to Brimm that perhaps he himself had inherited a predisposition of some sort from his father. While his father had been a full-blown alcoholic and a suicide, Brimm, one generation removed, had suffered a kind of passive detachment from life. In any case, had Muriel not interrupted his conversation with Deirdre on the screened porch, he might have explained to the girl that if you took any human trait or emotion—willfulness or anger or cleanliness or avarice or disappointment, anything really—if you took it to an extreme, you had mental illness.

"What are you doing out of bed?" Muriel said to him, standing in the doorway to the kitchen.

"I'm having a nice talk with Deirdre," he said.

Muriel looked at Deirdre and said in the same scolding tone, "He has a flu."

"It's my fault," said Deirdre. "I practically ambushed him. I didn't know he had the flu."

"It is not your fault," said Brimm, "and I do not have a flu."

Muriel moved to the table and placed the back of her hand against his forehead. "You're still running a fever," she said. "If it's not a flu, what is it?"

"I don't know."

"What do you mean, you don't know? And why do you say it like that, as if you're proud of it?"

"I simply mean I don't know," Brimm said. "But it's not a flu."

"I forgot my ring again," said Deirdre to Muriel, holding up her ring finger. "Can you believe it? What do you think it means?"

Deirdre soon went home, complaining of fatigue.

"What an extraordinary young person," Brimm said once she'd gone.

"You don't know a thing about it," said Muriel, in the foulest of moods.

Detective Sergeant Connie Shoulders phoned to say that he was going to be tied up the rest of the day, and Muriel, preferring to see him in person, assured him that what she wanted to talk to him about could wait.

This was fine with Brimm. Any urgency he'd earlier felt in that matter had completely dissipated.

"I don't like this aura of mystery you have about you," Muriel said to him as he began backing out of her drive, on his way home. "You can't entirely fool me," she said, narrowing her eyes. "You're up to something."

"I'm not up to anything," he said out the car window.

"You go straight to bed when you get home," she said, "I'm going to phone you later and make sure you're in bed."

"I'll look forward to your call," he said.

But it was early in the afternoon on a lovely, late August Sunday, and once he was back at the cottage, Brimm didn't go straight to bed. Instead, he poured himself a snifter of the good Armagnac and sat in his armchair for the longest time, at peace, making the most of his low-grade fever and his slightly altered state. Everything he thought of seemed to have a wonderful, dimensional vividness. When the aged bronze statue of Hernando de Soto, over the tunnel entrance downtown, crossed Brimm's mind, it was as if he could close his eyes and reach his hand out into the room and touch it. This same intensity caused him to shudder when he thought of the dismembered girls buried in the sand traps of the golf course, washed up on the banks of the Yustaga.

He recalled having gone to the Raphael School once during a visit home, walking through the great majestic hall beneath the bell tower on his way to the library to meet Muriel. In the long marble hall there was row upon row of enormous glass-doored cabinets, housing the things of the world, so that blind students might feel these things and know them through the sense of touch—seashells and coral, a stuffed rooster, an owl, an oboe and a French horn, a hammer and a wood plane—and it seemed to Brimm, the photographer, as he sat now in the armchair, thinking of things with his eyes closed, that images came to him this way, intimately, through his fingertips: Muriel's bedroom furniture, the bed, the chest, the vanity with the oval mirror, the same furniture she'd had as a child—was it maple or oak? The warm hard-softness of wood . . . Florida's diversity of trees: the red maples, beeches, tulips and hickories of the North, the broad oaks, cypresses, palms, and mangroves, the noble pines . . . The strange liquid feel of Muriel's satin sheets . . .

"I wonder what happened to the baby?" Brimm heard his sister say, and he recalled the lovely scent of grass that evening on the golf course, when they'd seen the Labrador digging in the distant bunker . . .

Then the grand Cajun magician Jean-Louis Galhemo took to the armory stage, bringing with him a volunteer from the audience and astoundingly removing the man's dress shirt with one clean yank of the collar, leaving the man's sportcoat undisturbed. It had been the last trick before intermission, and when Frankie rushed to the men's room in the armory lobby to pee, he found the man in there, the volunteer, putting his shirt back on. To Frankie's astonishment, the man was in tears. "I don't know how he

129

did it," the man said to him. "How'd he do it?" Frankie stepped up to the cavernous porcelain urinal, not knowing what to say. "It must've been real magic," the man said, shaking his head, buttoning his shirt. "But how in the world did he do it?" He took a handkerchief from his trouser pocket and blew his nose.

After a long while, Brimm rose from the chair and went out through the kitchen door to the garage. As he entered the garage through a side door, he said aloud, with a mock-ominous tone, "Red touching yellow, dangerous fellow"— not for any particular reason, just that it had entered his mind, and he was trying to honor as best he could everything that entered his mind.

He poked through some paper sacks on a shelf above the work table until he found the one he was looking for, the bag from the seed store. He chose packets of seeds for lettuce, beets, spinach, turnips, things you could plant in the fall and still expect to harvest. He found a spade and loaded up a wheelbarrow with bone meal and peat moss.

He had to take his time, going easy. The hardest part was clearing the grass away from a small patch out by the kitchen stoop, exposing the soil beneath. Again and again he had to stop and sit until he could catch his breath. But once he'd got that done, the turning up of the soil with the spade and adding in the peat and the bone meal came easier. He got down on his hands and knees, working the dirt with his fingers. He recalled having read somewhere that the first ancient Native American groups had entered northern Florida some ten thousand years ago. Farming arrived around 500 B.C. The late afternoon sun was hot on his back, and Brimm felt mysteriously connected to this ancient history. He would have eagerly removed his clothes and worked naked had it not been that Claudia Callejas, next door, already had grounds on which to have him arrested, and he figured he'd best not push his luck.

When he was done, he put away the things in the garage and soaked the new, modest vegetable patch with the gar-

130

den hose. He went inside and washed up at the kitchen sink. Afterward, he looked up the Ottos' number and phoned Ned. "Ned," he said. "I'd like very much to take that deep-sea fishing trip you mentioned."

"Of course, Frank," said Ned. "When would you like to go?"

"I think soon," he said. "I think it would be a good idea to go fairly soon."

"Okay," said Ned. "I'll arrange it right away and let you know."

"Good, good. That'll be fine."

"Are you all right, Frank?" Ned asked. "You sound sort of . . . I don't know . . . dreamy."

"I'm fine, Ned," said Brimm. "I was just thinking about it. About the fishing trip. That's all. Thinking about the sea, the water, you know."

Muriel phoned at around six. "How do you feel?" she said.

"I feel sick," said Brimm. "But not at all unpleasantly. I've had a remarkable day."

"I hope you're taking care of yourself."

"I am, I am. Don't worry."

"Frankie," she said. "I don't know what's going on. Something happened today, didn't it, something out in the grape arbor?"

"Yes," he said.

"It's okay," she said quickly, "you don't have to tell me. I just want you to know that I'm a bit more of a human being than meets the eye. There's more to me than I let anyone see. I've been in love and experienced real passion, for example. You didn't know that, did you? In those years after Mother died, and I was living here with Daddy, mopping and cleaning up after him, hauling him into bed at night, taking off his shoes . . . I was deeply in love with a merchant marine. He was about as romantic a lover as anyone could have had, complete with frequent farewells and promises of return. Somewhere upstairs there's a packet of poems I wrote during that time—love poems, and I think some of them are probably not too bad. I want you to know there's more to me than you think. You've never really trusted anyone in the world and neither have I. We have that in common. And sometimes I wonder if we couldn't make something of that. Make something of that shared thing we have."

"Muriel," he said, "you almost overwhelm me. Someday I'd like to see those poems."

"I'll have to think about it," she said.

He hadn't even a hint of an appetite and went to bed early without eating anything at all. He carried to bed with him another snifter of brandy, but hardly touched it before falling into a deep, solid sleep. He was awakened before dawn by the crying of the gulls out on the golf course. When he opened his eyes and rolled onto his back, all he saw was a plain white ceiling, like any other plain white ceiling, the world over.

Fifteen

"I HONESTLY DIDN'T think much about it," says Muriel, in her imagination, to the kind psychotherapist. "I didn't really stop to consider anything like fear."

It was early Monday morning. Deirdre had arrived and was running the vacuum. In the back yard, Muriel had pulled a chaise longue into a triangle of shadow cast by the roof of the screened porch. Her eyes were closed.

"Still," she hears the therapist say, "you seemed to know instinctively to take a friend with you."

"That's right," says Muriel, feeling pleased about that. "I asked Billie to help me."

"And who went up the stairs first?"

"Come to think of it, Billie did. I even let her get all the way to the top, and then she turned to me and said, 'Well, aren't you coming?' "

"But you weren't feeling afraid?"

"Not consciously," says Muriel. "But here's the interesting thing. The whole time we were up there looking for pictures, I never went into any of the rooms. I let Billie do that. I stayed out in the hallway, rummaging through the old cedar chest."

"So you felt you were protecting yourself from something?" asks the therapist.

"I don't know."

" 'I don't know' is not much of an answer."

"But I really don't know."

"Do you want to look into the rooms again—in your imagination?"

"No," says Muriel, "I don't think so. Not today."

"Muriel, dear," said a voice.

She opened her eyes and could see, in silhouette, her deceased mother looming above her, blinding beacons like bolts of lightning discharging from either side of her head. It was the dark tunnel with the bright light at the end that Muriel had so often heard about, and her worst nightmare had come true: her mother was there, in the tunnel, to greet her.

"You've fallen asleep, sleepyhead," said Billie. "You're getting as bad as Ned."

"As bad as Ned . . . ," Muriel mumbled, and then the world came back to her.

Back yard.

Billie.

The sun.

Monday morning.

Still alive.

"Come inside," said Billie. "Get a cup of coffee and we'll play. You do want to play, don't you?"

"Play," said Muriel. "Oh, the piano. Of course. Yes."

As they gained the porch, Muriel said, "My goodness, isn't that odd? I was out cold."

Over coffee in the kitchen, Billie said, "Frank called Ned yesterday, did you know?"

"Ned?" said Muriel. "Why?"

"Said he wanted to go deep-sea fishing, which of course tickled Ned to death. He's been looking for somebody to go with him for over ten years."

"Deep-sea fishing?" said Muriel. "Francis has never been a fisherman."

"Well, he said he wanted to go. Ned said he sounded dreamy."

"Dreamy?"

"That's what he said. I thought Frank had the flu. I thought it rather strange of him to be calling about going deep-sea fishing when he had the flu."

Deirdre, looking pallid, appeared in the doorway.

"Deirdre," said Muriel. "You don't look well."

"I'm fine," Deirdre said, not at all convincingly, almost bitterly. "Can I use the phone?"

"Of course," Muriel said. "Billie and I were just about to play the piano in the parlor. Why don't you close this door behind us so you won't be disturbed."

Muriel noticed Billie eyeing Deirdre suspiciously as they left the kitchen.

Once they were in the parlor and seated at the piano, Billie said, "Something's not right with that girl, Muriel. I'm sorry . . . I know you like her, but something's not right."

"Billie," said Muriel. "Deirdre is pregnant."

"Pregnant?"

"Yes."

"And unmarried."

"Right."

"Oh."

"Shall we play?"

They began the way they always began, with their favorite March Militaire. Halfway through, Muriel thought she heard Deirdre's voice from the kitchen, shouting. Note by note, Muriel and Billie began to falter, until no sound any longer came from the piano. They both sat facing forward, listening, in shock, to what was coming from the direction of the kitchen.

"Not fucking fair? You're going to talk to me about what's not fucking fair, you shithead? You wouldn't know fair if it came up and fucked you in broad daylight."

There was a pause, during which Billie looked at Muriel, her eyes wide.

"Excuse me," Muriel said.

Just as she pushed open the kitchen door, she heard, "No, no, no, no. Wait a goddamned minute. That's not what you

135

fucking said . . . Oh, am I? Well, let me tell you something, you sack of shit—"

Their eyes met. Deirdre's face was ashen, streaked with tears, the anger in her eyes stunning.

"I can't have this, Deirdre," Muriel said to her very quietly.

"*You* can't have this?" the girl shouted, then rammed the receiver into the cradle on the wall phone. She covered her mouth with her hand and went running past Muriel without a word, into the powder room under the stairs, and slammed the door.

Billie stepped to Muriel's side.

The next thing they heard were wrenching heaves and moans coming from the powder room—Deirdre's vomiting, violently, endlessly.

"Oh, dear," whispered Billie.

Neither of them moved.

At last, Deirdre, accompanied by an acrid stench, emerged from the powder room. "Sorry," she said to Muriel.

"I think you better go, dear," said Muriel. "I'm sorry too."

"Go?" Deirdre said. "But I still have to—"

"I can't have this kind of display."

"Display?"

"Especially when I have guests."

The girl shook her head and laughed through her nose. She turned into the entryway, grabbed her bag, and was out the door, gone.

Stepping to the dining room window to watch her go, Billie said, "Probably the father—on the phone, I mean."

"Probably," said Muriel, not stepping to the window but experiencing the first whispers of what would soon become a full-blooded ache of remorse.

They couldn't very well sit down and play Hungarian Dances after that.

Billie completely understood, felt the same way, and soon left. Muriel saw that Billie could hardly wait to get home and tell Ned everything that had happened.

Why, oh why had she used the word *display*? What a pompous, cold-hearted word to use. Surely she hadn't been thinking of the vomiting when she used it; she was thinking of the swearing and shouting on the telephone. But still, a very poor choice under the circumstances. On the other hand, didn't she have a right to want domestic help who did not bring their personal problems to the workplace? And wasn't this the sort of thing that always seemed to happen if you let yourself get emotionally involved with people who worked for you?

She resolved to apologize for her poor choice of words, on Thursday, when Deirdre returned to clean. And in the future she would maintain a bit more distance.

She went into the kitchen to load her Ezy Dose Pill Reminder for the week. This task accomplished, and the morning's medicine swallowed down, she wandered into the dining room thinking what an odd morning it had been already, another of those days that started out one way and then suddenly changed. She found herself in the entry hall, presumably en route to the parlor, but for what? Was she bound for the window seat? Should she sit in the window seat, watching out the window and stroking the cat? She stood still for a moment, at sea, wondering when she had so thoroughly lost anchor. (There it was again, that maritime imagery—her mind was virtually rife with it.) She placed her hand on the newel post's carved pineapple and looked up the stairs, thinking, Well, why not? Perhaps at times, she thought, courage is born of simple indolence.

That was as far as things got, however, for when her foot had touched the first tread, the telephone rang—Sergeant Connie Shoulders saying he would drop by in five minutes if that would be convenient.

She told him it would be more than convenient, surprising herself with the extravagant tone in her voice.

She made a fresh pot of coffee. When he arrived, she chose to receive him in the darkened parlor, which seemed more suited to what she had to say than the sunny screened porch. She noticed that he wore the same wheat-colored suit he'd worn the last time, and, as before, a dress shirt that was too large in the collar.

"I like this room," he said, taking one of the club chairs.

"Why, thank you," she said, honestly pleased. "No one ever compliments me on the house anymore."

"Well, they should. You have very good taste."

"And you," she said, "have very good manners."

"I guess we could start a mutual admiration society, couldn't we?" he said.

"Yes," she said. "I think we could."

Muriel watched as he added an extraordinary amount of milk to his coffee, then drank the whole thing down like an athlete fresh off the field. Something about the way he placed the cup firmly back into the saucer suggested that he had spent his morning's ration of small talk, so Muriel took the cue.

"Actually," she began, "Francis insisted I get in touch with you."

"You've had another of those calls?"

"Oh, no," she said. "Not that. Nothing, I'm afraid, quite as concrete as that. You see, I think I know who may have murdered those poor girls."

She noticed that his Adam's apple moved up and back down, just slightly, but otherwise he returned to her an utterly neutral face, at a moment when she could have used at least a nod of encouragement. She found herself wishing that she had rehearsed. She took a deep breath and said, "Joe Letson."

This, too, he received with apparent detachment. He did not say, "Joe Letson?" or "Why would you think that?" or "Don't be absurd." Rather, he merely seemed to intensify his focus. At last he said, simply, "Please go on, Miss Brimm."

138

She interpreted this as a sign of their having recognized each other's intelligence. He knew that she knew all that was necessary for him to hear, so why insult her intelligence by prompting her with questions?

"Several days ago," she said, "and this was before Francis had found the bones, I encountered Joe Letson on the Little Yustaga Bridge. I was on my way over to Francis's. I knew Joe from my days at the Raphael School. I was librarian there for nearly forty years. I hadn't seen Joe in a very long time, so when I ran into him there on the bridge, I naturally waved to him. It's a very narrow little bridge. We were no farther from each other than I am to you now. He was walking, you see, with some students. I was in my car . . ."

It was at this point that Muriel felt as if all the air had been sucked out of the room. She had reached the spot at which the narrative went irrational, and she felt she was losing her nerve. "Don't you want another cup?" she asked.

He didn't even flatter the question with an answer. "You were in your car," he said.

"Yes," she said. "Well, this is going to sound crazy. Believe me, I know it sounds crazy, and I probably wouldn't have even mentioned it to you had Francis not forced me to. You see, I waved to Joe, he looked directly at me, and then quickly turned his face away. Pretended he didn't know me. It was most inexplicable. A few days later, after Francis had found the bones and so forth, it came to me that Joe Letson had something to do with the murder. Don't ask me why. It just came to me. I told Francis about it and we let it go. Then yesterday, when it came out that the murdered girls were in fact from the Raphael School, well I . . . that is, Francis thought I should tell you about it."

An unbearable silence followed in which Muriel thought she might cry. Silently, she prayed for God to dam up her tears. If she hadn't already completely discredited herself as a person of sound mind, crying now would certainly push her over the edge.

He said, "That's it?"

"I'm afraid so."

He appeared to go into deep thought. She fought back every impulse to do or say anything more. Finally he said, "I'm going to share something with you, Miss Brimm. We've had some federal agents draw us up what they call a profile of our killer, based on the evidence we've managed to collect. This is what these people do. They study the evidence and draw up a profile. It's their science, their area of expertise. And I have to tell you, Miss Brimm, that somebody like Joe Letson misses by a mile."

"Oh," she said, feeling as if he'd gently put her in her place.

"Now, you say you know Mr. Letson . . . from the school?"

"Yes."

"How well do you know him?"

"Not terribly well," she said. "I never saw him outside the school, not socially, if that's what you mean. He was an acquaintance, I guess you could say. I was well acquainted with him, you could say."

"And he with you."

"Yes, of course."

"So do you think Mr. Letson would accept a telephone call from you, for example? He would recognize your name and, assuming he wasn't too busy, he would answer your call?"

"I'm positive he would recognize my name," she said. "He *knows* me. I can think of no reason why he wouldn't speak to me on the telephone. But of course I don't know why he didn't say hello to me on the bridge, either."

"Well, that's what I'm getting at. I'm going to be candid with you, Miss Brimm. I think we've got ourselves two different mysteries here. We've got the big mystery of who killed those girls, and we've got the little mystery of why Mr. Letson didn't say hello to you on the bridge."

She rose from her chair. "I won't waste any more of

your time, Sergeant," she said, trying to control her voice. "This has been more humiliating than I imagined. More difficult in an already difficult morning."

"Now wait just a minute," he said. "Don't get your feelings hurt. Please sit down for a minute."

She sat, on the very edge of the seat cushion.

"I appreciate you telling me what you've told me this morning," he said. "You would've been wrong not to tell me."

"Now you're being kind," she said.

"Not at all," he said. "Here's what I suggest you do. Call over to the Raphael School and see if you can get Mr. Letson on the line. Then tell him who you are and ask him why he snubbed you on the bridge the other day. See what he says."

"What, you mean right now?"

"There's no time like the present, Miss Brimm. It's midmorning on a Monday. He's likely to be in."

She decided to use the kitchen phone. Once she'd dialed the number of the school, she looked up to see that Connie Shoulders had followed her and was now standing in the doorway, leaning against the doorjamb, glancing at his wristwatch. Joe Letson took her call without any apparent hesitation.

"Muriel!" he said, as if he couldn't have been more delighted to hear from her.

"Joe," she said, "how are you?"

"Well, Muriel," he said, "if you've been reading the papers, you can probably make an educated guess about how I am. I've been better."

"Yes," she said. "I can imagine."

She wasn't sure what to say next. The moment she had heard the sound of Joe's voice, his whole affable personality had come back to her, and she knew at once how preposterous it was to think of him as a murderer. Now she was going to have to hang up the phone and face the detective in her utter foolishness and embarrassment. This was Francis's fault—she would never have pursued this course had it not been for his urging, and how fitting, now, that Francis wasn't anywhere to be found.

"The way I've got folks breathing down my neck," Joe said, "you'd think *I* killed somebody. What can I do for you, Muriel?"

"Joe," she said, "the other day, on the bridge—"

"Oh," he interrupted. "So that *was* you. I thought it was. I'm awfully sorry about that, Muriel."

"Then you did see me."

"What happened was that I was on overload right at that minute," he said. "One of the girls had just told me that Linda and Sara had gone missing. Right at that very minute when you drove by, I'd just learned that nobody had seen Linda and Sara for two whole days, you see, and I started thinking the worst right away . . ."

Now it seemed inevitable that she would cry, but by some miracle she didn't. After she completed the call, she told the detective what Joe Letson had said, and he apparently intuited what the merciful thing would be—to leave as quickly as possible and not prolong her agony.

In the entry hall, she opened the door for him. "Miss Brimm," he said, "in my opinion, the world would practically stop turning if everybody quit playing their hunches."

"Thank you," she said. "That's nice of you to say. I was thinking the other day, when you were over before, how proud your grandmother would surely be."

"Yes, ma'am," he said, and shook her hand.

An experience of humiliation was always apt to set up an echo of similar losses, sometimes trivial, sometimes not so trivial, and once Muriel had closed the door, she sat down on the stairs in a posture of defeat. As recently as last Wednesday night, when she'd attended evening prayer at St. Matthew and the Redeemer, she had stood, not by choice but by fate, next to a certain gentleman named Charles Lindgren, a recent widower about her own age.

142

Since the death of the man's wife, Muriel had noticed his lingering glances in her direction. He sang in the choir, and at Sunday worship she would look up from her service sheet to find him gaping at her from the chancel. She was not the least bit interested. Charles Lindgren, a retired English professor, was prissy, dull-witted, and outspoken in groups, a ghastly combination of traits. With the nuances typical to such causes—the failure to return a smile, the choice of an evasive route out of church—she had rebuffed his attentions, and in turn, with similar nuances, he'd conveyed his wounded vanity. At evening prayer on Wednesday, they had been reading antiphonally from the Psalter. It was possible, Muriel had discovered, to read from the Psalter without once thinking about what you were reading and still not miss a single word. Her mind had wandered, and in the line from Psalm 11, "For see how the wicked bend the bow," she had said bow as in a ship's bow instead of bow as in crossbow, and Mr. Lindgren had giggled, quietly, triumphantly, snakelike. Certainly this event belonged to the category of trivial injuries, but lately it seemed that Muriel abided every one of these with more hurt than usual, as if she had lost any reserve of self-confidence that she might draw on at such moments.

She continued to sit on the stairs for some time. At least it felt to her that time passed. Some blankness occurred. There was a change in the light. Then she thought she heard the stairs creak behind her. A foolish old woman in a haunted house, she thought, a foolish old woman in a haunted house. Not long ago, a loose board in the floor, near the sill between the two parlors, developed a three-syllable squeak that sounded distinctly like "Mur-i-el." On her way to bed—or worse, on her way to the bathroom during the night—she would step on the loose board and hear her name spoken into the darkness by a basso profundo parrot. She never had got used to it, it unnerved her each time, but then, after a while, it ceased of its own accord. Over the years, she'd had to renew her vows about the house many times, about its wealth of noises; she knew that if she was going to stay there alone, and stay within the bounds of reason, she would not be able to react with alarm to every noise. In addition to the usual pops, yelps, clucks, and grunts of an old house settling, there were the soft stir- rings of lizards on the screens, martins under the eaves, and an assortment of clinks, sighs, and twitters, upstairs and down, that defied explanation. In any case, these sounds, belonging to an empty house, were preferable to those of an earlier age (the ice age) when Dr. Brimm had still been alive—that is to say, when he had still been undead.

Not long before his death, he'd bought a television set with a round cathode-ray tube, had it installed in his bed- room, and mounted an atrocious antenna to the widow's walk. (The antenna remained standing, its wires discon- nected, until hurricane Camille took it down in 1969.) Dr. Brimm drank and watched television. Every shift, tide, and turn of Muriel's life at home, her dressing and undressing, thinking, feeling, waking and falling asleep were accompa- nied either by badly orchestrated, melodramatic music or canned laughter and applause through the walls. She got him out of his armchair and into the bed by the whine and pale light of a test pattern bearing the image of a Cherokee chief in full war bonnet. Once, he'd broken the glass on the front of the set by throwing a rye bottle at it. Muriel couldn't remember why—something unacceptable about Gisele MacKenzie's dress on *Your Hit Parade*.

Before that, there had been the stumblings and rattlings of a somnambulant mother and the dark drone of her inces- sant prayer. But loudest of all perhaps was the dead silence between them. Yes, the house had been more haunted then, before they were in their graves, than it was now. When her mother died, Muriel experienced relief. When her father died, she experienced further relief. In the case of the fa- ther, the lifting of burden had been formidable, disorienting; she had thought of ants living under a rock, the apparent panic and scattering that set in when the rock was suddenly lifted. She wandered the streets in a state of anomie. Contradictorily, her sense of doom took the form of sinking down rather than floating away. Walking in Bonifay Square, she expected the paving stones to part and for the earth to swallow her up. On the beach, she expected quicksand.

But nothing of the sort happened, of course, and after a while she began to breathe more easily, to sleep more soundly, heady in waking hours with a sense of her own survival. She had survived the tragedies of two love affairs (the unrequited one of her youth, with Captain Fayson; the one in middle age, with McGavern, the merchant marine), she had survived her mother, and she had survived her father.

About a month before he drove his car off Milligan's Bridge into the lagoon, she'd been roused from sleep by her father's voice calling her name. Even before she reached his room, she could tell that something had badly frightened him. She found him sitting in the big red armchair in a state of terror. Instinctively, she looked to the room's murky windows, knowing windows to be potential portals of danger. (In a recent nightmare, a matador wearing a black fedora with small black pompoms hanging from the brim had stood outside her bedroom window, tapping his long, clear-polished fingernails against the glass.) The television made a sound like gas escaping from a valve, its screen filled with white snow, the only light in the room. Her father pointed to it, saying, "Do you see that?"

His cheeks glistened with tears. She looked at the screen. "No, Daddy," she said. "I don't see anything."

"You don't see that?"

"What, Daddy? It's only a blank screen."

"Oh, God," he said, covering his eyes, shutting out whatever horror it was.

Then he looked again, bravely, hopefully, and began to weep. "Oh, God," he said, "it's *me*, Muriel. Don't you see it? That's *me*!"

* * *

Muriel did not at all like the direction Monday had taken. Hoping to steer it back on course, she had decided to go walking and to show up for the noontime Eucharist at the church. The temperature, having already reached ninety by eleven-thirty, had required her going slow.

Besides herself, there were only five others present at the church, four women and one man, all over sixty, all probably alone in life, all obviously retired or unemployed, none of whom she recognized, and that was always a bit dispiriting; but naturally she knew Mary Whiteside, the celebrant, and as Muriel and the rest of them joined their voices with angels and archangels and with all the company of heaven, the brilliance and vigor of the Holy Eucharist began to work its mystery on her, despite everything. At the rail, however, as the six communicants knelt to receive the bread of heaven and the cup of salvation, someone, not Muriel, broke wind, and the chancel filled with a malodorous vapor that might genuinely have originated in hell. The result, the sacrament administered under the pressure of such foulness and sidelong glances, was confusing. The day, she decided, refused to bend, and afterward, when she saw that storm clouds had moved in during the service, that she would be caught in a downpour on the long walk home, that she would be thoroughly soaked by the time she reached her door, and that in this way God would provide an antidote after all (with water rather than wine), she took heart. The first drops of rain struck her on the shoulders, wrist, and nape of the neck, about a hundred yards from the churchyard gates.

Sixteen

A MEMORIAL SERVICE was to be held for the two murdered and dismembered girls, Linda Briscoe Wayne and Sara DiMatteo, at eleven o'clock in the gothic chapel of the Raphael School for the Blind. It was Wednesday, the first of September, the kind of cool, intensely brilliant day that sometimes caused Muriel to think of factory smoke, hydrocarbons, acid rain, and carcinogenic force fields, and to wonder what all the fuss was about. Her windows, from the inside, blazed with light, even those facing west (the gleam of Billie's white clapboard wall). The stupefied cats lolled and stretched—Henry's deep fur parting and closing like the bellows of an accordion—and slept in the sunny bay window behind the kitchen sink. The fine weather, thought Muriel, that unfathomable blue dome of the sky, would surely seem to mock the girls' friends and families as they emerged sorrowful and squinting from the dark chapel.

After breakfast, she phoned Francis to see if he would accompany her to the service, but got no answer. She had tried phoning him on Monday and Tuesday as well, to check the progress of his flu, but also with no success. She recalled, now that she had been reminded, that he was prone to this sort of disappearing act. He'd done it in their correspondence again and again, for months at a time. He'd even done it once when she had visited him in New York, gone for two full days and nights without so much as a message, so that she had to return to Pines without saying goodbye. Actually, if you thought about it (at the kitchen sink, rinsing out a coffee cup, gazing absently at the sleeping cats), Francis's whole life had been a disappearing act.

She decided to get ready for the service early and drive by his cottage on her way. She chose her simplest and best black suit, black cloche, pearls, black heels. You would certainly see every variety there (a memorial service, a secular chapel, the middle of the day), but she intended her costume to respect the gravity of what had happened. As she sat in her slip at the vanity mirror and applied her makeup, she thought she would tell Francis, the next time she saw him, that his whole life had been a disappearing act—it captured the exact flavor of Francis's long nomadic history. She would tell him, that is, if he'd managed to shake the dreamily vulnerable state he'd acquired in the grape arbor on Sunday morning.

Whatever had happened in the grape arbor, it had accomplished a subtle change in Francis's face and in his manners as well, but now, three days later, Muriel couldn't quite summon all that, nor could she summon the effect it had had on her. What she recalled was feeling moved to reach out to him with more than the usual amount of empathy, revealing to him the love affair with the merchant marine, the dusty packet of poems, the not really trusting anyone. She thought for a moment about empathy, about how empathy was more than a capacity to participate in another's feelings, that it was also a willingness to share one's own, and then suddenly she understood precisely what had happened: she had managed to touch Francis with Sunday evening's telephone call—she had finally *reached* him—and in response he had dropped from sight. She wondered: Had Francis chosen a nomadic life because it was his nature to bolt whenever anyone came near him, or had his choice to live a nomadic life turned him into someone with that nature? Probably she would never know. Probably it was not a question that he himself could answer.

On her way to Francis's she had a happy, uplifting thought—perhaps she would see young Detective Shoulders at the memorial service. If Francis couldn't be found, she might still have someone to sit with. Then, as she pulled the car onto the Little Yustaga Bridge and passed the spot where she'd seen Joe Letson, she had a horrifying vision of Connie Shoulders back at the station house, at the center of a circle of hairy-armed policemen, retelling his hilarious experiences with the dotty old bag whose brother had found the bones on the golf course. The policemen, straddling metal chairs, drink from Styrofoam cups and smoke cigarettes. "So then she says," Connie Shoulders gets out between attacks of laughter, "she says"—here he adopts a scratchy falsetto—" 'Well, I said hello to him, you see, and he didn't even say hello back. I'm just *sure* he's the killer.' "

Despite the paranoid character of this fantasy, Muriel decided it carried an important message. She would not seek out Connie Shoulders at the memorial service; she wouldn't want to embarrass him should there be any other officers around. That morning (it seemed so long ago now) when Francis had first called her over to the cottage and told her about finding the bones, she had scolded him about his apparent giddiness. Now she had to concede (if only to herself and to God) that she had been secretly hoping to put herself somehow at the center of things. What if her intuition about Joe Letson, now so clearly bogus, had proved useful and true? What, she asked herself, was the nature of this desire to be an instrument in the solving of Connie Shoulders's murder case? Her pursuit of this young man's company and regard smelled decidedly like the disgraceful folly of a lonely old woman.

When she arrived at the cottage, Francis was nowhere to be found. The doors were locked, front and back, and Francis's Jeep was missing from the garage. She noticed a patch of dirt by the kitchen door that looked as if it had been recently planted, and she stooped to feel with her fingers the cool soil, which must have been watered earlier in the day. She also noticed that a quilt and a pillow had been

149

left under a chinaberry tree that stood in the middle of the small back yard. She made a mental note to suggest to Francis that he have the tree's three lower trunks cabled together; the Ottos had had a chinaberry of about that same size in their back yard several years ago, and it had split right down the middle during a thunderstorm. Muriel rose and walked next door, where she rang the bell.

"Hello," Muriel said, pointing in the direction of Francis's cottage, "I'm Muriel Brimm, Francis's sister."

"Yes, yes," said Claudia Callejas, seeming to recognize Muriel.

"I was wondering if you had seen my brother."

"Seen him?" said the young woman, and uttered the two or three opening notes of what might have become a musical laugh. Then soberly, she added, "No, I am sorry. I have not."

Muriel thanked the woman and walked away, wondering what the meaning of that mysterious, truncated little laugh had been.

Both parking lots at the Raphael School were completely full when Muriel got there, and she had to find parking on a side street in a bordering neighborhood and walk the considerable distance to the chapel. As she neared the front entrance, which was an inner door made of glass and metal, a college-aged woman was escorting a boy out, a boy Muriel immediately judged to be deaf and blind. Muriel went to hold the door open for them, but the woman pushed it open forcibly and spoke sharply to Muriel. "Move away!" she said. "He'll try to grab you!" Muriel did move away and allowed the two to pass, feeling surprised and unwelcome.

Inside, all pews were taken and people were already standing in the side aisles and in the rear. Detective Sergeant Connie Shoulders, who was seated about four pews in from the chapel's small narthex, spotted Muriel and motioned for her to join him. He stood and smiled as she approached, and at first it seemed that he would give up his place to her. Once she was seated, however, he squeezed in next to her. "Miss Brimm," he whispered, "you're the best-looking white woman here today."

"Tell me, Detective Shoulders," she said, practically blushing with pride, "is your maternal grandmother living?"

"No, ma'am," he said. "She died about ten years ago."

"It's obvious," said Muriel, "that you miss her very much."

Through a side door near the front of the chapel, two women and a man appeared, all three well dressed and middle-aged, escorted by Joe Letson toward the frontmost pew, which had been ribboned off. Connie Shoulders whispered to Muriel, "The parents."

The night before, Muriel had wondered how the parents would look, how the horror of such a monstrous loss would show in their faces, but now, as she watched them enter the pew, it wasn't their faces that revealed their ordeal, but their postures. All three were extremely slump-shouldered and stooped, shamed in this public forum by the enormity of their loser status. One of the women wore a rather shrill cattleya orchid, which Muriel thought inappropriate, yet somehow touching in its inappropriateness.

A small string ensemble had been organized to play the weepy Albinoni Adagio in G. A young teacher from the school, a woman Muriel had never seen, said a few admiring words about the slain girls. Linda and Sara had been best friends, and the young teacher tried to comfort the mourners with the thought that the girls had been together at the end. This, of course, was only speculation, though it was fairly certain that they had been abducted together. Muriel experienced a pang of contrition when the teacher revealed that Linda Wayne had been a devoted horticulturist, cultivating magnificent orchids in the school's greenhouse.

There were no hymns sung, not even a prayer offered, and Muriel thought the tone of the service matched the stripped-down chapel itself—once a place of worship, when the Raphael School had still been connected to the Roman Catholic Church (until 1952), now picked clean of any religious artifacts, the chancel remodeled into a theatrical stage with a garish red velvet curtain.

Connie Shoulders seemed to have been badly affected by the service. Outside, they paused for a moment in the sunlight. "It's not going well, is it?" said Muriel.

"Miss Brimm," he said, "how can I put this so it won't offend your ears? We ain't got jack-doodoo. And don't go quoting me to the newspaper."

"I'm sorry," she said.

"And it's going to get worse. We've had a letter from Port St. Joe."

"What do you mean, a letter?"

"Tomorrow afternoon's paper," he said, abruptly excusing himself in order to hail down a uniformed policeman who was passing by.

She tried Francis twice more, in the afternoon and evening, without success. That night, she included him in her prayers, asking that God be with him, *wherever* he was; along with Connie Shoulders; the parents of Linda Briscoe Wayne and Sara DiMatteo; the souls of Linda and Sara; Linda and Sara's killer; Deirdre; Deirdre's baby; and Muriel herself, that she might be given strength and compassion in her talk with Deirdre the next morning when Deirdre came to clean.

But Thursday morning came and went with no sign of the girl. Around noon, Muriel dialed her number. A recorded message stated that Deirdre's line had been disconnected and that no further information was available.

She dialed Francis's number and still got no answer.

She went next door and knocked on Billie's back door. After waiting a full minute with no result, she returned home, feeling abandoned.

In a kitchen drawer she found Deirdre's address, scribbled on a scrap of paper, 28A Beauregard Street, a neighborhood near the college vaguely known to Muriel. It was within walking distance, and walking, she thought, was what she was called upon to do. She had behaved badly, and she needed to make amends.

Because rain had been forecast, she took an umbrella.

She found Beauregard Street with no trouble, its mouth flanked by square brick columns, painted white and peeling, and by a brief stretch of pointed steel pickets—meant, Muriel supposed, to suggest exclusivity. But sidewalks and curbstones had somehow been overlooked, and she was obliged to walk in the street itself.

The houses were part yellow brick and part clapboard, with pitched roofs and dormer windows—tract housing, Muriel judged, probably from the late forties. The builder, all those years ago, must have cut down every tree. As she walked along, she counted five different architectural plans. Each house had a concrete driveway leading to a single-car garage in back. She saw no children, though the evidence of them (particularly of young ones)—gym sets, inflatable swimming pools, tricycles—was recurrent, a neighborhood, she imagined, given over to married students and having the general run-down appearance of a district whose property was entirely rented out.

Number 28 was one of the most decrepit. She guessed that 28A would be found behind the house proper and began walking down the drive. As she passed the house, a curtain was pulled back in one of the windows, and the face of a child briefly appeared.

An apartment—28A—had been fashioned of the garage, though Muriel couldn't see how it could be more than one small room. There didn't appear to be any window other than the one in the short white door at the side. She knocked, though something about the silence of the place already told her that Deirdre would not be there.

She moved close to the glass in the door, cupping her

153

hands on either side of her face. It was too dark inside to
see much detail—a sink on the wall, a hot plate on a card
table, horrible green patio carpeting—but Muriel allowed
herself to envision for a moment Deirdre's bringing home
a baby to this place, and she was struck for the first time
by the severity of Deirdre's plight. She had thought of the
girl as unflappable, the self-proclaimed survivor, and she
had used Deirdre's optimistic spirit, determination to improve herself, and worldly-wise affect as means to dismiss
her. Satisfied with the surface, Muriel had not bothered to
look beneath, frightened by what she might find. Now,
chiding herself for failing to bring pen and paper, and more
generally, for having embarked on so futile (and finally
self-serving) a venture in the first place, she turned to go.

The screen door opened at the back of the house. A
young woman wearing very short shorts and a halter top
stepped onto the brick stoop, an infant straddled across one
hip. The child whose face Muriel had seen in the window—a little girl of about five, she could now see—
squeezed past and out the door, but was prevented from
going farther by a yank on the arm from her mother.

"Can I help you?" the woman called out with such hostility that Muriel thought she must have imagined it.

"I'm looking for Deirdre," she answered, moving slowly
closer to the house.

"Deirdre?" the woman said, as if the name were formal,
even ornate, and she herself knew Deirdre by Deirdre's gut-
ter alias. "Well, *Deirdre* ain't here."

"Oh," said Muriel, thinking that perhaps somehow she'd
come to the wrong address, and that Deirdre's actual place
of residence wasn't at all this desolate, and that the people
she really lived with were well groomed, hospitable, and
good.

"You a relative?" the woman said.

"No," answered Muriel, now having reached the stoop.
"I'm Deirdre's employer."

"Oh, really?" said the woman. "Her employer. Well, you

ain't been paying her enough is all I got to say. You tell her for me that if she don't have the rest of her shit out of there by this afternoon, it's going on the street."

The woman turned, pushed the child back through the door, and went inside.

Walking out the drive, Muriel decided that this woman, and not the father of Deirdre's baby, was who Deirdre had been shouting at on the telephone.

When Muriel reached the brick columns, Deirdre herself rounded the corner into Beauregard Street, a laundry bag slung over one shoulder. Deirdre stopped, obviously surprised. She let the bag fall to the pavement, then lifted it again and resumed walking.

"Deirdre," Muriel called out. "Don't."

The girl stopped again and turned. "I don't want to see you, Miss Brimm."

"I tried phoning you," said Muriel.

"Yeah, well, my phone's been disconnected. I've had a lot of doctor bills to pay."

"Deirdre," said Muriel, "I came to apologize, dear."

"Okay," said the girl. "Apology accepted. But I still don't want to see you. I have to be around people who . . . never mind. I just don't want to see you."

"But where will you go, child?" Muriel said. "Where will you go?"

Deirdre looked at her a moment longer. "Forget about me, okay?" she said, turned, and walked away.

That was the one thing Muriel would not be able to do. She was good and angry by the time she reached her own front porch, with its hanging deer ferns and tubs of caladiums. She picked up the afternoon paper and went inside. She had made a little mistake, chosen a wrong word at the wrong time. Was this so unforgivable? For this she was to be rejected utterly?

Exhausted, she went straight to the bed and lay down. She was glad to escape the humid air outside, with its swampy odor blowing off the bay. She opened the paper. In state news, another abortionist had been gunned down during a protest rally outside his clinic, and a spokesman for the organization who had staged that rally claimed to lament the slaying, while pointing out that the lives of several babies had been saved by it. A Haitian cab driver had been shot through the head by a fourteen-year-old boy and robbed of the nine dollars in his pockets. Another teenage boy, following a dispute with his father over the loudness of the boy's radio, seized a Mossberg pump-action shotgun, fired it into his father's face, pumped and fired again. In a condition described by the arresting police as "excited," the boy reportedly said, "I was Terminator, man, I was f——ing Robocop!"

Halfway down the front page, Muriel read this headline: "Crier Receives Alleged Killer's Letters." Beneath that: "Text on p. A12." The article was complicated and badly composed, and Muriel had to read it twice before she could understand exactly what had happened. She managed to decipher that two letters, both postmarked in Port St. Joe, about eighty miles from Pines, had been received by the editors of the *Crier*, the writer of the letters claiming to be the killer of Linda Briscoe Wayne and Sara DiMatteo. These were not the first such letters to be received by the newspaper, but when police were consulted, certain details revealed by the writer about the murders of the blind girls convinced them that this was indeed the actual killer. It appeared that these details (not made specific by the article) had been included by the writer as a means of establishing his authenticity.

The first letter was a kind of cover letter for the second, much longer one. In the cover letter—which contained the incriminating details about the murders and was not reproduced by the *Crier*—the "killer" requested that the editors print the second letter. He had also threatened, pretty straightforwardly, that if this wish was not met, he would "probably have to go hunting again." The article stated that both letters had been turned over to forensic laboratories. In the meantime, an ad hoc committee (composed of the mayor of Pines, the Pines chief of police, the editor in chief of the *Crier*, the deputy director of the governor's Crime Commission, and a professor of criminology at Pines State College) had conferred; the parents of Linda Briscoe Wayne and Sara DiMatteo had been consulted; and it had ultimately been decided to go ahead with printing the letter, purported to be the killer's "life story."

Preceding the text of the letter was a warning that it contained explicit material that might be upsetting to some readers. The letter itself read as follows:

I am sorry for the pain and suffering to the families. I am sorry I have caused fear in the citizens. I have no excuse for what I did, and I am not going to offer any. I do not regret it either. I thought about it a long time. When I was a boy, when I was nine years old, I had to pick up the eggs. I had six houses I was in charge of. I had to feed the chickens, clean the waterers, pick up the eggs four times and be ready to load the truck by 5:30. (I started at 6 a.m.) My daddy came around in the truck at 5:30 and if I wasn't ready yet he would sit in the truck getting madder and madder and waiting for me to get finished. The chickens pecked me every time I reached under to get the egg. Sometimes one of those hens would get hold of the skin on the back of my hand and I would have to pry her beak open to get it out. No matter how much this hurt, the only thing for me to do was to go and put my hand up under the next chicken and get pecked again. My hands and fingers would bleed and I would think I couldn't do it anymore but then I would think of my daddy coming with the truck and it was the only thing to do. I hated going to work, but I had to do it every afternoon after school and on every Saturday and Sunday. During the summer and on vacations I worked seven days a week. I had no say in this. Every morning at 5 o'clock I would be lying in bed dreaming of some-

157

thing nice and my daddy would knock on the door and say Get up!

When we got back to the house at night my mother would ask my daddy how I had done that day. They would go into their bedroom and discuss it. They usually decided I had to have a whipping. My daddy was fat and his belt was long and thin. He would call me into the room and tell me to drop my pants. My mother would stand on the side and watch. Then he would whip me all the time yelling Stand still! My mother would cry, and when he was done he would go over and hug her to make her feel better. I would go in my room and lie down in the dark. If he had whipped me hard enough to make me bleed, I didn't care if I got blood on the bed. After a few minutes he would come in and tell me to get up and drop my pants again so he could see what he had done to me. He would turn on the light and when he saw the welts on me he would be very sorry and call me "honey" and say he hadn't meant to hit me that hard. He would say "Oh honey" in a very sorrowful way and get down on his knees and cry over my welts, laying his head against me and sometimes kissing me. The next thing I would feel would be the vaseline and then he turned the light off and told me very businesslike to bend over the side of the bed. He did me like that and there are other details I won't mention and then he would leave me in the dark. When I went into the kitchen to get some supper my mother would be mad and upset and say Why can't you do a better job so we don't have to go through this practically every night? She said it hurt her just as much as it hurt me. She would make me eat my supper in the kitchen while they ate theirs in front of the tv.

I saved up some money and bought myself an old plastic Polaroid camera called a "Swinger" and started taking pictures of myself in the full-length mirror on the inside of the bathroom door. I would lock the door and take off all my clothes and turn so I could take pictures of my backside. Every time my daddy whipped me and then did me on the side of the bed I would go in the bathroom afterwards and take a picture of myself front and back. I kept these in a Dutch Masters cigar box and I still have them to this day. Then I would go back to my room and go to bed and dream about something nice until I heard Get Up! and it would start all over again. Sometimes I dreamed about Jesus. In one dream I used to have, Jesus baked me a key lime pie, and served me at a picnic table under a great big oak tree with Spanish moss hanging down.

This went on until I was nearly 14. Some time shortly after my 14th birthday, I started opening up chickens and that's all I'm going to say about cutting because that part's secret. That's about technique and what have you. My mother and father are still alive and when they read this they will know who wrote it. I am not worried about them going to the police. They know I could put them in jail a thousand times over.

This letter is not a work of art but there is no profanity and it is grammatically correct. I believe I have spelled everything correctly. When I don't know how to spell a word I look it up in the dictionary. I have read "The Elements of Style," a book on how to write in which it says to "avoid fancy words" and that "it is seldom advisable to tell all." It's funny. I've read this letter over a hundred times and I am smarter than it makes me seem.

Muriel had sat up on the edge of the bed and now she noticed that the newspaper was trembling in her hand. She laid it aside and stood. She walked through the front parlor to the foot of the stairs, feeling a kind of agitation in her chest that couldn't be accounted for by the simple beating of her heart. She thought to pray, but decided not to. She decided that she was on her own now. She walked up the stairs slowly, the way people do when they are afraid of falling, though she was not afraid of falling.

It was very warm upstairs, and the first thing she did was to open the hall window. She went straight to the end of the hallway and opened the door to her mother's room. Inside she saw her mother's bed and dresser. She walked to the dresser and opened the top drawer, where there were three books: a white leather-bound marriage manual, a small green book entitled *Manners for Moderns*, and her mother's huge, ancient Bible. She removed the Bible, which had figured so dominantly in her girlhood, from the drawer and passed her fingers across the ornately carved cover: depictions of David's lyre, the stone tablets, the sacred meeting tent in the desert, the Heavenly Jerusalem, Peter's sinking into the sea (inscribed with "Save Me Lord or I Perish"), Moses lifting up the serpent in the wilderness ("Look and Live"). She opened the Bible, thumbing through the black-and-white lithographs that were as familiar to her as if she'd seen them only yesterday—the famous one of Jesus holding a lantern and knocking on a door ("Behold, I stand at the door and knock"), the departure of the children of Israel from Egypt, the triumph of Mordecai. She remembered the old Bible's special features, including the parables of the Lord illustrated and explained; the comprehensive and critical description of the Israelitish tabernacle; the chronological and other valuable tables designed to promote and facilitate study; the natural history, containing descriptions of the animals, birds, insects, and reptiles mentioned in the Holy Scriptures.

And in the very back, just where she expected to find them, lying loose between the endleaf and the cover, several snapshots. She removed these from the Bible and held them in her hands. In one, a little girl of about eight stood at the edge of a corn field, wearing shorts and a cotton shirt, squinting and shielding her eyes with her hand. In another, the same little girl, this time in a white dress, sat on a concrete bench, deep sadness in her eyes. In another, the

160

little girl sat on the edge of a bed in what looked like a hotel room, wearing nothing but her white underwear, the same sadness in her eyes. And in another, taken from far away, she stood at the base of a huge statue of a woman, a giantess draped in copious robes and who appeared to be exposing her breast as an offering of nourishment. Holding these several snapshots in her hands, Muriel sank to the floor, bowing her head toward her knees, and wept.

Seventeen

BRIMM'S FEVER PERSISTED for three days, straight through Tuesday night, then went away as mysteriously as it had arrived. What remained past the fever's departure, however, was an absorbing, steady fatigue. Often when he moved—rising from bed, descending the few stairs off the kitchen stoop, even bending to tie a shoe—he grew light-headed. He spent much of his time lying on a quilt in the back yard, reading briefly, sleeping mostly. (Monday, he fell asleep in the afternoon, under the chinaberry tree, and awakened hours later in darkness.) He ate very little, mainly dry cereal and fruit. It was not, of course, the life he'd imagined for himself, but then no recent developments had quite fit that billing. He felt he had moved on to a deeper, more crucial tier of solitude, and once again he was impelled to reinterpret his coming back to Pines. The torpor he'd often experienced since his return, the vague inertia, hadn't been fundamentally spiritual after all, but merely a preamble to disease. How stupid he'd been not to recognize this weeks ago—he hadn't felt really good for a long time.

Occasionally Brimm was struck by the preposterousness of his situation, his fate, having retreated to the town of his youth (now it was clear) to die, an old man, a lifelong skeptic, granted, in his final chapter, visitations by an angel of death. He supposed it made some sense, and he even was able to construct at least a shaky logic for it: this important imagery, the girl in France, the village street, had entered his subconscious (along with its soundtrack), later to emerge meaningfully in his old age. Analyzed in this way, it didn't seem all that extraordinary. Then, alternately, he would be struck by just how extraordinary it truly was, and eventually, as he lay on a quilt staring up at the branches of the chinaberry, absently studying the random shapes of sky leaking through, his fate seemed to him both ordinary and extraordinary at the same time, a paradox that felt closer to the truth than any other formula he could contrive.

Nevertheless, he felt chosen again now, as he'd felt temporarily after finding the bones on the golf course; singled out for presage of his imminent death, he'd been elevated to a kind of clear distinction. He thought, too, that there was a practical benefit in his having been given time to prepare.

Immediately upon hitting on the topic of preparation, he recognized his presumptuousness. He hadn't really the slightest idea about date or time. He might die tomorrow. Or even that same day (Tuesday). It seemed dimly plausible that since he had discovered the real purpose of his vision on the ceiling, there wasn't much left to do but go ahead and die. He saw his revelation in the grape arbor as a kind of washing away of a sand dam, and thought that he would now be carried swiftly into the outbound current of death.

Brimm knew that Muriel—who was always looking for the pagan implications, the unsupportable assumptions—would not take any of this angel-of-death business in stride. He would have to present it to her in just the right way. He recalled his visit to the rectory of St. Matthew and the Redeemer and reminded himself that he had plenty of biblical precedence on his side in this matter, and that if worse came to worst he could always trot out the Reverend Mary Whiteside. What he hoped was that if he let it alone for a while, did nothing—and assuming he didn't die in the meantime—then a good plan for disclosure to Muriel would emerge. This, at least, was the reasoning he developed, all the while knowing that, at bottom, lurked the same thing

163

that lurked at the bottom of most procrastination, a kind of unspecified fear.

Wednesday, a magnificent, cool day, the first of September, there was to be a memorial service for the murdered girls at the Raphael School, and Brimm considered going. He finally decided, however, that since he hadn't known either the victims or their families, attending the memorial service would be hypocritical, with a voyeuristic edge. Only hours ago, of course, the voyeuristic edge would have guaranteed his presence at the memorial service. But he was changed now, directed inward.

Encouraged by the remission of his fever on Wednesday morning, he chose instead to drive to the beach. The beach, he determined, would be a place to think—or even better, a place not to think.

He drove to St. Thomas Beach, some nine miles outside of town, the closest, still unspoiled beach and the one he'd most often visited as a boy. There were dunes to climb (barefoot, as he'd left his shoes in the Jeep), but happily they were not as high as Brimm remembered. Still, the distance of about three hundred yards, through sand, from the nearly empty parking lot to the beach, winded him considerably, and twice he had to sit and rest.

The most remarkable trait of St. Thomas Beach was its timeless atmosphere. The dunes hid any view of the road or parking lot, and its neat crescent shape hid at either end any view of coast, any foul hint of civilization, such as a motel or seafood restaurant. There was the sand and the Gulf to behold, but no snack concession, no lifeguard platform, no public restrooms of concrete blocks. On a cool weekday such as this (no people to speak of, no beach umbrellas), and lacking a discernibly modern boat on the horizon, there was no positive suggestion of the twentieth century.

Today Brimm shared St. Thomas Beach with a red mongrel dog, who ran up to greet him once he'd descended the dunes, and the dog's apparent owner, a thin old fisherman who stood, fully clothed and wearing a wide-brimmed

164

straw hat, repeatedly casting a line in the water about twenty feet beyond the breakers. Upon the dog's first friendly barks, the old fisherman turned and acknowledged Brimm with a nod, a salient gesture even from a distance, given the straw hat.

Brimm had worn bathing trunks under his trousers, and now he removed his trousers and shirt and spread a blanket on the sand. Because of the cool breeze blowing off the water, he needed some of the blanket as cover, and so he lay on half and folded the other half over himself.

He soon fell asleep. In his dream, the old fisherman walked out of the water and came to sit next to him on the sand. Brimm noticed that the wind had stopped entirely and there was that kind of utter stillness that can be accomplished only in dreams. Brimm thought of this in the dream—that the utter stillness could be accomplished only in dreams—and he felt quite happy to be dreaming, to be held as it were in this dreamy, utter stillness. The old man was about Brimm's own age. The underside of his straw hat was pinned with several photographs of children. Down by the surf, the dog chased a yellowlegs, barking and barking.

The dog's actual barking was what awakened Brimm from the dream.

The fisherman was walking up the sand, the dog jumping excitedly around him and barking, trying to get him to play. He carried his rod in one hand and a creel in the other. His mustache was entirely white, his skin very dark and weathered. As he neared Brimm, he seemed to look deeply into Brimm's eyes, and then hesitantly nodded and moved on.

Brimm watched the man go. He watched him as he disappeared with each step, bit by bit, from the feet up, behind the crest of the dune, and once the man was gone, Brimm experienced a confusion in which he thought perhaps he had *only* dreamed the old fisherman and the dog. In any case, it seemed certain that the stillness in the dream was the stillness of death, and he was reassured by having enjoyed it so.

That evening, back home, as he lay under the chinaberry tree, he recalled the fisherman's hesitation, his brief but poignant stare, and he thought, Yes, it shows in my face. He shouldn't have to explain anything to Muriel. She would take one look at him and know.

Thursday afternoon, Brimm was asleep in his bedroom when the *Crier*, with its killer's epistle, landed on his front porch. Around six o'clock the telephone rang, waking him.

"Frank," said a woman's voice, "something's wrong with Muriel."

"Muriel?" he said. "Who's this?"

"It's Billie, Frank. Billie Otto. Next door. You know I wouldn't call you like this if I didn't think it was serious."

Brimm was feeling much worse. The fever had returned, and as he tried to sit up, something inside his head (not his brain, but something wet and heavy, like clay, just behind his brain) seemed to shift and pull him back down onto the pillow. At first he was confused by Billie's describing herself as "next door," when Brimm knew that the beautiful young concert pianist lived next door. Then, after a moment, he understood that she meant next door to Muriel.

Billie explained that naturally she and Ned had gone over to Muriel's after they read the afternoon paper, and that they'd found Muriel in a most enigmatic mood. This in itself was not unusual; Muriel was often in an enigmatic mood lately. But Muriel had been especially unwelcoming, and when Billie had simply expressed an opinion on the subject of the newspaper article, Muriel had asked her and Ned to please go. That, too, had happened before; Muriel had asked Ned and her to please go more than once in recent weeks, but never before with such vehemence. And all because Billie had merely said that she was sick and tired of seeing all this childhood abuse stuff every time you turned on the television or picked up anything to read.

Brimm said he hadn't the slightest idea what Billie was talking about.

"Frank," said Billie. "You have read the newspaper, haven't you?"

"Not yet," he said.

"Well, my goodness," she said. "No wonder."

She then explained about the letter in the *Crier*.

"Oh," said Brimm. "I'll go and read it now."

"And then you better call her," said Billie. "This is the worst I've seen her, Frank. She's been crying again this afternoon."

"Okay," he said.

"Frank," she said. "You don't sound so good yourself."

"I'm fine," he said.

"Well," she said. "Okay. But call her, okay?"

He fetched the *Crier* and returned to bed.

"I am sorry for the suffering to the families . . ."

Brimm's fever contributed some unusual effects to his reading of the letter: a scorching vividness to each of its nuances and at the same time a pure emotional detachment. Without any analysis, he knew the letter would have greatly upset Muriel. He put down the *Crier* and phoned her at once.

"Francis," she said, "where have you been?"

"Nowhere," he said. "I mean, I've been right here."

"No you haven't. I've tried calling you many times. I even came by the cottage on Wednesday."

"Wednesday I was at St. Thomas Beach."

"St. Thomas Beach?"

"But mostly I've been at home," he said. "In the back yard. I've just had a call from Billie Otto. She's worried about you. Says you're having some kind of trouble. I wondered if the letter in the newspaper might have upset you."

"Of course it upset me, Francis."

"Yes," he said after a pause, since she apparently in-

167

tended no elaboration. Then he invited her to supper, offered to make pancakes.

"Francis," she said. "You sound as if you're out of breath. What have you been doing?"

"Nothing."

"Are you still sick?"

"Yes," he said. "I think I'm running a fever again."

"What do you mean, 'again'?"

"It went away and came back."

"Well then, you must stay in bed," she said. "I'm very tired tonight myself. I'm thinking of taking a sleeping pill. What about if I come over and see you first thing in the morning?"

He said that would be fine. "Muriel," he added. "The sleeping pill is a good idea. Try not to dwell on things. Just sleep, and then we'll talk in the morning."

She agreed and quickly hung up, her voice breaking when she said, "Yes, Frankie."

By the next morning Brimm felt as if he lacked the strength to get out of bed—or at least the strength to stay out of bed.

When Muriel arrived he got up to let her in, still in his pajamas.

"Oh my God, Francis," she said. "You look terrible."

"Yes," he said. "I feel terrible."

He turned, motioning for her to follow, and went back to the bed.

When she saw his room, she said "Oh my God, Francis" again. "No wonder you feel terrible. This room would make anyone feel terrible. It's making me feel terrible already and I've only just set foot in it."

He sat on the side of the bed and looked around. "What's wrong with it?" he asked.

She moved to the window, raised the shade, and lifted the window. "Well, for one thing," she said, "there's no light. And no air. The sheets on that bed look as if they haven't been changed in six months. I don't know what all this clutter is on the floor—your dirty clothes? Is that *food*?" She pointed to an uneaten bowl of cereal on the night table.

"It used to be," he said sheepishly.

She walked to his side and felt his brow. "You feel a little hot, but not too bad," she said. "Let's get you out of here." She looked around the room with great skepticism. "Do you have a robe?"

Muriel made hot tea and got them situated in folding chairs, near but not in the shade of the chinaberry tree, insisting that what Brimm needed was sunlight and fresh air. Then she began rattling on and on—nervously, Brimm thought—about some story she had been trying to remember as she was driving over to the cottage.

"By one of those old New York writers," she said. "Not Salinger, but somebody like him."

"But there's not anybody like Salinger," said Brimm.

"I'm sure there must be," she said. "It was one of those stories where everybody's having a terribly gay time in New York and one group of people meets another group of people in a restaurant or a club . . ."

"Oh, that one," said Brimm. "Sure. Where one group of people meets another group of people."

"Don't be so smart," she said. "There were three young people in their late twenties . . . a married couple and an extra man—I remember the young woman's name was Jenny. And an older couple in their sixties. Everybody was getting on very well and being extremely charming. Do you remember this story, Francis, or not?"

"Naturally I don't remember it," he said. "I never read any such story."

"Oh, Francis, it was a lovely story. They all ended up leaving together and walking down to the river where they could look out and see stars in the sky."

"This must have taken place long ago," said Brimm, "when you could still see stars in New York."

"Of course it did," said Muriel. "And the old man kept

169

saying, 'You must all come up and have a drink with us, I insist,' and eventually it dawned on the others that he meant come up to Connecticut. Which meant that they should all come up to Connecticut and have a drink and then sleep over, and Jenny thought it the most wonderful night of her life.

"But you see, there was this little problem, which was this third wheel in the young couple's life, this other man . . . Frank was his name, like you, Frankie. It seemed that maybe Jenny was in love with Frank, but she was also deeply in love with her husband, and her husband loved Frank too—Frank was his closest friend—and it was all very complicated. And the young couple very much wanted to have children as Jenny was nearly thirty, but they needed to sort out this little problem of Frank first.

"Later it turned out that the old couple from Connecticut were so keen on the young people coming home with them because they themselves were missing their own grown children so much, who'd moved away long ago . . . It was all very touching. I remember the old man saying to Jenny, 'What do you drink, girl?' and Jenny said, 'I don't know. Tea, I guess,' because she didn't drink any alcohol, and there was this moment, as if a wet blanket had fallen over all the gaiety, and then the old man turned to his wife and said, 'Why, look here, Mabel, a girl who drinks my drink—tea.'"

Muriel fell silent. A breeze stirred the branches of the chinaberry. Brimm noticed that she gazed into her lap briefly and then out at the pine woods on the east side of the cottage. The tall pines leaned one way and then the other in perfect unison.

"But the best part," she continued, "was when Jenny was standing between the two young men, her husband and Frank, and she began trying to recall a story she'd once read—just as I myself am doing now—and she says to her husband, 'What was that story, dear? You know, where the man says to the woman, "What do you think you'll remember of this night thirty years from now?" ' And the woman says, ' "Don't talk to me about memories. *Give* me memories." ' And on the word *give*, Jenny sucks in her breath because just that instant one of the two men she loves has touched the small of her back in a certain way."

To Brimm's astonishment, tears were now streaming down Muriel's cheeks.

"Muriel," he said, leaning forward. "What is it? What's wrong?"

She looked at him with such sudden rage in her eyes that he actually felt his breath stop. "Oh, just look at us, Francis," she said. "Where are our children? Tell me, where are our grandchildren?"

For a moment, he found himself looking around the area where they were sitting. "What?" he said, though of course he had heard her perfectly well.

"Our children, Francis. Where are our children?"

After a pause, he said the obvious: "Well . . . we haven't any, Muriel."

"Right," she said.

"Muriel," he said after another pause. "What is this really about?"

"Surely you must know what it's about."

"No. I honestly don't."

"Well, what do you *think* it's about?"

Brimm recalled the first girl he ever confessed his love to. They were teenagers, her name Anna Jones. "What is it?" the girl had said in response to Brimm's sullen, cryptic humor, as he rowed them across the lagoon where years later Brimm's father would drown himself. "You know," he said. "No," she said. "Well, what do you think it is?" he said, finally making her say the actual words—incredulously, "Do you think you're falling in love with me, Frank Brimm?"—and his merely acceding to them.

"I imagine it's about Daddy," Brimm said at last to Muriel.

She did not lower her head but looked him straight in the eye and said, "Yes."

"Muriel," Brimm said. "He was a drunk . . . out of control . . ."

"Yes," she said again with something like hatred. "He had sex with me, Francis. Real, adult sex. For more than four years. It started on that goddamned trip to Iowa. I was *eight years old*, Francis."

A house sparrow flew down from the chinaberry and landed near Muriel's feet, appeared stunned to find itself there, and flew away again. Brimm, at a loss for words, reached for her hands, but she pulled away, averted her face.

"Well, what difference does it make now?" she said angrily. "I'm an old woman. What on earth can it matter now? I can tell you one thing. I can tell you what I refuse to do. I refuse to interpret my life in light of this. I'm not going to go back over my whole long life and see every one of my disappointments and failings as caused by this. That's what I'm not going to do."

She wore a long full skirt with big kangaroo pockets on either side. Now she reached into one of these, took out a man's white handkerchief, and wiped her eyes. Then she reached into the other and took out a small green book.

"I brought you a present," she said, tossing the book into Brimm's lap.

He turned it over in his hands. *"Manners for Moderns,"* he said. "I remember this."

"It's perfectly ludicrous," she said. "He used to read this garbage to us." She yanked the book from Brimm's hands. "Just listen to this," she said, quickly finding a certain page. " 'Using good manners is like putting money out at interest,' " she read aloud. " 'You get back more than you put in. If you don't believe that, you can try it for yourself. Get up some morning with the idea that you are going to be as pleasant as you can to everyone all that day. Smile! Act interested in everybody. Go out of your way to be agreeable

172

and do small errands for other people. Don't let yourself get into any arguments. Don't say a cross word to anyone. Use all the good manners you have ever heard of on everyone from your closest friend to the corner bootblack. Make yourself be cheerful all day. Go to bed feeling cheerful.' "

By the time she finished this passage, her voice shaking with rage, she had begun crying again. Brimm took back the book, gently. He could only begin to imagine what it must have been like for her, hearing Dr. Brimm dole out this kind of advice. On the book's cover was a picture of a beautiful young girl from the twenties, sitting upon a high pedestal. A man who looked like Valentino gazed upward at her, adoringly.

Eighteen

BRIMM DIDN'T AT all like the way Muriel had left him that morning. She hadn't permitted him even to begin to console her, and he wouldn't have known how, even if she had. He thought his helplessness was at least in part due to his being physically impaired. At bottom, he was so preoccupied with the course and nuances of his illness, his mind was working at a great disadvantage. During the time that Muriel had spent attempting to retell the story about the old couple from Connecticut and the young people they met in New York, Brimm had been thinking all the while, It's going to be soon—by which he meant that not only was he going to die soon, but he was going to die very soon. Under the circumstances, he couldn't share this intelligence with Muriel. Her disclosure had preempted his.

How had he known that Muriel's agony that morning concerned Dr. Brimm's molesting her as a child? There had always been a bit of telepathy between them, him and Muriel. That could have played a small part, he supposed, but it was more than that. Had he always known? Just as she surely had always known? He'd recognized immediately, when he read the letter in the *Crier*, that the depiction of sexual abuse would distress her deeply. And when she said to him, "What do you *think* it's about?" he recalled the incident in the rowboat with the young Anna Jones. Then, moments later, when Muriel had left him so abruptly, another memory, all of a piece—a night when, as a child of four or five, he'd awakened in the wee hours, left the nursery, and walked down the hallway to Muriel's room. He couldn't remember what he had intended that night, but when he pushed open her door he saw Muriel, a delicate girl in the fourth or fifth grade of elementary school, reflected in the vanity mirror. She lay in her bed, awake. Her open eyes met his in the mirror's oval. Dr. Brimm lay across Muriel sideways, on his stomach, sound asleep, snoring. Brimm had stood like that in the doorway for the longest time, not moving, the two of them, he and Muriel, staring at each other in the mirror.

It was not a definitive memory—he had not seen any sex—but the discovery had been strangely powerful and bizarre, and certainly troubling, too, since he'd apparently buried it away for all these years.

Brimm decided that the questions of when he had known and what he had known and how he had known defied analysis. The truth was this: when Muriel had said, angrily, squinting in the bright sun, "What do you *think* it's about?" the answer had simply occurred to him—it was one of those inexplicable mental confluences—and once the answer occurred to him, he saw that it possessed a kind of authority, borne he imagined on the wings of reason. Given who Dr. Brimm had been, given who Muriel had become, it made sense.

What made less sense, he thought, still sitting in the back yard sun where Muriel had left him almost an hour ago, was this anthropological attitude of his. Well, there was the great distance (as Muriel herself had acknowledged) between that particular past and the present, the dulling impediment of many, many years. And Brimm was in a sun stupor, he imagined; every five minutes or so it had been dawning and redawning on him that he should move into the shade, but somehow, so far, he'd not been able to summon the will for such an enormous change.

Now when he closed his eyes, he witnessed (no better word, for the sun's lasers on the top of his head had incised his meditative faculties into any number of separate departments) the following scene in his mind's eye. He's standing—the small boy, Frankie—in the hallway just outside Muriel's bedroom door. Dr. Brimm, a snoring corpse, has Muriel pinned to her bed, wide awake. Something about young Muriel's eyes, and maybe the angle of her head, has conveyed to Frankie to stay put, not to come any closer, and for the last minute or so he and she have been having this staredown in the dark, rather like Davy Crockett and the bear. Mrs. Brimm, buttoned up in something like a white shroud, comes along the dark hall and turns Frankie, by the shoulders, away from the door. She quietly pulls the door to, then escorts Frankie, still by the shoulders, but gently, back to his own room and into his own bed. Once there, under the covers, Frankie asks her why Daddy is sleeping on top of Muriel. "Because your father had too much to drink," Mrs. Brimm answers, "and he fell into the wrong bed."

When Brimm opened his eyes, it seemed more likely that he had only seen Mrs. Brimm having one of her bouts of sleepwalking—and perhaps on a different occasion altogether. This stuff, this childhood memory stuff, was like debris from a shipwreck—whole pieces, intact, floated around in a general area, but which piece connected to which? And what was the meaning of this or that piece, unconnected to a discernible whole? And wasn't it the very nature of the mind to mix memory and imagination? Didn't one imagine things and then recall them many years later as having actually happened? Surely his mother's exchange with him about Dr. Brimm was more a product of imagination than of memory.

Lab work, thought Brimm of his own speculations, a chemist breaking down a compound. Where he might be feeling something like horror, if only on Muriel's account, he experienced the old familiar (and therefore comforting?) detachment. For the first time ever, it occurred to him that he might have developed this hard journalist's composure in his boyhood, stranded as he'd been on that island of madness and abomination in Pines. When he'd pondered it before—this fine objectivity of his—he had imagined it bred in the practicing of his craft, but now he saw it as the personal aptitude he had brought *to* his craft, the bedrock that had allowed him poise while shooting the public humiliation of the young head-shaven mother in Normandy, the Yugoslav father gathering the broken body of his son from under the wheel of an army truck, the soldier who'd been lost for weeks in a Southeast Asian jungle and so ripe with jungle rot that he could squeeze a whole cup of pus from his right calf. There it was, thought Brimm (now engaging the aural department of his mind), the clicking of the shutter, the glassy insect sound, the chitinous staccato of a species surviving the holocaust.

He rose from the chair at last and went slowly into the house. He looked up the number of Muriel's Dr. Van Buren and dialed it, standing at the kitchen counter. From there he could see, out the window, the boy Nicolás standing on the back stoop of the house next door, playing with a bright yellow yo-yo. Brimm watched as Nicolás stepped off the stoop onto the grass and expertly executed an around-the-world. He spoke the boy's name softly—"Nicolás," pronouncing the syllables and the vowels in the Spanish style, as Claudia Callejas had done that Sunday on the porch when Muriel had accused Brimm of "transforming" in the face of the young woman's beauty. You see. He was capable of connecting sometimes. To a young woman's beauty. To a vague longing at seeing a boy with a yo-yo. Brimm began to explain himself to the receptionist who had answered the telephone at Van Buren's office, to describe the symptoms of his illness. But the receptionist interrupted him halfway through, turned him over to someone else, a nurse, and he had to begin all over again.

Nineteen

AFTER LEAVING FRANCIS'S Friday morning, Muriel experienced an odd confusion that reminded her of the time when she'd been taking the drug Aldomet. As she drove the Volkswagen over the Little Yustaga Bridge on her way back into town, she was aware of an agitation in her mind (it would be wrong to call it thinking) that was like the most explosive point of an enormous waterfall: the white, brilliant, fragmented water near the top that overshoots the main body. As she tried to reflect on her visit with Francis, and on its substance, she found one would-be thought so quickly displaced by another that she was unable to bring anything into focus. She pulled the car into the unpaved turnaround on the opposite side of the river, came to a stop, and said aloud, "All right, Muriel, now *think*."

After a moment of silence, a more familiar, less churning sensibility returned. She found she could recall with ample clarity the events of her visit with Francis, but they seemed to have happened long ago and to someone else. She knew she had disclosed to Francis, her only living relative, that their father had sexually molested her as a child. She had felt rage and sorrow and cried many tears. But now, only minutes after the fact, she couldn't quite think why she had been so upset. After all, the abuse itself had occurred almost seventy years ago, and the effects of it, if there had been any, had long died their natural death in company with her father. Her extreme emotional reaction had been theoretical and disingenuous, based on ideas she might have had about how one ought to react to such a thing. Unwillingly, for reasons she probably would never understand, she had dredged up and acknowledged some early buried memories, and on this side of that dredging up, she felt much the same way as she'd always felt. Life went on. New awareness had brought no earth-shattering consequences. The image of herself kneeling on the floor of her mother's bedroom, holding old photographs in her hands and weeping, seemed not like weakness to her now, but like insanity, and Muriel was glad to have it behind her. The distance she now felt was undoubtedly an early sign of repair.

She knew, as she sat in the car by the bridge, that she had not been able to paint a complete and satisfying picture of things, but at least she had composed herself and brought a bit of order to her thoughts—which had the practical result of enabling her to remember that she needed to pick up her dry cleaning.

At the cleaners, she was greeted not by Mr. Peerless himself but by the college-aged son, whose name was Sonny, and who emulated to a tee his father's eloquent manner.

"How very nice to see you again, Miss Brimm," Sonny said to her as she entered.

Paying her bill, Muriel asked after Mr. Peerless.

A look of great sympathy overtook Sonny's face— sympathy for Muriel—and he said, "I thought you might have read in the papers, Miss Brimm. My father suffered a heart attack last week and passed on."

Stupidly, Muriel said, "That's not possible."

Sonny smiled at her, again with sympathy, and said, "He was a great, honorable man, Miss Brimm. He gave us much more than love. He gave us values and pride and a vision of what life can be. I already miss him more than I can say."

Muriel left quickly, feeling strangely overcome by grief. During the five minutes it took to drive home, she fought back tears, and she was pleased with herself for having

179

done so, for when she arrived, Billie Otto was waiting in the swing on the front porch.

Cheerfully, as Muriel mounted the porch, Billie said, "You forgot our book club meeting this morning, didn't you?"

"Oh, my heavens, I certainly did," said Muriel, determined to return Billie's cheerfulness. She apologized to Billie and invited her in.

Once they were inside, Billie looked on as Muriel hung the dry cleaning in the hall closet; she said, "You've been to the cleaners."

When Muriel turned to face her, Billie said, "Muriel, what's wrong?"

"Mr. Peerless has died," Muriel said, and began to cry outright. She allowed herself to be taken into Billie's arms.

"Goodness," Billie crooned, pulling Muriel's head onto her shoulder, patting Muriel's back. "I'd no idea you were close to old Mr. Peerless."

"I wasn't," Muriel said.

After a pause, Billie went on patting Muriel's back and said, "Oh," as if she understood something, which of course she did not.

Later, after Billie had returned home to Ned, assured by Muriel that she was only overtired and wanted a nap, Muriel sat in the window seat and began to gaze across the sunny boulevard. Now that it was September, Muriel thought she could already see something different about the light, the angle of the shadows cast by the crape myrtles. Soon both cats joined her, the big one, Henry, claiming Muriel's lap while the Siamese curled up on the cushions near enough to be a part of things but far enough away to indicate that he didn't care who sat in Muriel's lap. Had Muriel not forgot her meeting of the book club, they would have discussed three stories by James Joyce, stories that were already known to her but that she had reread in the early part of the week, including the long famous one, "The Dead." Now, looking out at the vacant lot across the way,

180

Muriel recalled the haunting effect of that story's ending. "His soul had approached that region where dwell the vast hosts of the dead," it said of the character Gabriel. "He was conscious of, but could not apprehend, their wayward and flickering existence. His own identity was fading out into a grey impalpable world"—a perfect description of Muriel's own recent state of mind, or so she had thought around Monday or Tuesday. And, at the very end of the story, Gabriel's standing at the window, watching the landscape fill up with snow; it was like an important dream that lingered long after the dreaming. The rhythm and grit of the language had been so beautiful that Muriel had tried committing some of it to memory.

All at once, thinking of snow, looking out at sunlight, an intense physical strain seemed to wash over her. She couldn't recall when she had last slept, though she knew she had been taking her sleeping medication. She acknowledged a sharp pain behind her eyes, a pervasive aching in her shoulders and elbows and the balls of both thumbs. A motor of anxiety hummed inside her chest, near her heart, and for a moment she actually experienced a fear of taking the next breath. She thought, I am losing control, which suddenly struck her as comical and terrifying, a morbid understatement. It occurred to her to pray—she had been trained to turn to God and God's word in times of trial—but some low-pitched resentment bubbled up inside her, a defiant voice that whispered of the need for self-reliance. The stairs creaked, she turned away from the light of the window, and the dead Mrs. Brimm came walking down from upstairs, dressed in the same outfit Muriel had worn on Wednesday to the memorial service at the Raphael School. Mrs. Brimm moved forward with an exaggerated world-weary look on her face, brushed the Siamese cat off the cushion distastefully, and sat opposite Muriel in the window seat. She stretched her mouth into a thin line and sighed heavily.

She had a sickly sweet smell about her, and Muriel calculated her to be about half her own age.

"Those are my clothes," Muriel said to her mother at last. "That's my hat."

Mrs. Brimm closed her eyes and shrugged, not to be engaged on the subject of the borrowed clothes. "You're a very, very confused girl, Muriel," she said, shaking her head slowly. "It's not at all what you think."

"And you're dead," Muriel said, pulling rank.

"He was a drunk, I'll grant you," said Mrs. Brimm. "But Muriel, darling, you've let your imagination take flight. You're lonely, dear. Lonely and old, that's all. You need something to grab hold to. But frankly, dear, I would have thought it below you to jump on the sexual abuse bandwagon. And at your age! Isn't it just a little bit embarrassing? You were always highly suggestible. What was it we called you? Impressionable, yes."

"Shoo," said Muriel. "Shoo, shoo."

Mrs. Brimm shrugged again, stood, and returned to the foot of the stairs. Before beginning her climb, she turned to Muriel and said, "Do you honestly think I would have permitted it? Use your brain, Muriel."

Muriel looked out the window again. The Fayson house stood where it used to be, exactly as it used to be, except that the hydrangea bushes out front were grown clear up to the porch railing. The twins sat on the steps lighting sparklers in what appeared to be the faint light of dusk. Captain Fayson came out the front door, quite dashing in his dress whites. He paused at the edge of the porch to unwrap a cigar.

Muriel stood and quickly drew the drapes. She went to her bedside table in the other room, and though it was before lunchtime, and though she'd taken at least one the night before as well, she swallowed a Seconal capsule and lay down on the bed, pulling a cotton blanket over her legs. She closed her eyes and noted that a word was forming in her mind, *oblivion*, and fleetingly she thought the *o* in it was the round entrance to a dark, sinister tunnel. This made her laugh a little, yet there was no real comfort in her brief laughter, and certainly nothing like joy.

Twenty

SO BEGAN A spiraling downward that would last the next several days. Muriel decided she was ill—perhaps she'd caught Francis's flu, though her temperature (which she determined several times a day with an ancient glass thermometer) was consistently normal—and took to her bed. She continued her three regular medications, for she found some solace in swallowing pills, but she also continued using the Seconal at various hours in order to escape the prison of living entirely in her mind. For the most part she had always lived in her mind—that was the kind of woman she was—but this had been a choice, based on the fact that her mind was a pleasant enough place to live. Now that her mind had changed, now that it had become such a bad neighborhood, as it were, she seemed to have no choice about whether to live there or not. The Seconal, the seeking after oblivion, turned out to be a spectacularly unsuccessful strategy. Disguised as a friend, the drug provided brief respites by knocking her out cold for a few hours; but then, as it began to wear off, it intensified her vivid dreaming before she awakened, and left her with little or no resistance to the more horrifying aspects her mind served up once she was awake. She soon became so disoriented that she felt, paradoxically, that the drug was making everything harder *and* it was the only thing in life she could really depend on. Over the course of about five days, she succeeded in practically reversing her sleep schedule, so that she slept a good deal of the day and was awake for most of the night. This development, she decided, was necessary in order that the nightly terror to which she was to be subjected could have full effect.

She had no appetite to speak of and ate very little. She did not go out for groceries, and there was no Deirdre to bring any in. Fear hung over the prospect of any sort of excursion, including attending church services. She understood this apparent agoraphobia as a concentrated mutation of a lifelong pattern. She had spent her life in the town where she was born, she had continued to live in the house where she grew up; it made sense now, at the nadir of her life, that she was unable even to leave the house. This drawing in was perhaps the form her death would take—she would be found dead, alone, crouched in a corner of the cellar closet.

Sometime Saturday a note was slipped through the mail slot from Billie Otto, stating that she and Ned were taking the bus up to Satsuma (Alabama) to visit their daughter and her children and would be away for a few days. That was good—Muriel wouldn't have to deal with the Ottos. The newspapers continued to sail onto the porch in the morning and afternoon, and she brought them in (so the house wouldn't appear unoccupied) but left them unopened in the entryway. What mail arrived was unexceptional. No one telephoned, certainly not Francis, who'd undoubtedly been frightened into his escapist hibernation by her visit on Friday.

She noticed that in Deirdre's absence the house was gradually becoming untidy, which seemed to fit nicely with the general direction of all things. It occurred to her that she was suffering a deep depression. It even occurred to her that the sleeping pills were aiding and abetting the depression. But these insights were incidental and fostered no change. She tried reading Sunday's Bible lessons Monday night, but her heart had become a cynic's heart. The Hebrew Scripture and the Epistle were platitudes—God would deliver his people, bring forth the usual springs in the desert; one must live the Word, not just hear it—and the Gospel passage from Mark (Jesus heals a deaf and speech-impaired man) depicted crowd-pleasing and unnecessary pyrotechnics near the Sea of Galilee, with Jesus putting his fingers in the man's ears and spitting and touching his tongue. Muriel thought the evangelist Mark would have done an equally good job of chronicling the life of, say, Harry Houdini, or Evel Knievel.

Despite these reactions she was strangely moved when Jesus said to the afflicted man, *"Ephphatha,"* a word that meant "be opened." This bit made her see Jesus in her mind, and she realized that most often when she saw Jesus in her mind, who she really saw was the young Bavarian who had portrayed Jesus in the Oberammergau Passion play that had been held in the old Pines armory all those years ago. She recalled the fair young man pacing backstage, his head bowed in allegiance to his role, his beautiful hands folded at the small of his back; she recalled watching him as he paced, and the feeling of mystery, awe, and some other, unnameable thing he inspired in her; and she recalled a moment when he happened to look up and see her watching him, how he'd met her eyes and smiled. Smiled to her, only to her, and oh how her heart had leapt! She had pondered that moment for hours afterward, wondering whether he had smiled at her as Christ or as a young actor in a Passion play, and she had judged precisely that ambiguity to be truly Christlike. The actual Jesus must have radiated that identical God-or-man confusion with every gesture, surely with every smile.

Very late on Monday night, in depression and drug haziness, Muriel thought of this man, this German actor, of how old he would be today were he still alive. Ninety at least. She imagined a snowy cabin in the highlands, flames in a hearth, his telling his great-grandchildren of the time long ago when he'd played Christ in America, and this fire-lit portrait caused her such a sharp ache that she believed, mistakenly, she had maybe touched the bottom of her loss.

186

By Tuesday night it seemed the house, her refuge, had turned against her. Around midnight she thought she heard footsteps on the front porch. She went from her bed to the window seat and drew back the edge of the drape a fraction of an inch. Out on the street a police car cruised by, which made her think of Connie Shoulders, of her foolishness regarding him, and, for the first time since last Thursday, of the blind girls' killer, the deranged prophet, author of (among other things) the famous line "What's buried ought to stay buried."

No one was visible on the porch, but that didn't mean there hadn't been someone there a moment earlier. Seeing the police car approach, the intruder might have quickly withdrawn into the azalea bushes. The grown-up child who'd been tortured and defiled by his own parents and who'd penned the words "I am sorry for the suffering to the families" might have decided that the old woman mentioned in the newspaper was in some way responsible for some of his grief. After all, she had been important enough for him to telephone her that night. It was easy to imagine that he'd taken her up again as a subject for obsession. Who knew what went on in a mind like that?

Muriel went to her desk in the parlor, found pen and paper, and wrote, "Wed., 12:05 a.m., footsteps on front porch." She went into the kitchen and checked the lock on the back door, which was secure. Through the door's window, however, she could see that the latch to the screened porch, which she was sure had been hooked earlier, was now undone. A knife blade slipped between door and jamb could have easily unhooked it. She went back into the parlor and wrote down, "12:09 a.m., found screen door unhooked." Though melodramatic, making these notes gave her the satisfaction of having taken action, since she was not about to go onto the porch and latch the screen door.

She returned to bed and imagined that the young man who had scraped the flesh from Linda Briscoe Wayne's bones would turn up at the door—not at the front or back door but, already inside, at the door to her bedroom. Muriel would be sleeping and would wake up to find him there, a good-looking man in his twenties, standing quietly and peacefully in the doorway. He would smile. "Hi there, Miss Brimm," he would say with that terrible backwoods twang. "What's wrong with you anyway—been taking too many of them pills?" She would reach for the telephone, but of course the line would be dead. "Oh, I took care of that," he would say, winking. "I didn't want us to be disturbed." But in the end she would not be harmed, for Detective Sergeant Connie Shoulders, who had been trying to reach her, and who had determined through the telephone operator that Muriel's line was out of order, would arrive at the house at the last minute.

This fantasy shamed her, not in its B-grade trashiness but in its concise grasp of her two great needs: to suffer and to be rescued.

"You see, Muriel, dear," she heard her mother's voice saying, "you're just a lonely old woman, trying to put a bit of significance into your lonely life."

Last Thursday, after reading the letter in the *Crier*, Billie Otto had said, "I am so sick and tired of this childhood abuse stuff every time you turn on the television or pick up a magazine. Every star in Hollywood, every singer, every talk show guest. Why, you would think there wasn't a man, woman, or child who wasn't molested by their father, mother, or priest. Now the *criminals* have joined in the whining!"

At those words, Muriel had envisioned herself with her hands around Billie Otto's throat, her thumbs pressing down on Billie's windpipe. Without really intending to, she had thought what a pleasure it would be to see Billie's eyes bugging out, and Muriel had been frightened by the prospect that she had more in common with the homicidal maniac who'd dreamed of Jesus serving key lime pie under an oak tree than she did with her old friend and neighbor.

* * *

"Why don't you tell me about the dream," says the kind therapist, pulling a chair up close to the side of the bed.

It was Wednesday night at around 10 P.M. Though she had been awake only for about half an hour, Muriel had just swallowed another Seconal. She lay in bed, still distraught after having awakened in tears. She embarked on another of her imaginary conversations with the imaginary therapist, but now she was so far gone that it seemed to her that she could actually hear the therapist's words, and see her (an attractive, simply dressed woman in her fifties) with the same vividness that had characterized her mother's visitations.

"Zacchaeus," says Muriel, aloud, into the dark room. "I dreamed about Zacchaeus."

"Zacchaeus in the Bible?" asks the therapist.

"Yes," says Muriel. "He was a tax collector, and rich, and hated by all the people in Jericho. Jesus was passing through, and because Zacchaeus was very short, he climbed up in a sycamore tree so he could see Jesus. And when Jesus came to the tree, he shocked everybody by looking up at Zacchaeus and saying, 'Zacchaeus, make haste, and come down; for today I must abide at thy house.'"

"And?" says the therapist.

"And that's all," says Muriel.

"Muriel," says the therapist, "why does that story make you cry so?"

"I don't know," says Muriel. "I don't know."

Soon she was out again, and slept dreamless for five hours. As the pill began to wear off, she dreamed again of Zacchaeus in the sycamore tree. Only it was she, Muriel, who waited in the tree for Jesus to pass. In the dream she was both a child and an old woman, slight of stature, and undistinguished in every way. Uncelebrated, unloved, and unremarkable except for some private, extraordinary pain in her stomach. Waiting in the tree, she was full of hope and dread, for though she wished to be recognized by Jesus, she

also knew that, recognizing her, he would know her through and through. He would apprehend the pain in her stomach, and he would see to what degree she was responsible for it. When Jesus finally appeared, he was dressed in tropical paramilitary garb, like Fidel Castro, and he rode in the passenger seat of a Jeep driven recklessly by another man, similarly dressed. This was a surprise to Muriel, something she hadn't prepared for. The Jeep cut a path through the people in the street below, rather like a bowling ball cutting a path through tenpins, and raced beneath the tree and out of sight, affording Muriel only the briefest glimpse. She tried to cry out, but her mouth was filled with dust. Still, some lower-animal sound escaped her throat, a wailing of air, an appalling rasp that shook her awake, and to her relief she realized that she had fallen asleep in the sycamore tree while waiting for Jesus and had only dreamed about the Jeep and the rest. Luckily she awakened just in time, for when she looked down, she saw him standing beneath her, looking up. "Muriel," he says, "make haste, child, for I must abide with you tonight." He reaches his hand up toward her, and as she touches his fingers, the pain in her stomach melts away and she is a girl of twelve or thirteen again. "You've done nothing wrong, Muriel," he says, reading her thoughts, shaking his head, "you've done nothing wrong," and now she is walking beside him, barefoot, somewhere near a lakeshore, a warm gentle breeze blows her hair, the light in the sky lovely and pale blue. She can see that the clean clear lake swarms with fish, and as she and Jesus walk along, the fish swim up to the water's edge to be nearer them. Soon they come to a kind of tall white gazebo, something like the bandstand downtown in Bonifay Square. Jesus indicates that she should climb the stairs up to the dance floor, and when she arrives at the top her father is waiting for her, serene and handsome and happy to see her. As they begin to waltz on the wooden floor high above the lake, she notices that her father's missing arm has been restored, he has both his hands, and there
190

is absolutely no danger in them. To the contrary, he is a physician, possessing the gift of healing, and those strong, able hands are in the world precisely to protect her. He leads her away from the dance floor, back down to the shore, back to Jesus's side, and, falling into step, safe and perfectly loved, Muriel thinks that this is how it was in the beginning, when God used to come in the evenings and walk in the Garden with his children, this is how it was in the beginning . . .

She was startled around dawn by the sound of the piano in the next room, single arbitrary notes, but she could see, turning her head on the pillow, that it was only Henry, walking along the keyboard. A great, viscous sorrow began to enclose her, the violent remorse of having returned to the world from the dream of the lake, and she reached for the amber bottle of sleeping pills. She sat up on the side of the bed, struggling with the bottle's plastic cap, and when it popped open the small red capsules seemed to explode from the bottle, falling to the floor and scattering in all directions. "Oh, no," she heard herself say, in a voice she did not quite recognize. There was nothing for it but to get down on her hands and knees, which she eventually accomplished, bracing herself on the side of the bed.

She had not bathed or changed clothes in five days. She had not eaten any food in at least . . . she wasn't sure when she'd last eaten. She did not feel hungry, though there was something satisfying, like answering hunger, as she plucked not one but two, then three capsules from the floor and put them directly into her mouth. She did not bother to gather the rest. She maneuvered herself into a sitting position, her back against the bed, and reached for her water glass on the nightstand. "Come over here, Henry," she said to the cat, who had leapt down from the piano and now sat staring at her. Yes, she thought, I am a curiosity, but Henry just continued staring at her a moment longer with an impeccably detached wisdom, then walked away. It occurred to her that

191

the cats were probably hungry, but she did little more than glimpse this negligence. She discovered that the wood beneath her felt pleasantly cool, and slowly she allowed herself to slide downward until she lay fully on the floor. She suddenly had a strong feeling that she was not alone. She sensed another presence in the house, and in a fragment of a dream or hallucination (she couldn't tell which) she lifted her head off the floor and saw two middle-aged nurses in crisp white uniforms, fiddling with some oxygen tanks in the parlor.

Frankie, a beautiful long-haired boy of ten, sits in the swing on the front porch. He doesn't know she is just inside, in the window seat, and can hear him singing. He sings the Gershwin tune "Bidin' My Time," but with complete innocence, and to her utter delight he's got the words all wrong. "I'm bitin' my tongue," he croons. " 'Cause that's the kind of guy I am . . ."

Four burning questions. What day was it? Why was she sleeping on the floor? How had her kimono got so wadded under her? How was she to get to the bathroom in order to urinate when she felt so unable to move or wake up?

The phrase "burning questions" passed through her mind. She actually seemed to see the questions burning in a fire. None of them, she realized, had the least bit of importance, none of them, she saw clearly, counted for a goddamned thing, and with an oddly satisfying surrender, she allowed herself to urinate right where she was, a physical sensation that felt a little like bleeding.

Years ago, there was an old blind woman by the name of Irene who used to frequent the Raphael School library. The official story was that Irene had been left blind by suppurative meningitis in early childhood, but she was fond of telling people that her father had blinded her when she was a girl. The business of her father's culpability was clearly
192

an obsession. Checking out a book in Braille, she would stare off into space dramatically, as if she didn't know where Muriel was in the room, and say, "My father blinded me, you know."

Muriel would say, "Irene, you had meningitis as a child. Dr. Rush told me."

"Who's that speaking?" Irene would say.

"You know perfectly well who it is. It's Muriel Brimm, the librarian."

"Well, don't call me Irene. I don't know you."

"Yes, you do."

Once, after this same, usual exchange, Irene tried to reach across the circulation desk and throttle Muriel. "What do you know about me?" she said fiercely. "What do you think you know about me, Miss *Prim*? I'm telling you my father blinded me."

"All right," said Muriel, trying to calm her. "He blinded you."

Irene stood stock-still, breathing hard, audibly. "He blinded me, I say."

"I said he blinded you. Okay."

"That's right. And you remember it, too."

Muriel, temporarily taken aback by Irene's anger, quickly recovered her mischievousness, and then said, "Only Irene, if he blinded you, how did he do it?"

Irene, calm now, and not to be ruffled again, said, "I haven't worked out all the details."

At first Muriel took this remark as a surprising admission of Irene's inventiveness regarding how she'd come to be blind. But there had been something strangely unprotected about Irene when she said it, the kind of overt vulnerability that lets you know a person is telling the truth.

The next time Irene came to the circulation desk, she said, "My father blinded me, you know," and Muriel, because she had been touched by the old woman in a way she herself couldn't have explained, said, "Yes, Irene, I know."

One day, years later, Muriel had entered the front door of

the Raphael School on her way to work and had seen Irene, distraught, standing in the middle of the lobby. There was an inlaid star, inside a circle, in the marble floor of the school lobby, and Irene stood at the very center of the star. Off to the side, a nurse, a middle-aged black-haired woman, struggled with a ring of keys, trying to unlock the door to a washroom. Her back was to Irene, and over her shoulder she shouted with great contempt, "You *hold* it, you hear me! You *hold* it!"

"I can't, I can't," Irene cried.

Muriel spoke up and said, "Irene, whatever's the matter?"

"Who's that?" said Irene, shocked, and a stream of urine began to splash onto the marble floor between her feet.

In the dream, Irene walks across the Little Yustaga Bridge, tapping her red-tipped cane against the stones. Muriel, in the Volkswagen, tries to roll down the window on that side of the car, but she can't get the handle to turn. She begins to tap on the glass. Irene turns toward the sound and begins to speak words that Muriel cannot hear.

The foul stench of the bay had entered the house through the air conditioner, as it sometimes did. Oh, how she hated the sea and everything about it! Here she had lived in a coastal town all her life, and she hated everything about boats and fishing and ocean life. She hated seafood, and she especially hated the crazy zeal so many people seemed to have for horrid things like shellfish, slimy gelatinous flesh oozing from hard prehistoric carapaces, the things nightmares are made of.

Staring up at the ceiling, a blank page, she urinated again.

A few light taps on the pane made her turn to the window. It had begun to snow again. She watched sleepily the flakes, silver and dark, falling obliquely against the lamplight. The time had come for her to set out on her journey. Yes, the newspapers were right: snow was general all over Florida. It was falling on every part of the dark central plain, on the treeless hills, falling softly upon the Bog of Allen and, farther westward, softly falling into the dark mutinous Shannon waves. It was falling, too, upon every part of the lonely churchyard, on the cold granite pietà, filling the lap of the Savior. It lay thickly drifted on the crooked crosses and headstones, on the spears of the little gate, on the barren thorns. Her soul swooned slowly as she heard the snow falling faintly through the universe and faintly falling . . .

The horrible woman in the shorts and halter top steps to the edge of the stoop, one arm roughly wrapped around the shoulders of a young child. "It's his *penis*, you fool!" she shouts. "Don't you know anything at all? You're dreaming about his *penis*."

Bright lines of light glowed around the edges of the windows, which seemed to suggest a daylight hour, and the windows themselves seemed to suggest that she was looking at the windows inside her own house, the house where she had grown up and lived all her life. But that was impossible, because if she were in her own house, then she must be the woman who lay on the floor in the stink of her own urine.

The bright lines seemed to grow softer, fuzzier, but they still delineated what was unmistakably the windows in the parlor. The acrid odor that stung her nostrils was unmistakably that of her own urine. She lay on the floor amid strewn red capsules, without a clue as to what time of day it was, or for that matter, what day. Frantically, she sat up and reached for her prayer book on the nightstand, upsetting a water glass, which crashed to the floor, glass shards mixing with the red capsules. She jerked open the prayer book to a page marked with a purple satin ribbon and began to read aloud, fast, without pause, one prayer after another. "Almighty God," she read in a weak and hoarse voice that was not her own, "whose son had nowhere to lay his head: Grant that those who live alone may not be lonely in their solitude, but that, following in his steps, they may find fulfillment in loving you and their neighbors; through Jesus Christ our Lord, Amen. Look with mercy, O God, our Father, on all whose increasing years bring them weakness, distress, or isolation. Provide for them homes of dignity and peace; give them understanding helpers, and the willingness to accept help; and as their strength diminishes, increase their faith and their assurance of your love. This we ask in the name of Jesus Christ our Lord, Amen." The next prayer was for a birthday, but she went on and read it anyway, without pausing. "O God, our times are in your hand: Look with favor, we pray, on your servant—" Here she broke down, speaking her own name into the room. "On your servant Muriel as she begins another year. Grant that she may grow in wisdom and grace, and strengthen her trust in your goodness all the days of her life."

Unable to go on reading, she pulled herself up and got to the powder room under the front stair. The flesh on her face felt as if it had been removed, poached, and pasted back on her skull, not quite in all the right places—and she dared not look at herself in the medicine chest mirror. Her eyes fell instead on something in the soap dish. She lifted it out and held it up close to her face: a small silver ring, set with a single amethyst.

Part II

"HERE'S WHAT I remember of my childhood," says Deirdre to Brimm.

She sits in a dark maroon wingback chair, positioned so that she can prop her feet on the edge of Brimm's bed, and from which she has been reading to him. They are in the bedroom at the back corner of the house in town, upstairs, two rooms down the hall from Brimm's boyhood room, the nursery, which has a window seat and an alcove for a crib, and which therefore has been assigned to Deirdre herself.

It is a morning in late December, the week between Christmas and New Year's, and the windows in Brimm's room are shut against the winter chill. Deirdre is quite visibly pregnant as she sits in the chair, one hand splayed over the dome of her belly, one hand holding the open book off to the side. She and Brimm are wearing the Christmas present each gave to the other, Deirdre a long baggy sweater (selected for Brimm by Muriel), Brimm a pair of pale blue cotton pajamas. Physically, Deirdre feels good now, and from time to time she has even wondered what the big deal was earlier about being pregnant. She has noticed with delight that as a result of a surge in hormones, her hair has grown thick and shiny.

"This is my childhood in a nutshell," she says to Brimm, who has interrupted her reading again with a question. "When I was four or five years old, my old man was on the early shift at Eglin, doing systems testing, and he'd get up around four in the morning to go to work. They had an old-fashioned gum machine out at the base, the kind that takes pennies, so if I got up before he left for work and gave him a penny, he'd bring me home some gum from out of the machine. Little Chiclet things, two little white tablets wrapped in cellophane. So I remember stumbling into the kitchen at around four-thirty, half asleep with a penny in my hand, and he'd take the penny and lift me high into the air and nuzzle my face with his beard."

She pauses.

"That's it?" says Brimm, opening his eyes for the first time since she began speaking.

"I guess it was something that probably happened a lot of times," she says, "but over the years it's kind of congealed into one memory—you know, as if it only happened once."

"That's all you remember of your entire childhood?" asks Brimm. "It wasn't all that long ago, you know."

"I've blanked most of it out," she says. "That's my one good memory, see? Sometime after that, after the time when I was getting up and giving him pennies in the morning, he started giving me quarters in the afternoon to take showers with him. And after that, things get hazy. Then my memories are more like feelings. Sadness, self-loathing, fear, stuff like that. So if you ask me do I think it really happened to Muriel when she was a little girl, I tell you I have absolutely no doubt about it. It happens all the time."

Brimm, an entirely neutral expression on his face, recenters the back of his head on the pillow, closes his eyes again, meditatively, and says, "Continue."

Deirdre returns to the book and begins again: *"Moers was an unassuming man, thin as a rail, whose suit always needed pressing. He had been at the Quai for so long that it was impossible to imagine Criminal Records without him."*

For a while now it has been clear to Deirdre that when Brimm actually listens to her reading, which is seldom, it's a transitional tactic: he wants the story to push aside his thinking so that he can drift to sleep. Most of the time, however, he doesn't really listen at all but uses the sound of her voice as a kind of white noise on which to float his various thoughts. (He has let it be known to her that he likes the sound of her voice. She can recall vividly the afternoon several weeks ago when he said to her, "You have a mellifluous voice," and how, surprising herself, she had blushed, even though she didn't at that time know the meaning of *mellifluous* and had to go look it up afterward.) It seems to Deirdre that Brimm thinks an awful lot, perhaps too much, though she admires the way he embraces thinking as a worthy pastime. She also admires his analytical abilities, and she has noticed that, for a man, he has remarkably good insights. "Things happen," he said to her on another occasion. "And then you have to make sense of them." That, he explained, is what a photograph is all about—it stops things, freezes things so you can think about the implications, so you can "contemplate the ramifications."

"He was always ready for work," Deirdre continues, *"whatever the hour of day or night. True, he was a bachelor and there was no one waiting for him in his student's lodgings in the Latin Quarter.*

" 'One fact is already clear,' he answered in his rather monotonous voice. 'Quite recently, yesterday afternoon probably, all the furniture has been polished, all the doorknobs wiped, the ashtrays, even the smallest object . . .' "

She stops reading and looks at Brimm, listens to his breathing, which has become deep and regular. "Oh, Frank," she whispers very softly, "you look positively bleached."

She is referring to his extreme pallor, and she thinks for the first time—or rather, for the first time she acknowledges thinking it—that he will not last until February.

Sometimes, when she watches him sleep, or watches him as he appears to sleep (for he is prone to extended, closed-eyed periods of an unknown variety), she is filled with a

201

weird longing. It seems to be attached to what began as Brimm's desire and then later became her own: that he should stay alive until the baby is born, in February. But she knows it's also about her feelings for him, a subject that has been given a lot of play in her head these last few weeks. She considers his presence in her life only one part of the larger miracle of *her* presence in this house—warm, fed, busy, needed, even loved.

Back in August and September, when she had been exhausted and sick so often and then got kicked out of her apartment and (probably foolishly) quit her job with Muriel, she had been reduced to spending some time in a public shelter for women, a frightening, hopeless place run by a frizzy-haired woman named Bobbie Towers, who seemed to have nothing but contempt for the people she was helping—contempt for the people, Deirdre observed, who were providing Bobbie Towers a livelihood. Bobbie Towers never missed a chance to present herself as someone who had a wide range of experience, who had been everywhere and knew everything. She drew elaborate distinctions among the plights of the women in the shelter, based on the degree to which their plights were, in her opinion, of their own making; she had been particularly contemptuous of Deirdre's pregnancy. "Some of these black girls I can understand," Bobbie once said to Deirdre. "But you, white, you should know better." The odd thing, Deirdre noticed, was that when Bobbie criticized, she seemed envious of the person she was criticizing, as if she were jealous of the attention even the sorriest woman was getting.

Deirdre prayed daily for a way out—out of the shelter and out of the tribulation that had landed her there. She went to her twelve-step meetings and talked about what was going on, about her loneliness, her fear of the future, and about the oppressive Bobbie Towers. At least twenty or thirty times a day, it seemed to her that nothing was wrong with her life that couldn't be fixed by a good stiff drink, a few tokes on a joint, and an uncomplicated roll in the hay with a horny oil rigger on shore leave. In the past, she had found that this particular mix of diversions usually did the trick. During her meetings, when she suggested this as a solution to her current predicament, everyone laughed empathetically. Nightly, in the shelter, she reconsidered abortion, worried and worried again the old points of debate—wasn't it morally preferable to abort this life than to bring it into such chaos and uncertainty? And when she considered the chaos and uncertainty, her opinion of herself sank far below anything Bobbie Towers might have bestowed. In the dark of the night, none of Bobbie Towers's insults could hold a candle to those Deirdre heaped on herself. When the shelter lights went out, and the crying started up all around her, she would think, "I brought myself here," and, "This is what I deserve." Long after she had given up hope, however, she continued going through the motions of a hopeful person, and out of the blue one afternoon, Muriel Brimm showed up at the shelter door with Deirdre's amethyst ring.

Deirdre could see right away that something had happened to Miss Brimm, something had changed her. Miss Brimm didn't beat around the bush. She said right out that she wanted Deirdre to come live with her. There was that huge house with all that wasted space upstairs, and Deirdre could earn her keep by helping out with some light cleaning and cooking, shopping and running errands. Was Deirdre still in school? No? Well, then they needed to make that a goal, make sure that Deirdre was back in school by the following September—the baby would be six months old by then, and they would figure out some child care. Billie Otto next door was an expert with children—she'd raised three of her own—and would be happy to help out. Deirdre would need to do some fixing up of the old nursery, and the upstairs bathroom needed work too, since it hadn't been used in so many years. She had tried making everything sound businesslike, but in the moment of Deirdre's hesitation (Deirdre had only been overwhelmed), Miss Brimm lowered her eyes and said, "I know it will take some time for you to forgive me fully, Deirdre. But I need you." Then she paused and said quietly, almost whispering, "I need you in order to work out my salvation."

These last, very strange, biblical-sounding words from Miss Brimm cast a kind of voodoo net over Deirdre. She had no idea what the old woman meant by them. But here was the point: Deirdre had been praying for a way out, praying as a would-be taker, on the receiving end of a favor from above, and never had it occurred to her that the answer to her prayers would come in the form of an opportunity to *give* something. She accepted at once, feeling almost dazed.

Then, after Frank Brimm was diagnosed with this rare blood disease that left him progressively dependent on the help of others, and after he moved, early in October, into the old house as well, richness for Deirdre grew richer still. She had been unable to resist interpreting this turn of events fatalistically. Somewhere in the back of her mind she knew that Frank Brimm had not become terminally ill in order to fulfill some purpose in her life, but given that these matters were way beyond comprehension anyway, she didn't see how anybody was harmed by her indulging in a little private egocentric interpretation. This, she thought, was only human.

Once she began to notice that fond feelings were developing between her and Frank, the first thing that came up for her was fear, fear of getting involved in something, no matter how trivial, that might prove smutty or pathetic. He doted on her, and in the beginning it seemed to her that he liked her mostly because she was young and because he considered her pretty. He told her she had a mellifluous voice, things like that, flattering things. He was weak, very sick, and sometimes despondent, and his spirits noticeably improved whenever she came into the room. His obvious infatuation embarrassed her again and again, partly because she recognized it as a cliché, like a sick old man's flirtation with his young nurse in a television soap opera. But then, after a short while, the boyish adulation stuff just stopped. It was as if he had to get it out of his system before he could begin treating her like a normal person. And with that change she began to appreciate some other qualities that had been there, obscured, from the start: many of his compliments were sincere, and she honestly felt flattered by them; she had never felt even the slightest hint of judgment from him about her being young and unmarried and pregnant; he talked to her about what was on his mind, and never condescended to her, he asked her questions about things—like what was going on with Muriel—as if he truly valued her insights.

Once these issues were resolved between her and Frank, she discovered a surprising pleasure in caring for him. She has begun to feel that a sort of healing is taking place between him and her—certainly not a healing of his disease; in fact his symptoms have worsened in the last few days— but a psychological or spiritual healing of some kind. It occurs to her occasionally that she romanticizes all that happens in the Brimm house, and she wonders if this might not be another result of hormones, like the more lustrous hair. In any case, most mornings she wakes up grateful for the day that lies before her, and at night, before falling asleep, she has what she calls her "quiet moments," in which she meditates and sends positive energy to the baby. Through amniocentesis and ultrasound, Deirdre already knows that the baby is a boy, and that he is normal and healthy. The positive energy she sends during her quiet moments with the baby is a kind of nebulous encouragement to grow and be happy, not to be afraid, and to know that he is wanted. One thing she loves is the way the baby sleeps when she's moving around and then wakes up and moves when she rests. She hasn't been able to put her finger on why this delights her so. *Cute* is the word she comes up with most often. It's cute. It's like kids sleeping on a car trip and waking up at the moment of arrival. It's like all the waiting that kids do in some dreamy stasis until the adult business is finally over and it's time to play.

But sometimes when the baby moves, her fear gets triggered, and she starts to obsess about what a terrible mother she'll be, and how she won't know what to do when the baby cries in the middle of the night or gets sick, and how she's probably totally fucked up her body with all the drugging and drinking she's done in the past and how she probably won't be able to make breast milk, and how the pressures of motherhood will probably make her go back to drinking and she'll be too drunk and hung over to take care of the baby, and how she'll probably end up abusing the child, and how, even if none of that stuff happens and everything goes beautifully and she loves the baby perfectly and to distraction, someone will probably steal it in the drugstore while she's turned her back for a minute to choose a pair of pantyhose ... And then, if she's lucky, she'll open her eyes and look around at where she actually is, and she'll think of Frank and Muriel and how God has brought her to this place and to these people. She'll think of helping Frank down the stairs and how they both have to pause at the bottom to catch their breath, and how Frank, his hand to his chest, will smile and say, "Bad blood," his chronic, comic reference to his illness. She'll think of finding Muriel in the window seat in the front parlor, lost in one of her reveries, and how Muriel, seeing her, will pat the cushion next to her, inviting Deirdre in without hesitation. She'll recall what Frank's doctor said, that the promise of the baby is the main thing that can help Frank, that Frank's wanting so badly to stay alive to see the baby born is the main thing in his favor—that there's always the chance of spontaneous remission as long as Frank can just stay alive. She'll think of Muriel shopping for the baby already, coming home with washcloths and blankets and sleeping shirts, buying for Deirdre Dr. Spock's book for Christmas and then sitting in the window seat and reading it herself. And with these thoughts Deirdre is lifted out of obsession and greatly comforted. She doesn't care if the Brimms are functioning as substitute grandparents. She doesn't care if she finds herself seeking their approval and wanting and relishing a kind of parental love from them she never got from her own family. She just wants it to be healthy. She doesn't want it to be smutty or pathetic. She doesn't want it to be twisted. When she sometimes watches Frank sleeping and feels that weird longing, she thinks maybe it has to do with her finally getting something in life she has desperately needed, and that her getting it calls up actual desperation and need, the way the smell of food can call up hunger. She doesn't know for sure. She thinks the longing might also be attached to the probability that Frank is dying already, and that Muriel, at her age, won't be around forever either. She thinks this great, bright, wonderful comet has finally crossed her sky, and here she is trying to grab after the tail.

Her message delivered and received, Brimm's baldheaded angel did not come again.

It occurred to him, shortly after being diagnosed with aplastic anemia, that she needn't have come at all. Wouldn't every outcome and evolution have been the same, with or without her? He would have begun to feel sick at some point, he would fail to improve, he would seek the advice of a physician. The physician, noticing spots (purpura) on Brimm's shoulders and ankles that Brimm himself had not noticed, would refer him to a second doctor, a hematologist, who would prescribe a battery of tests (blood work, marrow scans, MRIs), and Brimm's red cells, white cells, and platelet counts would all be found to be below normal levels. Eventually the hematologist would call Brimm into her office and ask him many mysterious questions about his possible exposure in the recent past to certain chemicals or to radiation. This blind alley briefly explored, she would inform Brimm that he was suffering from what seemed to be a self-perpetuating fatty replacement of the marrow, a loss

207

of hemopoietic cells, and pancytopenia. Brimm naturally would ask her what that meant, and she would explain that he had a rather rare, insidious, and in this case idiopathic bone marrow disorder, the course of which would most likely be a rapid decline, three to six months, perhaps a bit longer. Brimm, grasping after a moment's pause that the doctor meant he had three to six months left to live, would ask about treatment. Unfortunately, the only potentially effective treatments were extremely aggressive, marrow transplantation and immunosuppressive therapy, practicable only in much younger patients. Transfusions could prolong life, especially if there was anything Brimm particularly needed to stay alive for, but ultimately transfusions were of limited value and could also result in an iron overload. Unless Brimm's bone marrow were to begin making blood cells again—which did happen in some cases, for reasons no one could explain (spontaneous remission)—Brimm would grow weaker and weaker, in time an infection would occur, such as the one that brought him to the office in the first place (no namable organism, no explicit focus), and Brimm would be too compromised to fight it off. He needed to have his family arrange to look after him, for soon even the smallest task would prove a considerable challenge. There might be some unpleasantness along the way—obscure fevers, lesions in the mouth, lesions around the rectum. He should take pains to avoid infections by washing frequently with an antiseptic soap; he should switch to an electric razor in order to reduce the risk of nicking and causing a hemorrhage, and he should start using a stool softener and a soft-bristled toothbrush for the same reason. Having been told all this in the hematologist's office, Brimm would then know that he was going to die, and soon. A prophetic vision on the bedroom ceiling, an enigmatic head-shaven angel of death, hardly seemed necessary.

That day in September, driving himself home from the hospital where the hematologist's office was located, he stopped in the turnaround at one end of the Little Yustaga

Bridge. There was a narrow path there at the corner of the bridge, leading down to the water's edge. It was a warm day with hazy sunshine and no conspicuous hint of autumn. Brimm took off his shoes and socks, rolled up his trousers, and waded into the shade under the bridge, where the gentle babble of the river had an echo. He sat on an old concrete pier and dangled his feet in the water. Sharp bends in the river, both upstream and down, created what felt to Brimm like a pertinent effect: the water, carrying with it the light of the sky, emerged from an unseen birth out of the dark upriver trees and disappeared into the still darker trees downriver, to an unseen end. He did not think ironically of the times during the course of his life, both home and abroad, when he had thought he would surely die, though there had been a few. He thought instead of a particular woman, a woman he had met in a subway in New York over thirty years ago.

Today, many weeks later, as Brimm lies propped up in bed, listening to Deirdre read a murder mystery, he has begun to think again of this woman from the past; but Deirdre, the young woman in the present, has stopped reading, the lovely sound of her voice a necessary pedal point for the success of his daydreams. Without opening his eyes, he says, "What did you say, Deirdre? Why did you stop?"

"Oh," she whispers, startled, "I thought you were asleep."

"No," he says. "Please go on."

" '. . . to remove fingerprints,' " she reads. " 'The only prints we lifted were those of the tenant, Manuel Mori, whose card I found in Records, and those of the cleaning woman, who did go to Square La Beryère yesterday afternoon . . .' "

The name of the woman in the subway was Nora. That day under the bridge, following Brimm's diagnosis, she paid him a surprise visit, the logic of which he would figure out later. Since then, he has sometimes invited her back, as a means of giving form to whatever sense of loss he feels about his own dying, a thing, he suspects, so large that it is a comfort to have it contained by her. He supposes every man who ends up the way he has, alone, has a Nora in his past, the woman who beckoned him down the road not taken. Nora, a book editor, not especially pretty, about Brimm's own age (forty at the time), was as unlike his other women as it was possible to be. It seemed to Brimm that she had been angry with him almost from the first moment they met. They were standing on the subway platform in Union Square, waiting for the express train to Grand Central, total strangers, unnoticed by each other, when a man standing between them, a good-looking middle-aged businessman, wearing a dark suit and hat and holding a briefcase, suddenly collapsed onto the concrete and turned a chalky white-blue. Nora and Brimm fell to their knees on either side of the man, Brimm quickly rolling him onto his back. "Loosen his collar!" he heard Nora say as she began searching the man's jacket pockets for (she would tell Brimm later) nitroglycerin tables. Just then, a young Chinese man stepped from the crowd and knelt beside them. Brimm was sure he heard the young man say, "I'm a doctor," but what the young man did was to reach underneath the stricken businessman, lift his wallet from his trouser pocket, and run away down the platform and up some stairs. "Stop him!" Nora yelled, but no one did, and then an actual doctor appeared and began to initiate cardiopulmonary resuscitation. Brimm and Nora stood back and watched, but it was clear, at least to Brimm, that the doctor was working on a dead man. When it was all over, Nora looked at Brimm and said, "Why didn't you stop that thief? The poor man's dead. You could have at least . . ." She paused, gave Brimm the once-over, said, "Oh, never mind," and walked away, distancing herself from so shabby a specimen by about twenty feet. Soon the train came rattling in, and they boarded separate cars.

That was in the morning, a few minutes before nine. Around twelve-thirty the same day, one of those funny things that happen so frequently in New York happened: Brimm found himself sitting at a U-shaped lunch counter in midtown, directly across from the same woman. When their eyes met, Brimm gave her his cheapest, phoniest smile. She got up and walked around the counter to his side, apparently not quite done with him yet. But to Brimm's surprise, she took the stool next to him and said, "I owe you an apology. I was upset, naturally, and I'm afraid I took it out on you. Please forgive me."

Brimm did forgive her, instantly; a conversation ensued about what a terrible experience the whole thing had been; thus began their connection. They fell in love, Brimm went away intermittently on assignments, returned happily to her arms, and she soon wanted to be married, a desire, when spoken, that seemed somehow to spoil everything for Brimm. He disappointed her, broke her heart, possibly her spirit too, her consequent wrath the wrath of a woman who wanted deeply to have a family, who still wanted to have a baby, and who was running out of time. When next Brimm went away, he arranged to stay away for a period of several months, and that was that.

"*Each man knew what he had to do,*" reads Deirdre, and Brimm notices that her voice has begun to sound weary.

"Deirdre," he says, "stop if you're tired."

"No," she says, sounding tireder than ever. "This is good. *The articulated dummy that was used so often in reconstructions stood near one of the gable windows. It was used to discover, for example, in what position a man would be found if he had been struck by a knife . . .*"

All these years later, it seems to Brimm that he really did love this Nora, but that his half of their initial talk at the lunch counter somehow gave them a false foundation on which to build. They struck up a camaraderie based on a shared terrible experience, but about which Brimm was wholly artificial. Brimm, long inured to such things, had not found the businessman's sudden death on the subway platform a terrible experience. In a different setting he might have described it as interesting; undoubtedly, had he been properly equipped, he would have shot any number of pictures; the only unpleasant part had been Nora's scolding him for not chasing the thief. (The appearance of the young Chinese thief, posing as a doctor in order to rob the dying man, was interesting too. Over the years, when Brimm had occasion to think of Nora, it seemed to him that no other facet of their affair, not even the sex, which had been satisfying, ever matched the intensity of their original meeting on the subway platform.)

"Deirdre," he interrupts again, "what in the world is an 'articulated dummy'? Don't you think it sounds an awful lot like the new mayor?"

"Wait," she says, "listen to this. *He felt a little emotional just the same, as he did each time he left his wife for more than a day.* Isn't that sweet? I mean, it's kind of a surprise, isn't it? It doesn't seem like him, does it?"

"No," says Brimm, "I suppose not. Now explain to me where it is exactly that he's going."

"You *were* sleeping, weren't you?" says Deirdre, sighing. "He's going to this place, Bandol. For the burial. Do you want me to back up?"

"No, no," says Brimm. "Go on."

"*Once out on the sidewalk he raised his head, and he knew in advance that he would see her looking out the window.* Oh, isn't that sweet? It's just so sweet that you can tell they're so close."

"Deirdre," says Brimm. "How do you expect me to follow the plot with all this extraneous commentary?"

"*It was just as well that he did, for she was holding up the blue bag ...*"

Launched again across the drift of Deirdre's reading, Brimm recalls that when Nora returned to him in the minutes after his diagnosis, under the Little Yustaga Bridge, she seemed to say, "We could have been happy together," and now when Brimm calls her up in his mind, it is to hear her say this too: "We could have been happy together." The words have a certain effect on him. He feels an unintimidating sorrow, a remorse of manageable size and depth. But he also knows that his thinking about Nora, his using her in this way, is a coy, sentimental device, meant to hold at bay something larger and deeper.

From the beginning, he has not taken seriously the possibility of spontaneous remission. Fortunately, neither has Muriel or Deirdre—or if they have, they've been quiet about it. Brimm thinks that to hope for something so unlikely would be a waste of energy, energy that might otherwise be directed toward a reasonable goal, namely, staying alive until Deirdre's baby is born. Deirdre has acquired a midwife and intends to have the baby right here in the house, an idea Muriel frowns on, but Brimm is enthusiastic. He doesn't imagine that he would be present for the birth, but he has imagined himself lying in bed (where else?) and listening to the goings-on; he has imagined that splendid moment when the baby cries out. The desire for a reprieve is supposed to be, according to his physicians, an instrument for achieving such a reprieve, but now, when he thinks of Deirdre's baby's first cry of life, it fills him with apprehension. For the last couple of days he has been keeping a secret: he's pretty sure that he has a fever, and he's pretty sure that it's getting worse. He has three painful lesions inside his mouth, and he supposes that these could be causing the fever, but right now (and for the past few hours) he's much weaker than usual. It has occurred to him that he is bleeding internally, though he has no idea what that would feel like. In any case, he's beginning to feel overwhelmed by his disease. That in fact was one of the words the hematologist had used to describe aplastic anemia, *overwhelming*. "It can be brief and overwhelming," she had said. Brimm hasn't mentioned the fever to anyone yet because he's still hoping it will go away on its own and he'll never have to mention it. To mention it is to engage the hyperbolic side of Muriel's caretaking, the side most driven by her sense of duty. She will insist on rushing him to the doctor, he will have to endure her worried face, he will have to endure her twenty questions about what he might have done or left undone to have caused an infection. Meanwhile, throughout these passionate attentions, he'll be observing how unsuited Muriel is to this sort of thing, and braving the nuisance of having to be cared for by someone constitutionally opposed to caretaking but who feels duty-bound and probably secretly resentful. Thank God for Deirdre. Deirdre has been ballast to Muriel's torpedolike bedside manner. Brimm is deeply grateful to be where he is, attended by Muriel and Deirdre, but he makes a long-suffering show of the ordeal he's going through at Muriel's hands. "Go away," he has said most often to Muriel since moving into the house. "Go away, Muriel, go away." Even Deirdre has adopted this shooing tactic, though she employs it a bit more gently. "Everything's under control here, Muriel," Deirdre will say cheerfully, and, "We're doing just fine here, Muriel." But inevitably, frustrated, Deirdre will look to the bed, to Brimm, who'll say, "Oh, Muriel, just go away."

Muriel, on the advice of the Reverend Mary Whiteside, and with the hearty support of Deirdre, has begun seeing a therapist, someone she describes as "a kind, older woman, very mature," and is engaged in what she describes as "making progress." This phrase, "making progress," is all she will say to Brimm about it, but he has a sense that perhaps Muriel talks to Deirdre. Brimm, when he feels up to it, has tried to assess the change Muriel has gone through—or the change she continues to go through. She no longer asks him any questions about the past. He no longer asks her any. He knows that he lacks the details, but his general feeling is that Muriel is studiously going about something. She has had an extraordinary experience—the emotional detonations set off by her acknowledgment of the sexual abuse (which for lack of sound options Brimm takes at face value)—that has brought her to a sort of climax, and she is on the downside of it, changed, and made busy by all that is leading away from it. He sees in this a parallel to his

214

own experience since returning to Pines, and he likes the apparent, larger order implied. Taken as a whole, the experience—and here Brimm means everything, himself, Muriel, Deirdre, the angel of death, even the erotic tableau of Claudia Callejas in her window—seems to have a shape. It's as if he's being allowed to glimpse a blueprint, held up for him at some distance. He can discern order and an intimation of purpose—that is, he can discern *design,* even if not the niceties. Though he feels slightly annoyed when Muriel says, "Making progress," and though he feigns more annoyance than he actually feels, in truth he believes her.

The same cannot be said for the case of the two girls from the Raphael School for the Blind, who were so gruesomely murdered last summer and whose bones Brimm found on the golf course. He thinks about the girls from time to time, but that tragedy, like many such tragedies, lacks a satisfying outcome, lacks a final chapter. In November, elections were held in the town of Pines, and a new mayor, a man by the name of Hansom Bower, was elected. Bower's campaign made good mileage out of the unsolved murders of Linda Briscoe Wayne and Sara DiMatteo. Back in September, when the *Crier* ran the letter purportedly written by the girls' killer, many readers, including Hansom Bower, were outraged, not only by the graphic depiction of sexual abuse the letter contained, but also by the fact of its having been printed in the newspaper at all. Hansom Bower, then a lawyer and a Pines town councilman, charged that the decision to run the letter (a decision made by the current mayor and the chief of police, among others) had been tantamount to negotiating with terrorists. He declared his own mayoral candidacy in the same breath. In such matters every action causes a reaction, and yielding to pressure from the mayor's office, the Pines chief of police made a scapegoat of the sharp young detective who'd been heading up the Wayne-DiMatteo investigation, Sergeant Connie Shoulders, and took him off the case. Some black leaders in the community had charged that Shoulders's dismissal was racially motivated (it came out afterward that the DiMatteo family had been disappointed to find "a Negro" in charge of their daughter's case), and the usual tensions resulted, tensions that seemed to culminate in the election of Hansom Bower a month later. During that month between Connie Shoulders's removal and the election, no new evidence was uncovered in the Wayne-DiMatteo case. But there were also no new murders, and by December, though it was still officially open, the case had moved out of the spotlight. People in Pines have for the most part forgotten about Sara DiMatteo and Linda Briscoe Wayne. Brimm imagines that a kind of folksy mythology will grow up around the murders, bred and borne mostly by children, riverbank sightings of headless corpses and so on.

Connie Shoulders has turned up two or three times at the house for short visits, but none since Thanksgiving. Brimm has noticed that Connie does not talk much about the murder case—probably, Brimm thinks, because there's not much he can say that doesn't sound spiteful—but he has conveyed more than once his feeling that the killer will never be caught. Brimm has also noticed that he, Connie, seems to have an eye for Deirdre, but that Deirdre is having none of it. The young policeman's visits seem to cheer Muriel, however, though she appears ill at ease during them and immediately afterward. Muriel bought and wrapped a Christmas present for Connie, but so far, since she has never arranged to deliver it, it sits lonely under the tree in the front parlor. Brimm thinks maybe Muriel was hoping Connie might pop in at Christmastime, and only wanted to be prepared.

On Christmas Eve, the sappy, disagreeable notion crossed Brimm's mind that this would be his last Christmas, but since then he has carefully avoided dwelling on it. These days, when he thinks about dying, he mostly wonders what lies ahead, much the same way he used to anticipate an assignment in a faraway city. He has been trying to cultivate a healthy attitude toward dying, and he indulges in quite a lot of fantasy about what awaits him. He actively opposes the viewpoint that nothing lies ahead. He figures if that's the case, he won't know about it, because nothing is nothing, no knowledge, no consciousness, certainly no disappointment. He doesn't expect to be greeted by Muriel's Jesus at any sort of literal gateway, and he equally rejects the bright light at the end of a tunnel as lacking originality. Layer upon layer, or brick by brick, he has been constructing an afterlife for himself, based on a seed provided in a dream, and developing it most successfully when his subconscious is active, when he's drifting into sleep. He considers it his art project, his occupational therapy

" 'Then he asked me if you were angry,' " Deirdre reads, " 'and that time I said no.' She sounded like a child swollen with sleep. Oh, that's nice, isn't it? Swollen with sleep. I like that a lot."

"Deirdre," says Brimm, "please don't comment. You know it confuses me."

"You just don't like me to comment because it brings you out of your dream world," says Deirdre.

"My dream world is the only world I have left," says Brimm. "And I'm not complaining. I prefer it."

"Thanks a lot," says Deirdre.

"No offense intended," says Brimm.

"None taken," says Deirdre, "believe me."

What Brimm is most proud of is the degree to which he has been able to leave open his imagination to the suggestions of his subconscious. There have been many aspects to his constructed afterlife that, though it is a composite of places he's actually seen, he would not voluntarily choose. In fact the whole place—a huge, sprawling seaside bathhouse—is not especially pleasant. Men of all sizes, shapes, ages, and races wander tiled halls naked and in varying states ranging from bewildered to bitter to resigned. It is an all-male environment, the result, Brimm supposes, of his having lived a life so dominated by the influences of women, a life so dependent on the generosities of women.

217

The bathhouse has an eclectic architecture composed of yellow bricks and glass blocks, and myriad ceramic and terra-cotta tiles, reminiscent of no definite style or century but suggesting great amounts of history. Its proportions at every turn are bountiful. The weather is relentlessly fair, the sea tranquil. The tides ebb and flow inconspicuously. Looking seaward, one spies no land, though there is the occasional passenger plane flying noisily overhead, insinuating other destinations for other people, and even an ocean liner now and then, trembling on the horizon. No gulls in the sky, no apparent life in the water (save the birdlike, skinny-legged swimmers who wear the white rubber bathing caps and ridiculous goggles). Brimm has recently installed—that is to say, he has recently "noticed"—a bank of outdoor showers, convenient to the beach, intended, if the men will use them, to keep sand out of the indoor plumbing.

The men, Brimm has observed, are generally uncooperative in such matters, a little out of sorts. There is a rule, for example, about nude sunbathing—none is allowed—but since the rule states that "Swimsuits must be worn at all times," some of the men, especially the very old ones, the sun addicts with the russet, leathery skin, wear their trunks on their heads like turbans. In the gleaming white handball and racquetball courts abutting the beach, a brooding hostility pervades the games. Winners gloat, losers sulk. But mostly the men are silent, solitary, though some form of communication happens in the sauna, where it is close and quiet and rather uncomfortably intimate; newcomers show the most willingness to talk, often having questions about the facilities. A hugely potbellied, possibly Australian man who spends a lot of time in the sauna lists for the newcomers the swimming pool ("Too bloody cold, you can freeze your balls"), the weight room ("If you don't mind the smell"), the steam room ("Always too bloody hot, you can cook like a bloody lobster"), and so on. An American, a man known by everyone to cheat at chess, adds, "Oh, yeah, we got fucking everything. Everything but broads." This remark inevitably leads to someone's saying, "I knew a woman once who ..." and thus begins a story.

Broads are the great gaping absence at the bathhouse and therefore, in a way, an emphatic presence. There is the usual measure of homosexuality—clandestine exchanges of sexual favors in a utility closet—but when the men talk about women, when they begin "I knew a woman once ...," they are not expressing a physical longing but something more unmanageable than that, something much more uninterrupted than that. Occasionally they do digress into a kind of book-keeping, an accounting of the women they have had. Brimm confesses to hundreds, all around the world—and of course he has told the story of Nora from New York, and about the night that Claudia Callejas stood boldly in her window, daring him to step forward—but somehow he cannot quite keep it from sounding like a lament. The men know that "Everything but broads" reaches beyond sex. It reaches to the bittersweet and often unspoken suspicion that women are incalculably superior to men, the congenital defeat for which men are always trying to compensate.

Outside the bathhouse, Brimm has erected a high wall at either end of the beach, extending far out into the water. Women, though nothing much is known about them, dwell on the other side. If you stand near the wall, you can hear their voices, their maddening laughter.

Brimm opens his eyes just wide enough so that he can see Deirdre through his eyelashes, allows himself to admire her youth and beauty, allows himself to admire the musical sound of her voice. If there is a purgatory in which he's to burn off his worldly attachments, and if the burning off is to be achieved through prolonged deprivation from the thing to which one is attached, Brimm's chief task will be women. For some men it will be money, and other forms of power. For Brimm it will be women.

Muriel stands outside the door and listens for a minute.

"He saw the sea, flag blue, through the greenery," she

hears. *"Then he saw the beach where only a few people were sunbathing . . ."*

And Muriel thinks, Bandol, white, like Algiers. It is the murder mystery, recommended by her. She recalls perfectly the passage she overhears, the place described, and how it was likened by the author to Algiers, and how it is the one thing in the world she knows about either of these places, Bandol and Algiers, that they are painted white, and how most of what she knows of the world apart from Pines comes from books. She pushes open the door enough to see that Francis's eyes are closed, then waves her hand in order to get Deirdre's attention.

Deirdre stops reading and comes to the door.

"Asleep?" Muriel whispers.

Deirdre shrugs her shoulders and says, "I really don't think he has a firm grasp of all the facts in the case."

Deirdre is referring to the murder mystery, but Muriel laughs because it seems so suddenly metaphorical, a kind of general truth about Francis's compromised condition. "It won't be the first time," she says, and laughs some more. "His tray's ready downstairs, but if he's asleep—"

"What is that maddening laughter I hear?" says Brimm in an ominous voice from the bed.

"Oh, dear," says Muriel, entering the room quickly. "He's awake. I have your tray ready downstairs, Francis, if you want it." She punches the pillows behind him and then begins straightening the bedcovers. "Lentil soup and corn bread."

"Do I like lentil soup?" he says.

She freezes and looks at him, stunned. "How in the world would I know whether or not you like lentil soup?"

"Well, if you don't know whether or not I like it, why did you make it?"

"Francis, will you please open your eyes when you speak to me? You look like something out of a horror movie when you talk like that with your eyes closed."

"Don't try to cheer me up with flattery," he says, opening his eyes.

"Now," she says, "do you want lentil soup and corn bread or do you not?"

"I do," he says, and closes his eyes again.

Deirdre, taking her cue, leaves the room to fetch the tray.

"It's cold out," Muriel says, going to the window and raising the shade a bit higher.

"You've been out?" he says.

"Of course I've been out. It's Tuesday. You know I see Eleanor on Tuesday."

Eleanor is Muriel's therapist, an instrument of God's peace, a rank earned chiefly on the strength of her amazing resemblance to the therapist Muriel had previously fashioned in her imagination. She is connected in some way to Pines State, either clinically or academically, Muriel is not sure which. By the time Muriel first visited Eleanor's office—just the way she had imagined it, a nice room in Eleanor's home, comfortably dim, a leather chair like the ones in Muriel's own parlor—it was no longer necessary for Eleanor to do anything so directly experimental as walk Muriel through the upstairs rooms of the old Brimm house, which had seemed for a while to represent the past. Muriel had done that already, both actually and symbolically. What Muriel does at Eleanor's is talk, about anything and everything, about the past, about how she feels about things, about what's going on in the present, about her mother's haunted fanaticism and sleepwalking, her father's gloomy disappointment and drinking, about what she can recall of the sexual abuse, about Francis, Deirdre, Connie Shoulders, and even the Ottos, everything. She often loses her sense of purpose in this process, and it sometimes seems impossible that she is paying Eleanor to sit in a room and do little else but listen. Still, Muriel understands that Eleanor, in a kind, deliberately slow, and compassionate way, is leading her to and through her feelings. Eleanor asks clarifying questions, so that Muriel is forced to be precise; she asks for more detail, so that Muriel is forced to explore more than what is immediately available. Occasionally she even offers an opinion on a subject. Usually when she disagrees with Muriel, it's about some unmerited way that Muriel has judged herself. "I guess I disagree," Eleanor will say. "You don't strike me as a particularly meddlesome person." Or she encourages. "That sounds like a good idea," she'll say, as she did about Muriel's plan to throw her father's old doctor bag into the lagoon off the Milligan Bridge. "Have you thought about taking Deirdre with you?" Eleanor is always very pleased when Muriel cries, or when she gets really angry, and Muriel has to struggle not to stage these emotions just to please Eleanor.

When Francis asks Muriel about the therapy, Muriel says to him, "Making progress," knowing that the terseness of the response is meant to keep him at a distance, meant to keep him out. She's not sure about the reasons for this—she only knows that she feels, around Francis, a faint shame about being in therapy in the first place, that it's an indulgence, a way of getting attention, that she's too old for such things, that she's invented the memory of sexual abuse in order to dramatize a forbidden longing she may have felt for her father and for Captain Fayson across the street, that she should be able to work these things out by herself, that her long-championed religious faith ought to see her through, that she's a silly old fool, a lonely spinster who was never fulfilled sexually or romantically, all the dark fears. She has also noticed that "making progress" is an enormously faithful response. Faith-*laden*, she has sometimes thought, a requirement of the process, for the forward motion is not always apparent. What Muriel has told no one, including Eleanor, is about last September's brief, self-destructive, downward spiral that resulted in her waking up in the stench of her own urine. Jesus knows about it, God knows about it, and that's plenty for Muriel. She thinks she will take that one to the grave with her.

"How's it going?" says Francis from the bed.

"Making progress," says Muriel, turning from the window.

Deirdre is back with the tray, and Muriel, seeing her, rushes to the bed and begins pulling on Francis's arm, getting him to sit more upright.

"Oh, Muriel, will you stop," he says, brushing her aside. "Go away."

Muriel dips her index finger in the bowl of lentil soup and tastes it. "Good," she says, "still good and hot."

"Do you mind?" says Francis, sighing heavily. "It may just be very picky of me, but I prefer people to keep their fingers out of my food. Now will you please go away and let me eat?"

Muriel looks to Deirdre, a general inquiry.

"I think we have everything under control," Deirdre says to her.

"Go away, Muriel," says Francis.

Muriel leaves the room and slowly descends the stairs. She finds the window seat in the front parlor, where the cats soon join her.

Out the window everything is still, no traffic in the boulevard, no breeze stirring the barren branches of the median's crape myrtles. The vacant lot across the way is covered now with a straw-colored matting, summer's dead and decaying weeds and wildflowers.

Muriel knows that Francis endures her attentions only out of a sense of duty, that when she asked him to move into the house and let her take care of him, he felt obligated. Thank God for Deirdre. Deirdre has a way with him. If not for Deirdre, Muriel thinks, Francis would have made other arrangements. Or maybe he would still have felt obligated, would still have moved in, but everything would have been worse for him. She believes it was necessary for Francis to move into the house, that it was necessary for her to take care of him; it is part of what she means when she says, "working out my salvation"—just as it was necessary for Deirdre to come live there and have the baby.

She has felt guided by prayer in all this, just as she felt rescued by finding Deirdre's amethyst ring in the soap dish
back in September.

Sometime later in September—she can't recall exactly
when—she had another of her Jesus dreams, in which she
was with the disciples aboard a ship that had set sail in the
Sea of Galilee. Jesus was trying to escape the multitudes
again. During the night a great tempest welled up, and the
ship started taking water over the bow. Everyone was terrified out of his wits, and where was Jesus? Sleeping. He had
found the nicest, coziest stateroom below and was sleeping
through the whole thing. When the disciples went and woke
him up, he couldn't resist scolding them for their lack of
faith, but he took care of business: he rebuked the winds
and everybody got to the other side safe and sound. Now
Muriel has begun to think of God as often sleeping, as
someone who would sleep through anything, through practically any human peril, and as someone who has to be
waked up. So in the end she has felt guided, helped, but she
has to pray really loud, figuratively speaking. She can tell
that the metamorphosis that began with Francis's return to
Pines—and that her having got close enough to see some of
what had been obscured—has left her larger somehow, has
left her inner life more substantial, her seeing of the world
different, her connectedness new, her way of knowing
things more intimate. When Muriel thinks of Deirdre's
baby, for example, when she anticipates that first cry of life,
she feels as if she may be swamped by joy. At the end of
this blindered, isolated life, God has sent her a kind of family, something to draw out her goodness, people to love.

Today her therapist asked her how she felt about
Francis's dying. "I'm not at all sure that he is dying," she
said, and Eleanor gave her a quizzical look.

"The doctor says the disease could to into remission at
any time," Muriel added.

Eleanor was aggressively silent.

224

"Well, I guess it *is* a remote possibility," Muriel said. "At his age."

"How do you feel?" Eleanor repeated.

"Well, he doesn't at all seem like a person who's dying," Muriel said. "Except that he looks like hell. I mean, he's very clearheaded and—"

"How do you feel, Muriel?" Eleanor repeated again.

"I don't want him to die," Muriel said, and they sat for what seemed like a long time in silence.

Finally Muriel looked at her and added, "That's all I know."

When Deirdre reaches the bottom of the stairs, she sees Muriel pat the window seat cushion, an invitation to join her and the cats there. Gently brushing aside Henry, the big cat, Deirdre sits and says, "Eating."

She and Muriel have developed this kind of shorthand for the status of the patient. "Sleeping," Muriel will say, entering the kitchen at night as Deirdre prepares a cup of herbal tea. Meeting Muriel at the front door, on her way out as Muriel comes in, Deirdre will roll her eyes and say, "Impossible." "Thirsty," Muriel will say, pouring ginger ale into a tumbler at the kitchen counter.

"A little ornery," says Muriel now.

Deirdre nods, and says, "He's very weak today."

"More so than usual?"

"He couldn't walk from the bed to the bathroom. I practically had to carry him the whole way."

"Carry him?"

"Well, you know, hold him up."

"Deirdre, I don't want you doing that sort of thing," says Muriel. "We'll have to get somebody in if it's come to that. You can't be straining yourself."

"It wasn't a strain," says Deirdre. "What can he weigh, a hundred pounds?"

"Surely more than a hundred," says Muriel.

"I doubt it," says Deirdre.

225

"What does he say?"

"What do you mean?"

"I mean, what does he say about how he's feeling. About being so weak."

"He says what he always says, 'Bad blood.' Earlier this morning while you were out, I went downstairs for something and when I came back up, he had sat up on the side of the bed, you know, with his feet on the floor. He was like stuck there, waiting for me to come and lift his legs back up for him."

"We better get somebody in," says Muriel. "A man maybe. I was afraid it might come to this eventually."

"Something's going on," says Deirdre after a moment. "He's changing again."

"How?"

"I'm not sure. Getting sicker I guess."

Deirdre notices that Muriel's eyes have fallen on the book for Connie Shoulders under the Christmas tree, the present Muriel bought for him, and she's taken on a kind of vacant look, a look Deirdre has noticed before, whenever she says anything about Frank's getting sicker.

"We'll get somebody in," says Muriel, shaking her head and frowning as if she disapproves of Frank, letting himself decline this way.

Part of the richness of Deirdre's life today abides in what she understands. She feels filled up by all that she understands, and this has given her a sense of healthy pride. For one thing, she knows that Muriel thinks the detective, Connie Shoulders, patronizes her, sees her as a silly old woman, and possibly even goofs on her behind her back; but in fact Connie Shoulders comes around because he genuinely likes Muriel, because he enjoys his visits with her, and mainly because he's lonely. Deirdre knows that Connie is unpopular with the white cops on the police force, that the white cops are all racists, and that Connie constantly has to deal with their attitude.

Deirdre also knows that Frank is far sicker than Muriel acknowledges, that he is much closer to dying than anyone is saying. Frank has already decided not to undergo another blood transfusion—the last one took such a toll on him. Frank's doctor—his main doctor, the old man, Van Buren, who is also Muriel's doctor—comes sometimes to the house to see Frank. On one of these visits recently, the day after Christmas, Van Buren took Deirdre aside in the upstairs hall and said quietly, "Try to keep him comfortable." Van Buren had designated Deirdre as the one truly in charge, and he was telling her that Frank was dying, that he could go at any time, and that she should make things as easy for him as possible. Deirdre understands that Van Buren, a longtime friend of Muriel's, is protecting Muriel to some extent from the harsher realities. Deirdre also understands that Frank is protecting Muriel too, by telling her constantly to go away, feigning annoyance. Frank feels guilty about being a burden to Muriel; he thinks Muriel has taken over his care and moved him into the house out of obligation. But what Deirdre knows is that Frank is giving Muriel an enormous gift by being there, by dying there, a gift for which Muriel is grateful. Meanwhile, Muriel thinks that Frank would rather be somewhere else, a nursing home, but that he agreed to move into the house out of a sense of duty to *her*. But secretly Frank is deeply grateful to Muriel, grateful to have escaped the prospect of a nursing home. Deirdre understands all this, and more. She understands that Frank is more than resigned to dying, that he maybe even looks forward to it. She thinks of his dying as his entering a cold mountain lake, and she thinks that in his closed-eyed daydreams, he has been getting his toes wet.

Early in the morning, Brimm has seen young boys perched on the edge of the high wall that divides the men from the women. He has no idea where these children come from or where they go, where they disappear to. Sometimes he speculates that they are the younger selves of the men who

227

wander the tiled halls and sands of the bathhouse. Brimm
has decided that it is not necessary for everything to make
sense. This, after all, is an art project; it is not necessary to
apply logic to everything in a work of art. In truth, Brimm
doesn't even completely understand the premise of the
bathhouse. He has men complaining about the thermostat in
the steam room, complaining about the empty soap dispens-
ers in the showers, the sometimes clogged drains, complaining about there not being enough sinks and mirrors for
shaving. It seems that they are expressing a profound bitterness, a deep-seated sense of deprivation, of not having got
enough, and that it attaches to these mundane matters because the real thing is too vast and buried to articulate.
Brimm knows that the men must make peace with themselves here in the bathhouse, that somehow they must learn
a peace that releases them from the past and the future, releases them from remorse and fear and longing, and that for
himself and for these particular others, this peacemaking
has to do with their finding an identity apart from women,
which resides wholly in themselves.

Here is the irony: Brimm hopes that this peace, once
found, then passes him into the other realm, the glorious
one on the other side of the high wall, the heaven that in-
cludes women.

It is nine o'clock at night, a Thursday, four days after
Christmas, three days before New Year's. Brimm has been
sleeping for a while, and though he remembers no dream of
any kind, he has awakened with a couple of significant insights.

He is burning with the secret fever now—whatever the
infection (he thinks he has contracted infectious hepatitis),
it is full-blown, raging—and beyond weakness, so light and
brittle that weakness is not really a concern. He has summoned Deirdre to the room and asked for blankets. She has
brought him three, tucked him in tightly on both sides, and
now he feels warm and comfortably bound, as if he were

in a cocoon. At his request, Deirdre has raised the shade, and though only blackness fills the window, Brimm feels that he is letting in the night, a good thing. He can see the table lamp, the only light in the room, reflected in the window's glass, and something about this image, the shape of the lamp floating in the glossy dark, is consoling.

"My God," Deirdre says, touching her hand to his brow. "You're burning up, Frank. We better call the doctor. How long have you had a fever?"

She rises from the side of the bed, but Frank manages to touch her hand, and then, as she pauses, he grasps it.

"No, Deirdre," he says.

Looking at him, understanding, she sits back down. Tears well up in her eyes.

"Deirdre," he says, "there's something I have to tell you."

"I already know," she says with frustration. "Damn it, Frank."

"I'm sorry," he says.

"It's okay," she says. "It's not your fault. But it would have been nice."

"Yes," he says. "It would have been nice. Move a bit closer, Deirdre."

She is wearing the sweater he gave her for Christmas, and he places both hands on the wool that covers the globe of her belly.

Then she does something that surprises him. Looking quickly toward the door to the room, she lifts the sweater up so that he can feel the warmth of her skin. "Feel," she says, crying. "He's moving."

And Brimm can feel and even see the small eruptions in the dome. There is an odd distance here for Brimm—it is entirely physical, due to his illness—though he still knows and appreciates the extraordinary intimacy of the moment.

"He's moving," she repeats.

"He's moving," says Brimm, and laughs like a boy.

After a silence Deirdre says, "Frank, you know you might be wrong about this."

"No," he says, "I'm not wrong. You better fetch Muriel now."

Deirdre leaves the room. Aside from the clear insight that he is dying—now, this night—Frank has also awakened with a kind of clean slate regarding the thing that awaits him in death. All the speculation and fantasy, his occupational therapy, the bathhouse and the beach, have melted away, and what he faces in his mind now is a perfect blankness, free of brick and mortar, free of language and knowledge, free of everything known.

"Francis?" he hears Muriel say, something like terror in her voice, and a wave of fear passes fleetingly through him as well.

She is already dressed in her bedclothes, a nightgown beneath the blue kimono. She turns on the harsh overhead light.

"Turn that off, Muriel," he says quietly, and she does.

"Okay," she says, moving to the side of the bed. Now she sounds defiant. "What is it, Francis?"

"Sit with me," he says.

She starts to take the chair where Deirdre usually reads, but, patting the bed next to him, he says, "No, here."

She sits next to him and touches his face with the back of her hand. "Oh, Frankie," she says. "You're sick. I'll call Dr. Van Buren. You need—"

"Don't call Van Buren," he says. "I talked to him last time he was here. I'm not having a transfusion and I'm not doing any more goddamned antibiotics."

"Well, why not?" she says. "You're running a fever, Frankie."

"Don't call him," he says.

Then there is this moment, in which comprehension overtakes her face. "You mean you're giving up, don't you," she says, not quite angrily.

"No, Muriel," he says. "I'm just giving in."

"I'm sure I don't understand that," she says, her eyes clouding over. "I'm sure I don't understand this nice distinction you're attempting to make."

"Muriel," he says. "Quiet."

She takes a deep breath. "Quiet," she says.

"I want to tell you something."

"Well, what?" she says.

"Muriel," he says. "I always loved you a little."

"Well, Frankie," she says, fighting back tears, "I should have thought you loved me more than a little."

"No," he says. "I don't mean like that. I mean I was always a little in love with you."

"Don't be silly, Frankie," she says. "I'm not lovable in that way."

"You are," he says. "Of course you are. How else could I have felt that way?"

Brimm notes, with a good deal of detachment, that he has lost his sense of time. Perhaps it is an hour or more before she bends toward him and kisses him on the lips. "Frankie, my darling," she says, "are you in pain?"

"Maybe," he says. "But I don't think so."

"Well, I'm going to leave for a minute," she says, "but I'll be back, okay?"

"Yes," he says as she hurries from the room. "Come back and stay with me for a while," he says, but the door has already closed.

Toward morning he fell into a sound sleep. He dreamed that Muriel and Deirdre were just taking bread out of the oven, out of the giant old black woodstove from his boyhood, and afterward he climbed inside and had a nice steam bath there, lashing himself with a bunch of birch twigs. He slept for two days, though somehow he remained aware of most of what went on in the room; occasionally he even exchanged a few words with whoever might be passing through. Everything was entirely normal. There was some weeping in the hallway—Muriel, thinking she was sparing

231

him the burden of her grief, but not having the sense to go far enough out of earshot. Van Buren emerged from the darkness one hour, but it was clear that he had no inclination to alter the course of events. He unbuttoned Brimm's pajamas and touched his chest in several places with the stethoscope's cold, cold diaphragm. Brimm, an actor in an old war movie, said, "Hey Doc, warm that thing up a little, willya?" There seemed to be a great deal of talk about Brimm in the third person, as if he weren't right there in the room. He was certain at one point that he had an erection and hoped that it wasn't visible through the bedcovers to Deirdre, recalling that early in their friendship she'd been put off by his flirtatiousness. The oddest thing—though this, too, had an absolute air of normalcy—was the two soldiers and the sailor who sat in the corner of the room playing cards, all through the night and day. Every few hours one or the other would get up from the game, walk to the window, look out, and comment on the weather or the condition of the sea. For a long time the presence of these men, who seemed to be from a previous century, was a mystery to Brimm. But later, when two more sailors came in and carried Brimm out, when they had sewn him up in sailcloth so that he resembled a carrot or a radish, broad at the head and narrow at the feet, weighted him with irons, and brought him up to the deck and put him on a plank, Brimm understood that he must be dreaming the story about the old man who was buried at sea—the one in the book that Muriel had given him last summer. It was near sunset, and all around him stood the sailors and officers with their caps off.

"Blessed be the Name of the Lord," the priest began. "As it was in the beginning, is now, and ever shall be."

The sailors and the officers crossed themselves and looked away at the waves. Brimm had already begun to anticipate his brief flight into the sea, not unlike his father's brief flight from the edge of the old Milligan Bridge; he'd begun to anticipate the shoal of little fish, the harbor pilots, and the sudden underwater shadow of the shark. But when the man on watch duty tilted up the end of the plank and Brimm slid off head foremost and turned a somersault in the air, he realized that this experience did not belong to him but was borrowed, and the moment before he should have splashed into the lacy foam of the sea, he awoke back into the room of his childhood home.

Now, nearby, Deirdre sleeps in a chair, and Muriel . . . is it possible that Deirdre holds Muriel in her lap? No, it's a trick of the eye, Deirdre is sitting behind Muriel, in a different chair. In passing, Brimm is sorry to forgo the story's wonderful, rhythmic descent through the water, the balletic antics of the little harbor pilots and the shark. Out the window, however, he can see the sky and the sea, and to his delight, the clouds are massing together on the side where the sun is setting, just as they did at the end of the story, one cloud a triumphal arch, another a lion, a third a pair of scissors. From behind the clouds a broad, green shaft of light pierces through and stretches to the middle of the sky; a little later another, violet-colored, lies beside it; next to that, one of gold, then one rose-colored. The two women, Muriel and Deirdre, have moved to the open window and stand at the sill, their backs to him, waving as if they are on the deck of a ship and bidding farewell to the loved ones below who have come to see them off.

The sky turns lilac, and then something unprecedented happens. Francis begins to bleed—warmly, not at all disagreeably once he's used to it—from all the pores of his skin, and he is aware, in a way he has never before been aware, of his skin as a complete thing, a whole organ, a permeable sack in the shape of a man.

He sits up straighter and looks at Muriel and Deirdre, who have returned to their chairs, Deirdre asleep again. Muriel is alert, her spine rigid against the back of her chair, her eyes seeming to search his face, probably for a clue as to what's happening. He very much wants to offer an explanation, but he is keenly aware that he's only got a minute at most. Excited, he puts both arms out like a bird's wings and says, "This is something else altogether!"

He notes that Muriel has begun to smile quizzically, and he adds, "Know what I mean?"

She leans forward and says, "I think so, Frankie," yet she appears confused, and for a fleeting moment he fears his heart will break, leaving her this way, but he quickly understands heartbrokenness for the poor, earthbound concept that it is, not unlike gravity, not unlike parting.

Dennis McFarland

Part III

FRANCIS ELIOT BRIMM was buried the second day of January, not alongside his mother and father in the churchyard of St. Matthew and the Redeemer, but in St. Thomas Cemetery, a quarter hour's drive outside of town, about a mile from the beach he used to visit as a boy. The Ottos attended the graveside service, and Deirdre and Connie Shoulders as well, and to Muriel's surprise, Claudia Callejas and the young Nicolás. Claudia, beautifully dressed and striking as usual, seemed out of place the way sensual-looking women sometimes do at somber occasions, and Muriel saw that while Connie stole glances in Claudia's direction, Ned Otto almost never took his eyes off her. The day was damp and very windy. Claudia had worn a broad-brimmed hat and kept having to put her hand on the crown of it in order to keep it from blowing away. Each time she did this, Muriel thought the exotic-looking woman might break into a dance, and she thought how this would have pleased Francis.

Afterward, Muriel and Deirdre separated from the others, saying they would take a walk on St. Thomas Beach. But everyone said that would be foolish, given the wind and the chill off the Gulf. "What with Deirdre pregnant," said Billie Otto, "and Muriel, you . . ."

"And Muriel, you so old," said Muriel.

"Well, yes," said Billie. "Yes, Muriel, you are old, you might as well face it. Too old to be taking walks on the beach in January."

Muriel noticed that Connie Shoulders, overhearing these remarks, attempted to share a laugh with Claudia Callejas, but Claudia apparently did not see what was funny.

Finally Muriel and Deirdre agreed to drive to St. Thomas Beach and sit in the car and *look* at it rather than walk on it, but once they were there they could see only sand dunes from the parking lot. They took off their shoes, got out, and began walking up the nearby path—a kind of shallow trough running to the top and over the dunes—but the moment they gained its crest, from which they could see the churning water of the Gulf, the wind practically bowled them over. The sound of the wind and the surf was so loud that Muriel had to shout to be heard. "This was my idea, wasn't it?" she yelled.

Deirdre nodded, her hair plastered by the wind to one side of her face, and turned to start back, yelling, "Come on!"

Going down, Muriel thought this sight, too, would have pleased Francis, and seeing it through his eyes, she thought what a fine picture it would have made—two women, one old, one young and pregnant, both barefoot, wearing black dresses, slipping down the side of a dune in fierce wind.

When they were back in the car they began laughing, and once they'd begun, it seemed they couldn't stop. After a minute Deirdre asked if Muriel had seen Ned Otto ogling Claudia Callejas at the grave, and this sent them into further seizures, so much so that the pregnant Deirdre was soon in great distress and had to find the nearest public restroom.

In his will, Brimm bequeathed to Deirdre his Jeep and a mutual-funds investment worth a little over fifteen thousand dollars. Everything else, including the cottage and all its contents, went to Muriel. Muriel's grieving over the next several weeks was interrupted and diminished by the demands of bank officers, lawyers, accountants, movers, and real estate brokers sorting out Francis's estate; and early in

February, in the upstairs room that had once been Francis's, Deirdre, assisted by a midwife, gave birth to a baby boy.

After the arrival of the baby, whom Deirdre named Michael, it appeared in the beginning that he and Deirdre were one organism, the baby linked by its lips to her breast. Deirdre slept when the baby slept, woke when the baby woke, and sometimes even cried when the baby cried. It also appeared, given Michael's difficulty with sleeping, that Deirdre had given birth to a fiendish parasite who only wanted to be at the breast, night and day, and screamed when he was not. A little over seven pounds at birth, he climbed to eleven pounds in the first five weeks. The pediatrician acknowledged that this was a high rate of gain, but not unheard-of, and certainly no cause for worry. Muriel suggested they get a second opinion from a good veterinarian she knew, an idea that Deirdre, uncharacteristically, did not think funny. Gratefully, Billie Otto was around to help Muriel with the grocery shopping and the preparation of food for Deirdre. Muriel doubted Deirdre's ability to support the baby's ravenous appetite. She worried that one day she and Billie would return home from shopping and find Deirdre prostrate on the floor, skin and bones, as the baby, its head wedged beneath her, continued to suck, suck, suck.

But when the weather began to turn warm again, they discovered that getting Michael out into the air calmed him and helped him sleep better afterward. He very much liked going in the carriage, riding in the car, and being carried anywhere at all. Muriel, after a good deal of consideration, concluded from this that Michael, though sometimes fretful, was not hypertonic, since Dr. Spock said that hypertonic babies profited from leading quiet lives in quiet rooms. Lying on his back and looking up, Michael clearly delighted in a bumpy carriage ride, with its outdoor noises, changes of light, breezes, and especially, Muriel noted, the interesting, often swaying silhouettes of trees against the sky. Muriel discovered about herself that she enjoyed taking Michael for these carriage rides.

One sunny day in April, she was pushing the carriage along the sidewalk in front of the vacant lot across the boulevard, where the old Fayson house had stood. The cornflowers and goldenrod were returning to the lot, the crape myrtles in the median were full of buds. Billie Otto, who was sitting on her porch across the way, sang out Muriel's name and waved, and Muriel, waving back, felt great pride in having been seen pushing the baby in his carriage. She thought of the old Fayson house, gone, of that huge family, dispersed and gone, and of Francis, too, gone; the pride, she imagined, had to do simply with her having survived this long, as if life were a tedious, meandering spectacle—the halftime show in a stadium at a ball game, unsure of itself, amateurish, and she one of the few who had remained faithful enough in the bleachers to see it through to the last number, where, surprisingly, it redeemed itself.

It is a day in early May, a day that began with heavy rainfall at dawn and has now grown muggy and gray. Muriel and Deirdre have driven downtown with Michael, to Palmetto Street, to do some shopping. Later, Muriel will recall that she had meant to make a list, and—fatefully, it seemed in retrospect—when she went to the desk in the parlor, in search of a pen, she came across a scrap of paper on which was written, in her own handwriting, "Wed., 12:05 a.m., footsteps on front porch," and, "12:09 a.m., found screen door unhooked." She had wadded the scrap of paper into a ball and tossed it into a wastepaper basket. She will also recall that at breakfast that morning, sitting alone at the counter drinking coffee, waiting for Deirdre to get the baby dressed, she thought she felt Francis's presence, just as if he were sitting opposite her. Then she thought, No, not sitting opposite me, but about to phone, and she actually looked at the telephone on the wall, half expecting it to ring, half expecting to hear Francis's voice.

Now, in the Jeep, Muriel has been thinking about Michael, the baby; sometimes it seems that he has read

Dr. Spock and conforms to everything in the book, right on schedule. He is definitely a surpassingly healthy baby, despite his having been born with a small leak between two chambers of his heart (which has already healed itself) and despite his irregular sleep patterns. He still rarely spends two nights in a row on the same schedule, and often he wants to be awake for a couple of hours around 4 A.M., which is hard on Deirdre. Deirdre says it's lucky that Michael is cute; she says that in the middle of the night, when she asks him, "Why the devil don't you sleep?" in her most venomous voice, Michael grins from ear to ear.

Muriel has also been thinking about the Jeep that Francis left to Deirdre and in which they are sitting now. Muriel has noticed that when she rides in the Jeep, she feels vaguely uneasy, as if something still undetected has gone terribly wrong. Recently she mentioned this to Eleanor, her therapist, and it was Eleanor's theory that this nebulous anxiety Muriel experiences in the Jeep is grief, pure and simple.

"Grief?" Muriel said to her. "I don't feel sad, I feel anxious, fearful somehow. I think I'm just not used to being so high up. You know, so high up in a car."

But afterward, when Muriel thought about Eleanor's suggestion, she had to admit that she hadn't been entirely able to shake the feeling that Francis's dying was a breach of how things were supposed to have happened, that something had gone terribly wrong.

Several years ago, the four blocks of Palmetto Street that run between Bonifay Square and the Waterford Building (the town hall) were made into a pedestrian mall—closed to traffic, repaved with red bricks, planter boxes and ornate gas lamps installed, new façades on all the shops—a project meant to attract a better class of consumer to the downtown area, but which failed miserably to do so. Ironically, the rest of the street, the four blocks on the other side of the Waterford Building, where cars are still allowed and where rents have stayed low, has thrived: open-air produce markets; quirky discount dry goods stores with tables and wooden boxes of wares brought out onto the sidewalks in good weather; a Chinese take-out, two pizzerias; a decent coffee shop; a huge army-navy surplus store; a Furniture-in-the-Raw; the Pines Bowlarama, with its attached lounge, the Rhythm Room; a pharmacy; a hardware store; a Woolworth's. When Pines Merchants & Savings opened a branch downtown, they chose to locate it on this end of Palmetto rather than on the other, fancier end.

At midday, the traffic is unusually bad, and they—Deirdre behind the wheel of the Jeep, Muriel in the front passenger seat, Michael in back, facing backward and blessedly quiet—have been sitting in the same spot now for about two minutes while a man a few cars ahead negotiates a parking space.

Deirdre suddenly points to the left-hand side of the street. Astonished, she says, "Would you look at that."

On the sidewalk in front of Woolworth's, Muriel sees a young man, probably in his twenties, slapping a little boy in the face again and again. At first, as the boy tries to defend himself with his hands and forearms, it appears that they are only roughhousing; but when the boy collapses to the pavement on his back, and the man stands over him, straddling him, bending down and poking the boy in the chest with his index finger, then slapping him again, again and again, it becomes clear that this is no game. The young man is shouting something at the boy as he punishes him, but Muriel cannot hear his words.

Soon the man steps off the sidewalk and, coming right toward them, begins to cross the street. Muriel notes that he looks like a college student, rather thin and good looking, blond, wearing a light blue denim jacket, and apparently very angry.

Deirdre calls to the man out her window: "Hey, why don't you pick on somebody your own size."

This frightens Muriel, for she has already determined that

the young man is crazy; she puts her hand on Deirdre's upper arm as if to restrain her. The man pauses in the street and looks straight at Deirdre. "The little fucker was fucking with my dogs," he says rapidly in a voice that sounds oddly familiar to Muriel. "I'll teach him to fuck with my dogs." He continues across Palmetto Street, passing directly in front of the Jeep.

Muriel sees now that a black car—a large black car, something old, a Chevy or a Ford, or maybe an Oldsmobile—parked near where the man was striking the boy, has two German shepherds in its back seat. Then she sees something else: the little boy, the crazy man's victim, is Nicolás, Claudia Callejas's young nephew who lives next to Francis's cottage in Madison Heights.

"Oh, my God," Muriel says, already lifting her door handle, "That's Nicolás."

"Wait," says Deirdre. "Let me pull over there."

The street has cleared enough in front of them for Deirdre to execute a U-turn, and once she has done this, she double-parks the Jeep and they both get out. Nicolás is now standing again. A small black woman, a passerby, is attempting to comfort him. He is crying—and crying, he looks older than Muriel remembers him, almost adolescent. His face is red and splotchy, and Muriel can see that he's also a bit dazed. One cheek bears the clear imprint of the man's fingers.

"Nicolás," Muriel says to him, putting her hand on his shoulder. He looks up at her, stunned to hear his name, but with no apparent recognition in his eyes. "I'm Miss Brimm," she explains. "Muriel Brimm. You came with your aunt to my brother's funeral back in January. Are you okay, Nicolás?"

Nicolás appears too overwhelmed to answer this question, so Muriel tries another. "Nicolás," she says, "that man who was hitting you, is that your father?" She isn't sure why she asks this question—she is pursuing a hunch, what with the boy's separation from his family and so on—and she looks across the street and sees that the young man has stopped at the Merchants & Savings' automatic teller machine. Nicolás shakes his head, wipes his eyes, and the small black woman, who has planted a fist on each of her hips, says, "He says he don't know that man from Adam. He says he never saw that man before. If you ask me, somebody ought to do something."

Deirdre apparently intends to do something. She has found a pad and pencil in the Jeep and is now copying down the license plate number of the car with the dogs. Just as she finishes writing down the number, however, a huge man with a red beard appears next to her and says cheerfully, "Hey, what's happening?"

Now everyone, including Nicolás, looks at this new arrival, the man with the red beard, but no one says anything. Muriel is not so much fearful as confused. At first she thinks perhaps the man is a friend of Deirdre's. It even passes through her mind that perhaps the man is the vagabond father of Michael. But then the man touches Deirdre's pad with a finger and says, "Is that my license plate you've written down there?"

"Well, yes," Deirdre says, also clearly confused. "I guess so. Is this your car?"

"Last time I looked," the man says. "A nineteen seventy-nine Pony-ac Bonny-ville. She's loaded and runs like a dream. You wanna buy her?"

"And are those your dogs?" Deirdre asks, pointing to the dogs inside the car.

"Yeah, they're mine," says the man. "Pure-bred Alsatians. Retired guide dogs. You wanna buy 'em?"

Deirdre looks directly at Muriel, and they both shrug their shoulders. "Those aren't even his dogs," Deirdre says slowly, astounded, referring to Nicolás's attacker.

Muriel nods, thinking that she *knew* that young man was crazy. It occurs to her that the man with the beard is probably thinking something similar about Deirdre and herself. He stares at them another moment, a little wide-eyed, then waves his hand at them dismissively, unlocks the car door, and gets inside. Deirdre steps onto the sidewalk with the others, and they all watch as the man drives away.

"Those weren't even his dogs," Deirdre repeats to no one in particular.

The small black woman, who has not removed her fists from her hips and who seems determined not to be confused by anything, says, "Well, somebody ought to do something if you ask me."

"Look," Muriel says, for she has noticed that the young man, having finished his business at the bank machine, is now standing on the opposite curb staring directly at them. He suddenly turns and begins walking quickly away, looking once over his shoulder as he rounds the nearest corner and disappears.

"Let's follow him," Deirdre says, already headed for the Jeep.

Muriel begins ushering Nicolás toward the car. "Now, Nicolás," she says, "I hope your aunt has told you that you must never ever get into a car with people you don't know. This is an exception, because you and I have met before." Muriel turns to say goodbye to the small black woman, who still stands in the same spot on the sidewalk, her hands still on her hips. The woman, instead of waving to Muriel, nods her head approvingly, and Muriel gets into the front seat of the Jeep. Nicolás, who sits in the back next to the now sleeping Michael, has stopped crying, but still appears quite troubled; he begins cracking his knuckles. He looks around the interior of the Jeep, knits his brow, and says at last, "Whose baby is this?"

"Oh, that's Deirdre's baby," says Muriel. "His name is Michael. This is Deirdre, driving the car."

Deirdre pulls out behind a city bus, which stops at the next corner, blocking traffic to discharge passengers, and by the time they are able to move again and turn the corner where the young man disappeared, there is no sign of him.

"Where'd he go?" says Deirdre, hitting the steering wheel once, hard, with her fist.

They drive around the area a few minutes more, but to no avail, and eventually Muriel suggests they take Nicolás home. Nicolás seems extremely distressed by this idea. "What's wrong, Nicolás?" Muriel says.

Staring down at his lap, the boy says, "My aunt is going to kill me."

"Whatever do you mean?"

"I'm supposed to be in school."

"Oh, I hadn't thought of that," says Muriel. "Of course you're supposed to be in school. Why are you not in school?"

"I left after lunch," he says. "I hate school."

Absurdly, Muriel says, "You're probably just not used to it yet." Then she adds, "I'll make sure your aunt doesn't kill you. You've had quite an ordeal already."

She faces front, and after a minute she can hear the boy cracking his knuckles again. By the time they reach the river and the Little Yustaga Bridge, he has fallen sound asleep.

Claudia Callejas explains to them that her husband is out of town, that he is a scientist, that he travels a lot, and Muriel sees something dark cross the woman's face, heartache, anger, bitterness, something that causes her to conclude that Claudia Callejas's husband is having a love affair with another woman, perhaps they are even separated. Not only is this explanation of her husband's whereabouts disingenuous, but as a response to Deirdre's suggestion that they report the attack on Nicolás to the police, it is irrational. Balancing the baby on one arm while she fishes in her shoulder bag for a pacifier, Deirdre says to Claudia, "It's all right. We don't need him."

After a moment's pause, Claudia says that she will get her purse, and Muriel notices that she casts Nicolás another
246

just-wait-till-I-get-you-alone look, the third one of these since they arrived.

As they leave through the front door, Deirdre whispers to Muriel, "She's scared to death of the police."

But at the station, when they are greeted by a police-woman who has evidently emigrated from one of the Caribbean islands, Claudia Callejas visibly begins to relax. Soon she and the policewoman are engaged in a long, warm heart-to-heart in Spanish, during which Claudia grows tender and overwhelmingly maternal, ending up with tears in her eyes and her arm around Nicolás's shoulders. Muriel exchanges a knowing glance with Deirdre, but Muriel isn't at all sure that she and Deirdre are knowing the same thing; it is clear to Muriel that Claudia's transformation is genuine, that there is no pretense in the arm around the boy's shoulders, or in the tears.

Over the course of the next hour or so, statements are taken from Muriel and Deirdre about what they witnessed on Palmetto Street, and the policewoman removes Nicolás to another room for a while to talk to him alone. Their description of the perpetrator, seemingly detailed at first—they supply his approximate age (early twenties), approximate height (about five nine, Deirdre suggests), hair color (blond), and his dress (the blue denim jacket, high-top white sneakers)—turns out to be rather commonplace. The policewoman sighs and says, "Well, it sounds like about a thousand students over at Pines State, but we'll keep an eye out."

Muriel can tell that "Keep an eye out" is an idiom the policewoman is not at home with (she puts the emphasis on *out*), and she obviously doesn't have much hope of finding Nicolás's attacker. By the time they are finished, Muriel has come to feel that since Nicolás wasn't seriously injured, physically anyway, the case won't be given any attention. Before leaving, she turns to the policewoman and asks, "Is Connie Shoulders around?"

"No, ma'am, not right now," she says. "Is he a friend of yours?"

"Yes," Muriel says. "I only wish you could have been there this afternoon and seen what we saw on Palmetto Street. It was violent, frightening."

"Yes, ma'am," the policewoman says, then smiles broadly at Deirdre and says, "Your baby is adorable. How old is he?"

At first it appears that Deirdre doesn't intend to answer the question. Then she says in a grudging tone that perhaps only Muriel detects, "Almost three months."

Having returned Claudia and Nicolás to Madison Heights, Deirdre says, as soon as they are alone in the Jeep, "They'll never catch him."

"I know," says Muriel. "I know."

They pass Francis's cottage just as Muriel says this, and somehow the disappointment and the resignation she feels seems to attach to the For Sale sign that stands in the small patch of lawn out front. Furthermore, it looks as if someone has thrown a stone through one of Francis's porch windows.

Muriel retires to her bed quite early that night and tries to read, but she has difficulty concentrating. Her mind keeps returning to the horrible image of Nicolás lying on the sidewalk, straddled by the angry young man.

At around nine o'clock, Deirdre knocks on the door and steps inside. "I'm going up now," she says.

"Is the baby asleep?" asks Muriel.

"I just put him down," says Deirdre. "Finally."

"Deirdre," says Muriel. "I can't seem to let go of what happened downtown today."

"Yeah, me neither."

"Why do you suppose that is?"

"I don't know. Probably because it was a child involved."

"What do you mean?"

"Well, I know I always react more strongly to things that involve children."

Muriel thinks for a moment. "I guess that makes sense," she says at last.

Deirdre says good night and turns to leave. Just before going out the door she says, "By the way, Michael has his checkup tomorrow afternoon. I'm going to the cleaners and to the bank afterwards. Is there anything you need while I'm out?"

"No," says Muriel. "I don't think so."

Once Deirdre has closed the door, Muriel turns off the lamp, giving up on the idea of reading. She thinks how harrowing it must have been for poor Nicolás, and how the bizarre attack from out of the blue must have seemed to him a retribution, a punishment for having skipped school.

Some minutes later, having seen, in a piece of a dream, Deirdre and Michael standing in a line before a barred teller's window, Muriel sits straight up in bed. "The *bank*," she says aloud into the dark, "how could we have been so stupid," and reaches for the lamp switch.

"Deirdre and I were on Palmetto Street this afternoon," she begins once she has got Connie Shoulders on the line.

"I know all about it already," says Connie. "Somebody mentioned your name to me and I read the report. I was going to call you tomorrow to see how everybody's doing. Is the little boy okay?"

"Yes," says Muriel. "But here's the thing, Connie, the amazing thing we forgot to say at the police station. The man used the bank. He used the *machine*."

"When?"

"After attacking Nicolás, he walked right across the street and used the bank machine."

"You're kidding me."

"Of course I'm not kidding, Connie, don't be ridiculous.

He used the bank machine. Don't all those machines have cameras in them?"

"They sure do."

"Well, then he must be—"

"On the videotape," says Connie.

"Exactly," says Muriel.

"Mind like a steel trap, Miss Brimm."

"Thank you, Detective Shoulders."

The next morning Muriel undergoes a series of shocks. First she is shocked to see the clock: it is nearly eleven before she awakens, having had great difficulty getting back to sleep the night before.

After she has pulled on her kimono and walked to the kitchen, she is shocked to find Connie Shoulders sitting at the counter having tea with Deirdre.

They are both weirdly expansive when she arrives—and, of all things, grinning. "Well, good morning, sleepyhead," Connie says, not a way he has ever talked to her before.

"We were afraid you were going to sleep the whole morning away," says Deirdre.

Their behavior instantly puts her in a foul humor. "What's going on?" she says, stopping in the middle of the kitchen floor. She notices that Deirdre is strangely dressed, rather formal for so early in the morning, and wearing makeup. "Why are you behaving this way?"

"What way?" says Deirdre. "We were just afraid you would sleep the morning away. I knew you'd want some time to get yourself together for the reporters. Especially if you're going to have your picture taken."

For a moment, she thinks Deirdre has slipped and has been using drugs again, which prompts her to say in a suspicious tone, "Where is the baby?"

"He's upstairs," says Deirdre, almost singing. "Asleep."

Giving up on Deirdre, she turns to Connie. She sees that the thick lenses of his eyeglasses could use a good cleaning. Businesslike, she says, "Did you call the bank?"

"I did," says Connie.

"Well, did you find him on the tape?"

"We did."

"So you were able to get his name."

"We were."

"Well, who is he? Did you arrest him?"

"Sit down, Muriel," Deirdre interrupts. "Let me get you some tea."

"I don't want to sit down," says Muriel.

Connie takes a photograph from the inside pocket of his suit jacket and passes it to her. She looks at the man's face and for some reason a faint chill goes down her spine.

"His name is James Grimes," Connie says. "Jimmy Grimes. A very unhappy fellow living in a sad little apartment on Dean Street. Taking a few courses at the college . . . doing the work-study program . . ."

"Oh my God," says Muriel, feeling another chill, this one full blown. "It's him, isn't it?"

"We found a cigar box in his apartment, Muriel," says Connie, serious now. "A Dutch Masters cigar box with—"

"With pictures of himself as a child," says Muriel, and inexplicably, tears begin to fill her eyes.

"That's right," says Connie. "Polaroids. And we found a lot of other things too."

"Now I will sit down," Muriel manages to get out, and Deirdre has her arms around her.

"It's okay, Muriel," Deirdre is saying. "You're a heroine, sweetheart. It's going to be okay."

After Connie Shoulders leaves the house and Deirdre goes upstairs to tend the baby, she feels enormous relief at being alone, almost as if she can breathe again for the first time in a while.

At the end of this long day, she will recall how deeply and tangibly she missed Francis throughout, how she almost ached for him as she moved through the hours, meeting the day's unusual demands, appearing competent, perhaps even confident, to observers.

A week or so later, she finds herself approaching the front doors of the Raphael School. She has come to see Joe Letson, to whom she means to make amends; that telephone call of last summer must have seemed very strange indeed, and she feels she owes him an explanation. She has dressed simply for the occasion, a lightweight navy blue suit she used to wear at this time of year to her job in the school library, chosen this morning (though she acknowledges the absurdity of the notion) to make herself more recognizable. She notices that the school's gothic tower is now enveloped in a network of scaffolding, and high on one of the platforms, men are busy cleaning the stones. Down the large sloping lawn that leads to the riverbank—the lawn on which another commencement ceremony will soon be held—she can see through some apple trees, now white in blossom, the bright play of sun on water.

When she reaches the arched wooden door with its four rectangular panes of leaded glass, it is heavier than she remembers it, and she has to use both hands to pull it open. She passes through the circular lobby with its star inlaid in the marble floor. There is no other person in sight, and as she walks through the long hall, her footsteps echoing, she is suddenly overtaken by the oddest feeling. It is not something she has ever quite felt before, though she can tell that it connects somehow to time, to her own history, to the events of her life and their sequence. She does not feel inner peace, she does not feel inner turmoil, she does not feel the resolution of any of her sorrows or struggles; the nearest she can come to naming it is *balance.* In her mind she sees the depiction of Justice, the woman blindfolded and holding that set of scales, the one with the two plates suspended by chains.

She has arrived a few minutes early and decides to linger there in the great hall among the rows of glass cabinets that house the things of the world, a labyrinthine display she has taken entirely for granted in the past, passing it thousands of times on her way to the library without so much as a glance. The only light in this part of the hall comes through stained glass windows, so it is dusky in the narrow aisles between the cabinets. She discovers, however, that her eyes adjust quickly to the dimness, and as she moves slowly through these passages, she can begin to see what's inside, behind the glass: a stuffed barn owl, a bald eagle, a terrapin, an iguana; a collection of mounted butterflies; the fully assembled skeleton of a goat. Soon she begins to open the glass doors, to reach inside. She touches a pair of wooden clogs, a bust of Cro-Magnon man, the smooth face of a china doll, and she is transported by these things not at all away from the present moment but far more deeply into it. She holds in her hands by turn a starfish, a pale chunk of rose quartz, a column of petrified oak.

Part IV

NED'S BOY (AS Brimm thought of him, though the man was well into his forties) said nothing at all once they were under way. He climbed up a ladder onto the flybridge, took a seat at the helm, and seemed to become a player in something much larger than himself, a drama of mythic proportions, engaging real gods and quite beyond the mere mortals (Ned and Brimm) below—though, as Brimm reminded himself, all the man was doing was steering a boat, a boat with the unassuming name of *Sweet Sue*. He was as unlike Ned at that age as anyone could be. Where Ned had been an indoor type, a reader, a talker, the son had acquired the weathered skin, beard, faraway eyes, and seamanly reticence common to actors portraying fishermen and ship captains. He had looked so deeply troubled as he mounted the ladder to the flybridge—his last words to them had been "Watch yourselves now"—that Brimm leaned close to Ned's ear and whispered, "The horror, the horror." (No doubt Ned's boy's affect seemed the more ironic to Brimm, since the last time Brimm had seen him, Ned's boy had been wearing a soiled diaper.) When Brimm whispered "The horror, the horror," Ned, though obviously proud to have a skipper for a son, seemed to understand, and laughed.

Somewhere out in the Gulf, the coast a thin white line, Brimm figured it out: Ned had told his son about Brimm's recent diagnosis. No ordinary cargo, Brimm. He was a dying man. Death had come to charter the *Sweet Sue*.

A bit earlier, on the dock, Brimm had seen the son talking to another fisherman. As Brimm and Ned approached, Brimm heard the other fisherman say, "It's October, man. White marlin off Orange Beach." Just then, the man who was speaking caught sight of Brimm and Ned, gave them the once-over, and said, "Oh." These paltry things, these tattered coats upon sticks, would not be strapped into any fighting chair to mix it up with a major sport fish. So they had pursued the shallower waters of Pensacola Pass, where the redfish roamed.

It was in fact the fifteenth day of October. The previous week, Brimm had moved into the house in town with Muriel and Deirdre, his Mutt-and-Jeff geriatric nurses. Muriel had frowned on the plan to go deep-sea fishing— "the expedition," as she called it. "You're much too weak for this sort of expedition," she had said. "Much too weak." Brimm himself had almost called the thing off, for though he relished the adventure, the extreme departure from the sickroom, the sea air, he didn't think he had the strength for any fishing. He had spoken to Ned about it a few days before, in Muriel's front parlor, and Ned had assured him that the actual fishing was optional. "We can just ride," Ned had said in an exaggeratedly consoling voice.

Billie, who had overheard this exchange, said, "That's all Ned ever does when he goes out with Jerry anyway."

"That is not true," Ned said, insulted, his masculinity at stake.

"It is most certainly true," Billie said, and Ned, defeated, had stuck his tongue out at her.

Now, three days later, Brimm and Ned were positioned in the *Sweet Sue*'s cockpit, quiet, mesmerized by the boat's wake as Jerry steered them deeper into the Gulf. The sun was just up, the sky full of early morning cumulus clouds of various hues. The white of the wake had a golden-pinkish tint. The original impulse behind Brimm's acceptance of Ned's invitation to go fishing had been something like this: he was dying; he had never gone deep-sea fishing;

he would go deep-sea fishing. The rapid progression of his illness had altered that plan considerably, though the effect had been, already, much the same. He'd been transported out of himself. He'd become something other than a sick man, a man who was dying. The buried drone of the boat's engine, its deep, seemingly infinite vibration, had claimed Brimm's body, making him a part of the boat, so that he had become but another of the boat's features, another piece of equipment—the *Sweet Sue* had its outriggers, its gunwales, its gin pole, its Brimm. And it was good to be claimed so thoroughly. For the last five minutes or so he'd been aware of a new sensation his illness served up, something he was just beginning to get used to. It was recognizable as fatigue, but a variety of fatigue so primary and inward that it had passed right through heaviness to a kind of buoyancy, a biological surrender, a physical willingness to be tossed about.

After a long while he became aware that he'd achieved, under the influence of these remarkable conditions—the boat's reverberations, the cool sea air, the effects of his illness—a state of consciousness that would appear to an observer as normal sleep. This was understandable, as he was completely still, his eyes closed, his breathing regular. But very little escaped him. He was alert, for example, to the fact that Ned's boy had cut the engine, that in his taciturn way he had come down the ladder without voicing his intentions, that he had begun tying a jig to a leader. All this without Brimm's actually seeing. When quite a long time had passed, Brimm felt something heavy and woolly spread over his shoulders and legs; he felt sunlight on his face and on the top of his head. He heard Ned say, "I knew his folks. You don't remember them. Somber people. Dark, somber people. Thin as rails, both of them. Crazy, I think, if you want to know the truth. Forceful."

"What do you mean, forceful?"

"I'm not sure exactly. All I know is that the same thing that trapped his sister—kept her looking after that old man

259

till he died, kept her in that house when she had nobody—it was the same thing that sent Frankie thousands of miles away. Away and away and away."

"Least he saw some of the world," said Ned's boy.

A silence, followed by Ned's voice again. "Oh, yes," he said, "a good long life. Been everywhere, seen everything."

"Nobody's been everywhere," said Ned's boy. "Nobody's seen everything."

"*He* has," said Ned. "All *around* the world."

"But did he get it?" said the boy after a minute. "It's one thing to see it, but another thing to get it."

Here Brimm wanted to speak for himself, but he felt paralyzed by the same surprising constraint that prevents speech in dreams. After a moment Ned said, "Oh, I think he got some of it . . . He definitely got some of it."

Nearby, a gull cried. A small prop plane flew overhead and faded out of earshot. "Here you go," said Ned's boy. "Just drop that in and work it up and down." There was the sound of his grunting as he mounted the ladder back to the flybridge. "Let me know if he wakes up," he added, "and I'll get him situated."

But Brimm, listening carefully to everything, united with the boat's gentle roll, and pondering his blood—he could see his blood's red darkness in his eyelids—thought he couldn't possibly be more situated if he tried.

"Compelling and Beautiful . . .
SCHOOL FOR THE BLIND is an extraordinarily well-written book. . . . Like the best-loved novels of the past, it is full of voices, voices that create harmony and discord, voices that weave counterpoint. . . . It is a book in tune with itself that chimes in the resonant spaces of our common experience; every heart will return its echo. . . . A book meant to be read aloud, shared with someone you care about."
—*The Boston Sunday Globe*

"A remarkable book as rich in emotion as his previous effort, and as active and compelling—and hard to put down—as a classic whodunit . . . A comforting yet invigorating book that will linger with you like the best of memories—the kind that make you look forward to whatever's next."
—*USA Today*

"An honest, uplifting book, the most affecting and satisfying work of fiction I have read this year."
—*The Miami Herald*

"McFarland displays an extraordinary ability to describe both states of mind and the evanescent physical sensations that accompany them . . . . When he allows his language to soar into poetry, it is transcendent and beautifully moving."
—*Publishers Weekly*

*Please turn the page
for more glowing reviews. . . .*